Dearest Violet and Francine,

Do not trouble yourselves. Elithorpe Pemberton is not dead. Rather he has been injected with a paralytic drug that both deprives him of voluntary motor control and leaves him fully sensate. The effects of this chemical will not wear off for several hours. Until then, consider him your toy. Mademoiselle Lange along with Miss Spence and Miss Bates have been subjecting him to almost continuous genital massages. Mademoiselle Lange wishes you both to continue her experiments as she has been called away by other duties. Delight yourselves!

> Fondly,
> Dale Armsworthy

Also by TITIAN BERESFORD:

Judith Boston
Nina Foxton
The Wicked Hand
Cinderella
The Best of Titian Beresford

Chidewell House
and Other Stories

TITIAN BERESFORD

MASQUERADE BOOKS, INC.
801 SECOND AVENUE, NEW YORK, N.Y. 10017

Chidewell House and Other Stories
Copyright © 1997 by Titian Beresford
All Rights Reserved

No part of this book may be reproduced, stored in a retrieval system, or transmitted in any form, by any means, including mechanical, electronic, photocopying, recording or otherwise, without prior written permission of the publishers.

First Masquerade Edition 1997
First Printing August 1997
ISBN 1-56333-554-9

First Top Shelf Edition 1997
ISBN 1-56333-906-4

Manufactured in the United States of America
Published by Masquerade Books, Inc.
801 Second Avenue
New York, N.Y. 10017

Chidewell House & Other Stories

Chidewell House	**7**
Cecil Fothergill's Matron	**131**
A Dose of Chadwick's Sleeping Tonic	**149**
The Playthings	**167**
The Research Institute	**189**
The Secret Police Nurses	**205**
The Rubber Sanitarium	**225**

Chidewell House

Chapter I

Elithorpe Pemberton sat with his legs together, both pale hands resting nervously on the brown paper packet he had placed carefully across his knees. Whatever the packet contained, he was guarding it with a vigilance that bordered on the obsessive. His finger toyed with the twine that bound the packet as he turned his head to stare out the carriage window at the crowd milling about on the station platform. As he turned, for a moment his thick spectacles caught the light and became featureless opaque circles.

Elithorpe Pemberton despised crowds. He knew that sooner or later the door to his compartment would open and his privacy would be disturbed. Elithorpe Pemberton was a brilliant investigative attorney, but certainly no conversationalist. A mystery of vital importance to his most generous client had been solved—through a very substantial effort on his part—and he was pleased. Though his client would not be pleased at all! Indeed, at best, his client would consider his findings a gross betrayal of the highest order. It was ironic that clients very often paid more for bad news than for pleasant. Elithorpe Pemberton was going to deliver his findings to his client in person, supported with exhaustive details. After that he would reward himself. Elithorpe Pemberton was meticulous and analytical even in his leisure. He determined to allow himself two or three blissful, uninterrupted days in the museum library deciphering and assembling cuneiform fragments. Assyriology was Elithorpe Pemberton's secret vice. His hobby and his investigative work shared much in common. Both were based on pattern recognition and the exercise of keen deductive reasoning.

Elithorpe Pemberton noticed a woman in the crowd outside the window of his compartment. She was looking carefully in the rows of windows before her as if searching for the face of someone she knew or was to meet. He noticed her because of her striking height, though she appeared to have none of the awkwardness common to most tall women. He noticed that the woman had high cheekbones, a somewhat prominent nose, and a small mouth with full, pouting lips.

The woman's mouth was turned down slightly at the

corners. The overall effect was rather striking. Elithorpe Pemberton refused to recognize its attraction. He preferred to think of women as rather shallow creatures, given to pleasure and not interested in intellectual or high-minded pursuits. Suppose she was to enter his carriage and annoy him with nonstop mindless prattle the whole way? Rail journeys could be tedious enough with the jolting of the carriages and the soot.

Elithorpe Pemberton considered himself to be above the pursuit of romance and gave little consideration to the fairer sex. He preferred to believe that women ignored him because he was a man of formidable intellect with little regard for them in turn. Actually most women hardly noticed that the slight, nervous little man with the thick spectacles existed at all.

The woman's full lips with their slightly down-turned corners were saved from a permanent expression of petulance by her ability to smile radiantly. She was smiling now. Elithorpe Pemberton gave a start! She was smiling at him! This was absurd! Perhaps she was mistaking him for someone she knew because of the distortion from the glass of the carriage window. Elithorpe Pemberton knew that she was not one of his acquaintances. Indeed, striking women with dazzling smiles were scarcely compatible with the limited academic circles of which he was part.

Elithorpe Pemberton was flustered. He stroked his scant mustache, a habit he often exhibited when nervous. The woman was coming to his door now. His mind, ever observant and categorizing, noted subconsciously that her dark brown hair was worn in a short bob. This effect, combined with her notable features was rather striking indeed. She was wearing a duster of some lightweight material despite the warmth of the day. Perhaps a motorcar had conveyed her to the Charing Hollow station.

Elithorpe Pemberton loathed motorcars. He believed that their very existence—at least in private hands—was a gross prostitution of applied scientific intellect. Elithorpe Pemberton was a man well suited to be hidden away in an ivied university cloister, his bookish studies interrupted only occasionally by the chime of the college clock in the bell tower.

The door latch turned as the woman stepped up from the station platform to enter his compartment. He was scandalized! And without so much as a, "By your leave!" This was highly improper!

Elithorpe Pemberton found her appearance most distracting. She was gloveless and the duster covered her from calf to chin. But her boots were like none that he had ever seen! The heels of her boots were so high as to give her an affected and highly tiptoed stance. They were of gleaming black leather and laced so close through the eyelets that it must have taken a maid a whole forenoon to accomplish it. The woman clutched a battered portmanteau in her left hand and offered him her right in greeting, still maintaining her dazzling smile. He shook her hand rather limply, his face flushing hot at her forward intrusion.

"Hello, there! I am Miss Armsworthy, but my friends call me Dale!" Elithorpe Pemberton coughed as preliminary to groping for a suitable reply. But Dale Armsworthy did not wait. She swung her battered portmanteau up onto the plush velvet cushion of the seat beside him causing a merry dance of dust motes against the lacquered mahogany of the carriage sidewall. Then she spun about and slid the duster from her shoulders gracefully, tossing it onto the seat across from him. Then she turned about and knelt on the far side of the seat across from him to open the carriage window. She kept one knee against the compartment door as if to discourage others from entry. She peered over the heads of the crowd on the station platform and waved, as if beckoning distant friends to share the ride with her in her compartment. Elithorpe Pemberton was nonplused! She seemed determined to be alone with him!

Elithorpe Pemberton was also shocked at what Dale Armsworthy wore beneath her duster! Her boots were more outrageous than he had even imagined! And indeed, if truth were known, Elithorpe Pemberton had a weakness for ladies' boots. After his services were accepted by his present client—whose message he bore now—he had lingered outside a ladies' clothing shop for quite some time, admiring the high-heeled boots through the window. Finally a pair of pretty young ladies noticed his attentiveness and began sniggering at him. He had walked away slowly, his back ramrod straight with violated dignity and outrage.

Dale Armsworthy's boots terminated at mid-thigh! Never had he seen their like before! And the way they clung to every curve and turn of ankle, calf, and thigh was sheer artistry! She wore sleek white riding trousers that clung to every womanly curve of her buttocks and hips. Her ensemble was completed with a burgundy vest, a tailored white blouse with long sleeves and a starched round collar, and a black tie.

Kneeling there on the seat across from him, her posture emphasized and exaggerated the charms of her bottom, while her wickedly gleaming boots captivated him in the extreme. Elithorpe Pemberton adjusted the package on his lap and crossed his legs, acutely conscious that the sight had stiffened his male organ.

Elithorpe Pemberton still had a bit of willpower left. He looked away from the delicious sight before him and willed his erection to subside. Once his rigidity had abated, he determined to leave the carriage and find another to occupy. However, his efforts were rendered futile by a piercing whistle from the engine and, scant seconds later the clack and jolting of the carriages as the train pulled from the platform. Elithorpe Pemberton gave himself up to the sight of his luscious companion, and his erection returned at once. Dale Armsworthy then turned around and sat facing him, a pretty smile on her lips.

Chapter II

"The fiends!" Frederick Uxbridge was fairly bristling with rage. "Of all the wicked, diabolical machinations known to man!" He paused to collect himself for a moment, much to the relief of his companion, Ellen Cromwell, who feared the onset of an attack of apoplexy. Despite her advice to the contrary, he had produced the short note from his writing table and reread it. As on the first occasion of its reading, the little note from his investigative attorney had produced a fit of rage.

After another moment or so, Lord Uxbridge subsided. Ellen Cromwell stepped forward to lay a concerned and attentive hand on the sleeve of his smoking jacket. "Dear, do calm yourself. We can't save Cecil now unless we allow cool heads to prevail. Else we shall simply be at sixes and sevens, and they will have their wicked way with him and debauch the poor boy entirely, I shouldn't wonder…providing of course that the contents of this note are proved." At this, Ellen Cromwell looked somewhat pensive and uncertain, as if unable to believe that human beings were capable of the wickedness to which the note alluded.

"I have no doubt that Elizabeth is capable of such things. No doubt at all." Frederick Uxbridge had subsided somewhat at last, but was still smoldering with barely contained fury. Here he paused and allowed Ellen Cromwell to clip the end of a fragrantly expensive cigar he had produced from a small rosewood box. Then she flicked the silver lighter for him while he puffed agreeably. Ellen Cromwell sat on one arm of his plush leather wing chair and regarded him with fond concern.

Frederick Uxbridge drew on the cigar and puffed, wreathing his head with expensive smoke from his Havana. Despite his eccentricities, he was a determined and formidable man. His vast fortune made him a vital friend or lethal enemy. Despite his passion for motorcars and his fondness for Madeira—a wine out of fashion for nearly a hundred years—nobody took Lord Uxbridge lightly.

"Elizabeth would do anything to secure Cecil's fortune through guardianship. She has little time—he comes into his majority in scarcely eighteen months. I was dearly fond of my brother Oswald's first wife, Cecil's mother, but when she succumbed to her last illness, I could never forgive my brother for consorting with Elizabeth, then finally marrying her. She has controlled my brother's fortune ever since his own death and means to control it still after Cecil's twenty-first birthday! I'm certain of it!"

"But would she sink to such vile devices, even to secure Cecil's fortune?" Ellen Cromwell was finding it difficult to believe that a human being could be so wicked.

"Yes, I have no doubt, no doubt at all. That is why I disowned my brother Oswald when he took that wicked woman as his wife. That haughty blonde is as cold as ice and as greedy as a Paxton whore!" Frederick Uxbridge paused again, puffing absentmindedly. Ellen Cromwell stroked his brow with one white gloved fingertip. Her pert breasts were lifted, pointed, and emphasized by the tight bodice of her pale blue dress.

Lord Uxbridge handed her the note. "Read it again, if you please," he said quietly. Ellen Cromwell did so a bit reluctantly, fearful of precipitating another burst of rage.

> Dear Lord Uxbridge,
> I have news as to the whereabouts of your nephew Cecil. I will arrive at Chudleigh Green to deliver my findings in person. I believe that Elizabeth has procured the services of ladies to addict Cecil to unnatural vices in order to weaken his constitution

so that he may be declared her ward permanently. Thus she would have access to his fortune past his majority. I believe one of the women involved may be connected to The Sexual Temperance Union of The Ladies' Morals Society.

I shall present you with my findings when I arrive on Tuesday evening. Of course I shall provide you with supporting evidence as well. My deepest apologies to you for having to convey what can only be disturbing news.

As ever, your devoted servant,
Elithorpe Pemberton

Ellen Cromwell stopped reading and regarded Lord Uxbridge with an expression of mingled relief and concern. At least he did not have another apoplectic fit! He sat quietly, seemingly lost in thought. She followed the direction of his gaze through the panes of the smoking-room window and out across the gravel of the carriage-way. Lord Uxbridge's motorcar stood gleaming on the drive, its lamps and leather gleaming. It soothed him to look at it. Ellen Cromwell turned her gaze back to Lord Uxbridge and smiled.

Ellen Cromwell was herself Lord Uxbridge's third eccentricity. She was from a notable though impoverished family. He made no secret of his fondness for her and also of his intentions of marriage. Until then he gave no account of propriety whatsoever. Though always a perfect gentleman, he regarded the notion of a chaperone's necessity as beneath contempt.

Lord Uxbridge's fourth eccentricity, after Ellen Cromwell herself, his motorcar, and Madeira, was his estate of Chudleigh Green. The huge house with narrow lawns and gardens just off Ladysmith Park was dear to him. It had once belonged to the notorious courtesan Elizabeth Chudleigh and was said to have been used by her as a trysting place for young George III and his paramours.

Ellen Cromwell's reverie was broken as Lord Uxbridge spoke again. "I'm certain that neither Josie Glade or Georgie Carstairs would have a thing to do with so vile a plan. Absolutely certain, beyond all doubt!" He paused at length to stub out his cigar in the pedestal tray at his side. "I have known Josie Glade for years. She is a splendid physician, and I regard Georgie with the utmost respect. Both have labored long through The Ladies' Morals Society to be a chaste example to the population and to curb immoral impulses of all types; nipping them in the bud, as it were. Why, just a fortnight ago, Georgie Carstairs told me of the arrest of a printer and book shop owner in Mayfair, an arrest precipitated by a Ladies' Morals Society investigation. And Josie Glade has produced research papers highlighting the blight of Onanism and its unfortunate effects on young men who succumb to it. No, I cannot believe that they are involved. Perhaps a woman in some way affiliated with their fine organization to satisfy her own prurient appetites, may be involved. That is a possibility I shudder to think of.

Such a one could unravel the careful moral upbringing my brother engendered in young Cecil, and that in short order—I have no doubt."

Ellen Cromwell nodded in agreement. "That is true, Frederick," she said thoughtfully. "Why, just a few days ago, when you invited Josie Glade and Georgie Carstairs to a dinner party, you told them that you suspected Cecil's stepmother as the orchestrator of his disappearance. Both women were the picture of concern and seemed greatly relieved to learn that you had procured Elithorpe Pemberton's involvement in the case."

"Yes, indeed, I well remember their concern," Frederick Uxbridge sighed, helping himself to a bit of Armagnac from a decanter at his elbow, pouring it into a cut crystal snifter that Ellen Cromwell gracefully held. Ellen declined his offer of a glass of dry sherry. She was practically a teetotaler. Her disapproval of his somewhat enthusiastic appreciation for Madeira and Armagnac were perhaps Lord Uxbridge's only sources of irritation with her.

"I have often been surprised that both women have taken a shine to us, you know—well, at any rate, at least to me," Lord Uxbridge went on. "After all, with my reputation as a lifelong bachelor who has unattached young women about the house, I'm certain it must at times be a great deal for them to swallow. Yet we have become very close in recent months."

Ellen Cromwell nodded. She knew the other woman that Frederick alluded to was Roslyn Osgood. Roslyn Osgood was a young woman who was Lord Uxbridge's closest friend beside herself, though they were never romantically involved, or so inclined. Roslyn Osgood was not above doing a servant's work about Chudleigh Green on a warm afternoon, perhaps weeding the flower beds just inside the wrought iron gate. When doing this she often clad herself in a scandalously tight cotton slacks and seemed amused at the shocked reactions of passersby. Ellen's initial jealousy had quickly faded once she realized that Lord Uxbridge and Roslyn Osgood were just friends and nothing more.

Roslyn Osgood was from a wealthy family, and certainly did not befriend Lord Uxbridge in an effort to access a piece of his fortune. She, too, had her oddities. She despised Josie Glade and Georgie Carstairs, and refused to be present at all when they were guests at Chudleigh Green. Perhaps just as well, Ellen thought, the free spirit and the moralists would be at odds in no time.

"Ah yes, and Wednesday evening we will take the motorcar and pick up Josie Glade and Georgie Carstairs for our little dinner party, though I don't see how I can play the merry host as usual," Lord Uxbridge sighed with a shake of his head and a sip of fiery Armagnac.

"Don't worry," Ellen Cromwell soothed him, her brow knitted in concern. "Elithorpe Pemberton will present his findings to us tomorrow night and our course of action will become clear then."

"Yes, and good intellectual company often stimulates

ideas and clears the head," Frederick Uxbridge agreed, perhaps a trace of his customary good humor returning.

Dale Armsworthy had not been idle. As the train clacked and puffed on through the countryside, her plan had been unfolding quite on schedule. It was difficult enough to draw poor, pathetic Elithorpe Pemberton out of his shell; that was certain. But Violet and Francine had been right about the boots. If he was enamored of a simple pair such as those found in a common shop window, it was not difficult to imagine the adoration inspired by her own outlandish pair. It cost her employers a great deal of money to have them made in a little shop just off Portland Square.

Of course this was not to say that Elithorpe Pemberton had been rude, certainly not, at least not after his initial shock and surprise. She had even drawn him out enough to agree bumblingly with some of her pleasantries. But now it was time for the second phase of her carefully contrived plan. The addiction phase. Dale Armsworthy smiled her dazzling smile. Elithorpe Pemberton acknowledged it with what he thought was a casual grin of his own. The effect was most amusing. He would be her plaything soon enough. She laughed aloud as she stood up and slid her battered portmanteau down from the seat beside him. She could feel his eyes fairly stroke her booted legs with a look of covert desire.

Elithorpe Pemberton had wondered about Dale

Armsworthy's battered portmanteau. It was in great contrast to the immaculate spit and polish of the rest of her ensemble. And now she was opening it up. He saw that her portmanteau opened vertically, rather like a book, to reveal separate compartments, two to each side, secured with worn leather straps.

In the top left compartment was a varnished wooden box about eight inches square. It had small brass fittings on each side and a strange black bellowslike device extending upward from its top. It almost looked like a pump of some kind. Dale Armsworthy had sparked his intellectual curiosity—there was no mistake about that.

In the lower left compartment was a smaller varnished box connected—by means of its own brass fitting—to a coiled length of slim India rubber hose. What appeared to be a foot pedal extended upward from the top of the smaller box. In the upper right compartment of the portmanteau was a cylindrical India rubber sheath of some sort, which appeared to be contrived of two tubes, nested one inside the other. One end of the rubber sleeve was open. A short coiled length of rubber hose was attached to the other end of the sleeve. About two inches from the attachment was a junction fitting that terminated in a small graduated specimen bottle. In the lower right compartment of the portmanteau was a banded packet of dull brown envelopes. Perhaps photographic envelopes. Elithorpe Pemberton's curiosity was surely piqued now.

At length he mustered the courage to make his first inquiry of his bewitching companion. "Is that a scientific instrument of some kind?"

Dale Armsworthy looked up from her unpacking operation to give him another dazzling smile. "In a manner of speaking, it is. It was developed by a physician with whom I am personally acquainted." His expression of unfulfilled curiosity amused her. Now he was in for a shock! She continued. "It is a foot-operated manustupration pump!"

A smile teased the corners of her pretty lips as she watched the effect of her words on the timid little man. He started visibly and sat clearing his throat, tugging at the corners of his mustache with one pale hand. He was still clutching his paper packet tied with twine. No matter. She would have that soon enough.

The tone of her voice teased him. "I see you haven't the courage to ask about the use of the manustupration pump. Perhaps you find its existence at all shocking enough for one day? Hmmm?" Indeed, Elithorpe Pemberton was in shock, at least in a manner of speaking. His lovely companion with her tight high boots with their outrageous heels and her skintight riding trousers! Her bottom might as well have been bare!

And now she was teasing him! His erection returned with a vengeance, his sex organ rigid between his legs. Elithorpe Pemberton's cherished and long-held illusions crumbled. He seemed to be in a waking dream. He realized then, that for all his pretenses of superiority, he was but the plaything of any attractive lady who would choose to exercise him. It was just that no woman had ever bothered to exert her sway over him before. Before now. And now his lovely companion who had invaded his privacy with a vengeance was collecting her due. A sickening certainty came over him then. He knew she wanted the package he carried. He knew also that she would get it from him. But at her own timing. His mouth went dry.

Dale Armsworthy retrieved the banded packet of dull brown envelopes from the lower right compartment of her portmanteau. She stepped across the carriage and sat beside him, her rounded hip brushing his woolen trousers. She noted everything about him at close range. The gold watch chain running from his waistcoat pocket, the small dark mole on his right cheek, and the enlarged appearance of his eyes caused by his thick spectacles. He'd probably be blind without them! She smiled at him again and watched his Adam's apple bob up and down. He was pulling at his mustache frantically now. She undid the band and opened the first envelope. She withdrew the photographs and held them for his perusal with her right hand, resting her left hand casually on his thigh. For a moment she thought he would faint from her enticing proximity.

"I was recently a matron at the Clackton Sanitarium. Under the auspices of a female physician, certain experiments were carried out there in an effort to find a non-punitive way to render certain troublesome inmates docile. Such is the purpose of the foot-operated manustupration pump. Before its invention, we had to make do with prolonged canings!" Elithorpe stared at the first photograph, his mouth agape. He was seized with a mixture of peculiar feelings ranging from revulsion to excitement.

Chapter III

Francine Glade and her friend Violet Naughton stood before the cheval glass in the dusty attic. Both girls were clad in tightly laced thigh boots of gleaming leather. Both pairs of boots had heels so high that they forced the girls onto their tiptoes. Both girls wore white riding trousers of quite scandalous snugness. The riding trousers clung to the youthful, slender charms of the girls' hips and bottoms. Both girls wore tucked-in white blouses with highly starched round-point collars. Their ensembles were completed with immaculate white gloves and black ties—tied in precise half-Windsor knots.

Violet Naughton and Francine Glade had been practicing their toilettes all morning. They laced each other's boots over and over again until they got it right—according to Mademoiselle Lange's critical expectations. Then they practiced tying their half-Windsor tie knots. Finally they practiced walking about the attic room in their outrageously high-heeled boots for so long that they were getting a trifle bored. And, as young ladies of nineteen and eighteen respectively are wont, they became rather silly and foolish after their exacting efforts.

Francine Glade turned round and bent over at the hips, resting her gloved hands upon her thighs—presenting her bottom to the cheval glass coquettishly as she did so. She wiggled her bottom saucily. "If all the masturbators could see us now, Violet!" She giggled. Her cheeks flushed slightly. "Their addiction to unnatural vices would be reinforced!"

Her friend Violet stood prettily, hands on hips, as if in stern disapproval. "Neither my aunt nor yours approve of the term 'masturbators'! They regard it as vulgar usage, so I must sternly insist that you stop using it at once!" Violet sniggered and turned about before the cheval glass herself to mimic her companion's lewd antics before it. Both girls now stood side by side, wiggling their bottoms and looking over their shoulders to see their reflections in the glass.

"Oh, dear!" Francine Glade pouted, the perfect picture of exaggerated dismay. "If I cannot call them masturbators, then what is the proper and delicate term?"

Violet Naughton unsuccessfully attempted to suppress a giggle as she replied in the haughtiest tone she could muster. "Well indeed! We mustn't call them manustuprationists, certainly not! The term is far too cumbersome. We must call them 'Onanists'—a term fully alluding to the grave moral indecency of their vile habits, yet also a term of scientific accuracy, denoting a ray of hope for successful treatment...." Here both young ladies were too overcome with giggles to continue their playacting. They collapsed backward onto an old scroll-armed settee, transfixed with merriment.

In short, their conversation continued, as both young ladies sat crossing and recrossing their legs, then raising their booted feet high to view and snigger over their own alluring reflections in the cheval glass.

"I adore the boots!" Francine Glade purred. "I am so pleased with Dale Armsworthy finally persuading your Aunt Georgie to purchase us pairs identical to hers from that delightful old man in the shop off Portland Square!"

"Yes, and did you notice that Dale was rubbing the poor old fellow's trouser front in a most indecent manner as we were leaving the shop?" Violet Naughton observed as if fascinated with the whole idea. Then she went on, forgetting her own lecture from a moment before. "She probably made a masturbator out of the poor old fellow. After she had rubbed him so wickedly, he must have been tempted to relieve himself manually when next in the privacy of his rooms."

"Indeed!" Francine Glade added. "And your Aunt Josie

would consider it her solemn duty to reprimand Dale Armsworthy for her liberties!" Both girls giggled again, still raising their booted legs high in the air and shifting about on the old settee to examine the effect in the cheval glass. Both young ladies had pretty full-lipped faces and were the picture of good humor and good health. Both faces broke easily into broad smiles.

"Dale Armsworthy rewarded us with the boots because we made her job easier. After all, if we hadn't spotted that silly pathetic Pemberton thing drooling at the boot-shop window with a great lump in his trousers, it would have taken Dale a good while to plan his neutralization," Violet Naughton noted, her tone full of self-satisfied conceit.

Her friend agreed. "Poor little Cecil! And that poor pathetic thing—blind as a bat without his thick spectacles, I shouldn't wonder—is Cecil's uncle's best hope of snatching him from Mademoiselle Lange's hands!" Francine Glade arched her eyebrows suggestively and gave her friend a sideways glance.

Violet had well understood her meaning. "Or his uncle's best hope of snatching his male parts from Mademoiselle Lange's hands, at any rate!" Violet paused thoughtfully. Then her full, pouting lips broke into a secret smile. "Mademoiselle Lange herself let us watch some 'handiwork,' didn't she?"

Francine giggled. "I shall never forget when she let us watch Miss Bates perform Onanistic manipulations on poor Nigel Rollin while Miss Spence posed in a scandalously short dress and high-heeled oxfords. And Nigel was all snuggled up in his leather manustupration harness and quite helpless to prevent Miss Bates from abusing him manually between his legs!" Both girls sniggered at the recollection.

"They have promised that we shall be able to play such games with the experimentation subjects, too, and I simply cannot wait!" Violet breathed. Her eyes sparkling with anticipatory delight. "Dale promised that we could have a go with that poor old Pemberton thing—she said he would be a delight."

Her friend broke in. "Yes, and Mademoiselle Lange said we could fasten Nigel in his Onanism-prevention harness before he is put to bed tonight, and she said that we might be able to take Cecil about in the bondage wheelchair, perhaps around Effingham court." Francine stretched her supple form and wriggled. "Oh, I simply cannot wait! I do hope I shall remember all these things for my sketchbook and diary!"

Finally, came the bit of their new regimen that both young ladies dreaded most. Neither was fond—at least in this stage of their intellectual development—of scholarly or bookish pursuits.

Violet Naughton took a thin black leather bound volume from a dusty cherry end table placed handily by one arm of the settee on which they sat. "Well, I suppose it is my turn to read. We must do our obligatory chapter from your aunt's treatise to complete our daily training duties if we wish to become full-fledged members of The Sexual Temperance Union of The Ladies' Morals Society." Francine Glade leaned forward and nodded a reluctant agreement. She rubbed her gloved hand up and down the gleaming calf of her high boot, savoring the smooth gleam and shine of the leather clinging to her calf.

The narrow black leather-bound book was titled, *Onanistic Indulgence and the Physiology of Its Sorry Effect on the Young Male*, by Dr. Josephine L. Glade. Violet began to read.

"Book IV: Signs of Onanistic addiction frequently exhibited in the young male:

"The signs of Onanistic indulgence are many and varied though certain ones stand out due to their commonality and the frequency with which they are observed in subjects under treatment. These include a generally downcast aspect of personality. A markedly suppressed desire for wholesome interaction with other young males in the rough-and-tumble of the athletic field. The complexion of a slave to unnatural vice is often pale, with a marked tendency to blemishes as well. When an Onanistically inclined male is addressed or addresses another, there is frequently exhibited a good deal of notable blushing. Refined young ladies often observe such fellows hanging about, though never quite daring to address them directly. If such a young fellow is addressed by the young lady herself, he may well lapse into flummoxed silence—or even attempt social intercourse with a good deal of awkwardness and stuttering. The young lady may well feel that such a one is soiling her with his eyes, and she may become uncomfortable...."

Elithorpe Pemberton had never seen the like of the shocking photographs Dale Armsworthy held up for his perusal. Her hand rested enticingly on his thigh, and her proximity alarmed and confused him. She watched his reaction to the spectacle the photographs presented with an amused smile teasing about the corners of her lips. He stared at the first photograph with a mixture of fascination and horror. His mind was so occupied with what he saw that he barely heard her say something about Clackton Sanitarium being equipped with a dry-plate box camera—to be used to document both therapeutic and punitive treatments. The train had now begun descending a long downgrade about halfway along the route, between Blessing Hollow and Cheviot Glen. The clicks and rattles of the cars on the rails accelerated, causing Elithorpe Pemberton to feel he was careening to an unknown fate over which he had no control. In this he was entirely correct.

The first photograph depicted an inmate of Clackton Sanitarium clad only in a buckled straitjacket and naked from the waist down. The poor fellow stood on tiptoe, his head bowed in shame, his face contorted in anxiety. A pretty sanitarium matron stood behind him. The matron wore black patent leather oxfords with heels so high that she was forced on tiptoe. For the first time, Elithorpe Pemberton noticed that the affected tiptoed posture forced by the high heels emphasized the curves of a woman's hips, posterior, and calves most deliciously. The matron wore a gray wool calf-length dress with a high collar and a starched white apron. Each of her sleeves sported a row of five buttons that were used to fasten matching gray gloves to her uniform. The effect was a mixture of severe and suggestive overtones that he found most compelling indeed.

Elithorpe Pemberton gasped. In the photograph, Dale Armsworthy was smiling her dazzling, self-satisfied smile. But what her hand was doing between the asylum inmate's legs was terribly improper! She had the poor fellow by the scrotum, having reached through beneath his buttocks from behind!

Elithorpe Pemberton managed to quaver a question to the confident smiling beauty who held the picture for him, with her free hand resting indecently on his thigh. "What are you…doing to him?"

Dale Armsworthy's reply was as smooth as silk and very matter-of-fact. "I am simply exhibiting an invention of mine called the Clackton Sanitarium Mine-March. It is most effective in compelling inmates to go places they do not wish to go, and to experience what they do not wish to experience!"

Despite his shock and disgust at the situation the photograph conveyed so eloquently, Elithorpe Pemberton's sex organ pulsed in his trousers, stiff as an iron bar. His only comment was barely audible. "Oh, how cruel!"

Dale Armsworthy's hand left his thigh for a moment to shuffle the photographs and show him another one. In the second photograph, a pretty blond matron—clad similarly in a severe gray uniform dress with calf-length skirt, single piece gloves, and high-heeled oxfords—was seated on a parlor chair. Her left hand was raised and extended palm upward to cradle the bare genitals of another straitjacketed asylum inmate. The blond matron was sweet faced and smiling a carefree smile. The poor fellow, bound in a straitjacket, and completely naked from the waist down, was having his genitals displayed by the pretty little blonde to a group of three or four other matrons! His testicles lolled visibly in his slack scrotum upon the properly gloved palm that exhibited them. His sex organ reared above, fat and indecent with the excitement and shame of his helpless exposure.

Dale Armsworthy began to smile and rub Elithorpe Pemberton's thigh gently. "What is she doing to him?" he ventured at length.

"She is simply exhibiting his genitals to test his obedience and docility."

Elithorpe Pemberton's mouth was suddenly dry. His heart was pounding. "Oh, how wicked!" A straitjacketed inmate squatted "bottomless" in the third photograph, his scrotum dangling low and pendant. A manustupration pump—almost precisely the same as the one that Dale Armsworthy carried in her battered portmanteau—was affixed to his rigid sex organ. His penis was embedded in the two-piece India rubber suction sleeve. A thin suction hose led from the base of the suction sleeve to the pneumatic box with its top consisting of a black bellows within a glass cylinder. A semen extraction hose led from the tip of the rubber sleeve to a narrow graduated glass specimen bottle. Another rubber hose ran from the pneumatic suction box to a smaller box—also of varnished wood—containing the foot pedal that operated the device.

A pretty matron with lovely, refined features and her dark hair up in a prim chignon operated the foot pedal that worked the manustupration pump. She, too, was clad in a severe gray calf-length dress with built-in gloves and starched apron. Her feet sported the wickedly high-heeled oxfords that were the signature of the Clackton Sanitarium matron.

The sanitarium inmate's face was transfixed with an expression of extreme sensation, somewhere between pain and pleasure. It was difficult to say which.

Elithorpe Pemberton stared silently, imagining the poignant sensations the prim-faced matron was forcing the poor wretch to undergo. At last he spoke again. "Is the manustupration pump you have with you now capable of giving such sensations?"

"Indeed it is. But for a minor difference or two, they are the same device," Dale Armsworthy answered, her voice casual and matter-of-fact.

The fourth photograph's subject was an inmate bound rigidly in an overhead traction frame, his back suspended over the cushion of a high, narrow examination table, his limbs raised in the air by means of wires and pulleys. The poor fellow was completely naked. Four matrons stood about the examination table.

Apparently they were using a hand-operated version of the manustupration pump on him! One matron held a brass cylinder that was connected to a suction hose that ran to the pneumatic sleeve—attached to the inmate's erect penis. Another matron worked a plunger that protruded from the end of the cylinder to generate the suction necessary to stimulate the man's genitals. Two other matrons observed the procedure clinically, arms crossed primly, faces alight with scientific curiosity at the bizarre exhibition.

The naked inmate hung as limp as a rag doll in his bonds. To all appearances, he was completely senseless. "And, of course, we have developed hand-operated instruments as well," Dale Armsworthy said smoothly, her hand still rubbing Elithorpe Pemberton's thigh, her eyes noticing the great lump in his trousers.

"Is the inmate dead?" Elithorpe Pemberton's question was almost inaudible.

"No, he has simply fainted from the extreme sensations he was experiencing. Make no mistake, he will be revived in short order so that the experiment may go on!"

Elithorpe Pemberton was silent for some moments, his eyes digesting the spectacle presented by the photograph. "A dreadful fate! What wickedness!"

Dale Armsworthy was genuinely amused by the sad little man who quivered beside her. "No, being experimentation subjects is the only thing that gives their wasted, pathetic lives meaning!"

As Dale Armsworthy presented more horrific photographs of sanitarium abuse to Elithorpe Pemberton's shocked gaze, she kept talking to him. "The manustupration pump may well have uses outside a sanitarium's walls. Perhaps ladies of refinement could use these devices to settle the nerves of gentleman friends whom it would be most improper to relieve in any other way!" As she presented more mind-numbing photographs, Dale Armsworthy continued, "It is well and good to experiment on sanitarium inmates. But to have as a subject an articulate, educated gentleman of science—so that he might give observations as to the effectiveness of the instrument—that would be ideal." She paused and gave him her fetching smile. "Such as yourself, perhaps?"

Elithorpe Pemberton jumped as though he had been struck. "No, No! Absolutely not! It is unthinkable!"

"I see that only your timidity has overcome your scientific curiosity." Her voice was a silken purr. "So I fear I must insist. I have no desire for you to forgo a delightful experience and then always regret it!"

With those words Dale Armsworthy's hand slipped down from Elithorpe Pemberton's thigh and stole between his legs. He gasped and went rigid to feel her hand grasp him knowingly through his trousers and begin to knead him. He thought he was going to die of shame and he gasped, cheeks flaming at her outrageous impropriety.

Elithorpe Pemberton's sex organ reared and thickened, growing larger under her ministrations. Still kneading him, she bent forward and reached into the left pocket of her discarded duster. She withdrew a thick leather strap with a strong buckle at one end. "Come, now, be reasonable," she cooed. "This will take only a moment. The strap is necessary in order for you to experience the most authentic sensations."

Elithorpe Pemberton was now convinced that he was in a waking dream. He was trembling visibly and found himself quite helpless to resist his determined tormentor—in either word or deed. She stopped kneading him in order to remove his jacket. Then she pulled him up. Her fingers fluttered at his trouser buttons. In a moment, the poor fellow found himself naked from the waist down. He stood pale legged and trembling, clad only in shirttails and waistcoat, as Dale Armsworthy buckled his wrists behind his back with the leather strap. His scrotum hung low. His sex organ poked indecently upward through his shirttails.

Dale Armsworthy wasted no time. She stood up, now towering over Elithorpe Pemberton in her high-heeled boots. He unconsciously noted the narrowness of her waist and the smooth broadening curves of her hips. She took his chin in her hand for a moment to study him and then placed a hand on each of his shoulders to press him backward upon the cushions of the carriage seat. He started at the cool feel of the soft velvet of the seat cushion on his bare buttocks.

Elithorpe Pemberton sat frozen and watched Dale Armsworthy set to work assembling the manustupration pump. She withdrew each piece in turn from her portmanteau, assembling them with deft fingers. Elithorpe Pemberton looked with despairing eyes at the packet containing the messages of vital importance to his client that he had guarded so carefully. Dale Armsworthy offered no opportunity for his erection to abate. She knelt before him, her broad backside emphasized sumptuously by her riding trousers. Elithorpe Pemberton had a close-up view of the daintily high-arched soles of her boots and their wicked high heels.

Dale Armsworthy set the varnished wooden box with its suction pump in the center of the floor. She carefully fitted the airtight glass cylinder over the bellows so that suction could be built up and maintained. She attached a rubber hose to each side of the pumping box by means of its brass fittings. Then she fixed the sliding suction sleeve with its graduated specimen bottle to the right-hand hose. Her deft fingers then connected the box with the foot pedal to the left-hand hose.

Dale Armsworthy smiled up at him, noting that his penis was poking upward through his shirttails, all the more excited due to her improper posture and display. She reached into the right pocket of her duster and retrieved a pair of flawlessly starched white cotton gloves. "It would be highly improper for a lady to apply the suction sleeve to a gentleman's private parts without first donning gloves!" She slipped them on with a prim dainty smile, wiggling her fingers to snug them into the fingertips.

Dale Armsworthy took Elithorpe Pemberton by the arm and made him get down on the carpeted floor of the carriage and assume a squatting position. Her reply to his inquiry why such a posture was necessary was brisk and had to do with following standard Clackton Sanitarium procedure.

Then, to Elithorpe Pemberton's intense shame, Dale Armsworthy took his scrotum and slipped the suction sleeve over his penis. She drew back his foreskin as she did so to insure a proper tight connection. Then, as he remained squatting "bottomless" on the carriage floor, she sat upon the seat directly in front of him and placed her booted foot on the pedal. She smiled and began to work it up and down.

At first the sensations were subtle, but then they mounted most exquisitely. In a short while, he was gasping, fairly leaning forward to thrust his rigid organ more firmly into the machine to endure yet greater poignancy of the mechanical abuse. Dale Armsworthy watched him with laughing eyes, her face the picture of amused feminine curiosity.

Elithorpe Pemberton's face was crimson. Soon he was panting and grunting like a rutting pig in his helpless pleasure. At last he found the strength to gasp a few syllables. "Th-This pleasure must drive them mad!"

Dale Armsworthy laughed, her booted toes maintaining the rhythm on the foot pedal all the while. "Oh, it does so! Often!"

There was no sound from within the carriage now but Elithorpe Pemberton's heavy breathing and the click, hiss, and puff as the pump expanded and deflated within the glass cylinder. Dale Armsworthy paused for a moment. Her victim groaned at the cessation of the sensation that mastered and maddened him. She stood up and stepped across the compartment to retrieve his packet. Then she returned to her place, resting her booted foot on the pedal, but not working it just yet. Elithorpe Pemberton's spectacles were a trifle fogged from his heavy panting, and his brow was covered with perspiration.

"We have plenty of time, Elithorpe. There are no stops till Cheviot Glen. I could let you experience the full paroxysm of delight." Her booted foot worked the pedal a bit more. The manustupration pump reactivated with a click, hiss, and puff. Her victim's jaw hung slack in delight from the renewal of his addictive pleasure. Then Dale Armsworthy stopped pumping the pedal again.

Elithorpe Pemberton was totally enslaved to his new pleasure. He begged her to continue. Instead, she sat smugly, her foot once again poised above the pedal and opened his packet. She perused the contents, skimming them briefly. "Scandalous, I am sure! Flagrant falsehoods and distortions! These papers must be destroyed! I will continue your pleasures if you allow me to tear up the contents of this packet—Well, what do you say— Hmmm?" Her victim moaned and nodded his assent.

Dale Armsworthy's gloved hands tore the contents of the paper packet to tatters very slowly, as if she savored what she was doing. Then she leaned to the side to open the carriage window. In another moment, the shredded contents of the packet were fluttering down to come to rest on the sunlit blossoms of a summer meadow near the rail embankment.

Dale Armsworthy fixed Elithorpe Pemberton with an amused smile. Her foot began working the pedal once again. Again the sensations mastered him. "I fear you must close your investigative practice and come with me to Chidewell House, where our little experiments can continue." His bleary eyes remained fixed on the dainty pointed toe of her high-heeled boot as she pumped the pedal vigorously. He sagged forward weakly as the sensations between his legs reached their crescendo. Dale Armsworthy laughed as the spasming of his sex organ caused the India rubber hose to jerk and rear. She watched as his thick seed jetted from him to be captured in the specimen bottle. As he sagged forward in his pleasure, his spectacles slipped from his nose and fell to the floor. A moment later, Dale Armsworthy raised her other boot to crush them underfoot!

Chapter IV

Frederick Uxbridge's motorcar sped along the oak-lined avenue bordering Ladysmith Park. Ellen Cromwell rather liked the fantastic sensation of velocity of motorcar travel. They sped past hansom cabs and elegant broughams, along with the knots of pedestrians carrying picnic baskets, and the occasional cyclist. The motorcar rattled the planks of the eighteenth century arched bridge that spanned the east-west canal that bisected the park neatly and connected the two large ponds that made the park a favorite place for punters on a warm summer day.

They sped past the latticed two-story gazebo where The Ladies' Morals Society had been holding public assemblies of late to rail against the moral lack in all strata of society—especially the lower. They passed the rich green well-groomed embankments where intimate clusters of friends sat about their wicker baskets to enjoy cold poultry and perhaps a glass of chilled wine. Below, on the rich green fields of the park, several cricket clubs were holding matches well attended by parasol-twirling young ladies, ever vigilant to protect their complexions from the cheapening effects of the warm summer sun. Small pools dotted the park. Their cool, beckoning waters enticed even refined ladies to wade in the shallows barefoot, their skirts hiked up quite nearly to their knees!

Ellen Cromwell was concerned—but not alarmed—ever since the news that Elithorpe Pemberton seemed to have fallen off the face of the earth entirely. An inquiry sent by special post received but the terse and scant reply that the Pemberton Investigative Practice was closed and the whereabouts of its proprietor were unknown.

However, Frederick Uxbridge was a man of his word. Nothing could persuade him to cancel or postpone their scheduled dinner party with Josie Glade and Georgie Carstairs. Ellen Cromwell smiled. The streets between Chudleigh Green and Primrose Lane—the headquarters of The Ladies' Morals Society where they were to pick up their guests—were all neatly paved with close-set stones.

At least the more sedate pace of city driving and the paved roads made it unnecessary to wear the duster, goggles, and veiled hat that driving through the countryside warranted. Ellen Cromwell noticed that Frederick Uxbridge's driving was a bit more sedate than usual. And he wasn't nearly so free with his horn as customary. In fact, she had heard its Klaxon blast only once.

Ellen Cromwell pursed her lips and rubbed the plush green leather upholstery that lined the inside of the low passenger door at her side. The high two-piece windscreen kept her hair neatly in place. The afternoon sunlight glittered off the polished brass and glass of the running lamps that extended outward from the windscreen post before her.

She turned her gaze back to Lord Uxbridge and laid a gloved hand on his arm. "Remember what you said, Frederick. Good intellectual company often stimulates ideas and clears the head. Enjoy our visit with Josie and Georgie. Tomorrow we will plan how to extricate Cecil from his adverse situation."

Frederick Uxbridge set his jaw in a stubborn line, then gave Ellen Cromwell a sideways glance and a wink. Frederick Uxbridge's moods were like a tropical storm, quick to arise, spectacular to observe and quick to abate as well. Ellen knew that his formidable intellect could engage a problem even as he tended to mundane matters. The problem was that with Elithorpe Pemberton's disappearance they had no idea where to begin to set about Cecil's salvation. The only clue was in Elithorpe Pemberton's note. Perhaps a connection to someone in The Ladies' Morals Society itself, unthinkable as that seemed?

Lord Uxbridge shifted gears and turned into Primrose Lane with its rows of elegant town houses with their immaculate lawns. In a moment, he drew up beside the steps of the house at 29 Primrose Lane that served as the headquarters and meeting place of The Ladies' Morals Society.

Josie Glade and Georgie Carstairs were prompt, as usual. The motorcar had scarcely stopped when both women descended the steps, followed closely by a footman with their things. Georgie Carstairs was clad in a cream-bodiced dress with an intricate floral pattern and a black velvet vest. Ellen Cromwell had taken an immediate liking to her, almost from their first meeting. The rebellious lock of wavy chestnut hair that frequently fell down across her eyes gave her a rakish air. Ellen had expected the head of The Ladies' Morals Society to be a dour vicarette. Instead, she found an attractive young woman whose face broke easily into a fetching smile.

Josie Glade was also well liked by both Ellen Cromwell and Frederick Uxbridge. She wore a tight green dress of smooth satin with a high-laced square collar. Her clothing always emphasized her slender waist, and her overall aspect was one of aristocratic elegance. She had the fine straight nose and small pretty mouth that would have made her fit right in at Ascot or Balmoral. Her golden hair was up in a perfect swirl that was impeccability itself—not a single hair out of place.

The four exchanged greetings while the footman stowed Josie and Georgie's bags in the boot. As soon as Frederick had fastened the strap that secured the boot lid, they were off. It was difficult to believe that one of their carefree, smiling passengers was famous for her lengthy lectures on the evils of moral degeneracy while the other—as aristocratic and proper as she seemed—was not above treating the most hopelessly degenerate moral specimens herself, and had indeed written scholarly treatises on the subject. Both women were adamant in their determination to bring unnatural vice to an end.

Chapter V

Deep in the cellars below the street at 47 Effingham Court, just off Portland Square, a strange tableau was being enacted. The house at 47 Effingham Court was elegance itself, and even its discreet basement rooms were deeply carpeted and stylishly decorated—though in a most bizarre manner, to say the very least.

Mademoiselle Lange of The Sexual Temperance Union of The Ladies' Morals Society had assembled Miss Anna Spence, one of her assistants, and three female clients, who were to view the culmination of previous training performed on young Nigel Rollin. The three female clients were Claire Rollin, Nigel's young stepmother, Nancy Westercroft, Claire Rollin's pretty cousin, and Nikiko, Claire Rollin's lovely almond-eyed Japanese maid.

The center of the room was dominated by a manustupration apparatus! The apparatus consisted of a raised platform, on one end of which was a round polished dais about three feet across—partially surrounded by a circular brass handrail. On the opposite end of the platform was a strange chair, consisting of two parallel curving bars of thick lacquered mahogany. Between the chair and the polished round dais was a declivity shaped precisely to admit the lower portion of a smooth silver bowl. Beside the bowl, just at the front of the chair, a mahogany arm jutted up from the platform to support a stool upholstered with a blue crushed-velvet cushion.

Nigel Rollin sat upon the chair stark naked—if his posture, in any sense of the word, could be called sitting! He wore a leather harness that buckled about his waist and kept his forearms rigidly behind the hollow of his back in tightly laced cuffs. The harness also had straps that ran from the front of his belt up over both shoulders, then down again behind. Another strap extended from the rear of his harness to hook into the pedestal that supported his curving chair. Nigel Rollin's head hung low in shame. His face was flushed a bright pink.

Nigel Rollin's entire posture was one of unnatural contortion. His ankles were likewise bound with leather straps and secured to brackets extending from the base of his chair's pedestal. The overall effect was that his hips were thrust forward, causing his genitals to protrude through a ring in the front of his chair, whose top supported his abdomen. His legs were pulled upward and behind, while his upper body arched backward, at the limit of the strap which secured his harness to the hook in the pedestal of his chair.

Nigel Rollin's penis thickened a bit, despite his determined efforts to the contrary. His genitals had been shaved bald and his scrotum dangled low. The indecent exhibition of Nigel Rollin's nakedness was in full view of his stepmother Claire, Claire's cousin Nancy, and the maid Nikiko, who sat in three velvet upholstered parlor chairs scarcely five feet away. Mademoiselle Lange sat on the stool at Nigel's side, clad daintily in wickedly high-heeled oxfords, a plain black dress with white lace cuffs and collar, and a starched apron that covered her from breast to calf. Claire Rollin, Nancy Westercroft and Nikiko were dressed elegantly as if they were about to take tea, rather than watch a bizarre demonstration.

Anna Spence stood on the floor beside the platform, with one hand on the semicircular brass rail. She was clad in wickedly high-heeled oxfords along with silk stockings, a plain gray calf-length dress with turned-back cuffs, and a starched white apron. Anna Spence had an impudent upturned nose and a youthful face that was indeed very lovely. Her body curved generously in the area of her hips and buttocks.

Anna Spence's figure contrasted with the petite proportions of Mademoiselle Lange's tiny waist and feet. Her dark hair was up in an impeccable swirl. Her facial expression was one of sweetness, combined with an elegant continental sophistication. Mademoiselle Lange wore dainty close-fitting gloves of lushest satin.

Mademoiselle Lange spoke with soft, yet authoritative femininity. "You are about to witness the pleasing profitable results of a carefully inculcated addiction to manustupration, or, in the common usage, masturbation. This addiction to masturbation has been complemented with the inculcation of fetishism, so that the two, when combined, are far more addictive than either one singly." Here Mademoiselle Lange paused then said, "You may proceed, Miss Spence."

Miss Spence raised first one leg, then the other, to gracefully unlace her high-heeled oxfords. Then, after carefully placing them on the carpeted floor at the base of the platform, she stepped up to stand on the polished circular dais before Nigel Rollin's enraptured eyes. Resting both her hands on the brass rail, she stood on tiptoes, facing away from Nigel Rollin, her feet scarcely two feet in front of him and level with his genitals. Immediately Nigel Rollin's penis began to thicken yet more. His nineteen-year-old eyes were filled with worshipful adoration as he stared at Anna Spence's lovely stockinged feet. Both Nikiko and Nancy Westercroft flushed. Claire Rollin allowed herself a smile.

Mademoiselle Lange reached down with her satin-gloved hand to capture Nigel's penis and draw back his foreskin. Then she exhibited it to her clients as it lay across her palm. Seconds later, the poor boy was in full erection. Mademoiselle Lange continued to exhibit his penis as it lay across her palm, then resumed speaking.

"We have induced fetishism in Nigel, following the predisposed fault line of his natural predilection or weakness. We have inculcated a passion for ladies' silk-stockinged feet. Indeed, Miss Spence's stockings are of the sheerest, most transparent silk, and he would swoon but to worship them from afar. I fear he may find what is to come a trifle overwhelming." The three clients for whom the exhibition was held all laughed at this remark. "We believe he has developed a special passion for high heels and this arched tiptoed stance which she now assumes!

"Because Nigel has been masturbated repeatedly in the presence of his fetish object—specifically, ladies' tiptoed silk-stockinged feet—his fetish has become a passion, and his passion has been transformed into an addiction." Mademoiselle Lange then took Nigel's penis in her satin gloved hand and began to tug it gently to and fro, exercising it between her thumb and forefinger.

"To a hopelessly addicted male, the pleasure of being masturbated by a woman quickly supersedes that which can be experienced through normal coitus—indeed, as in our experiments here with Nigel." Mademoiselle

Lange's gloved fingertips ceased the gentle abuse of Nigel Rollin's sex organ for a moment. Once again she rested it across her dainty gloved palm.

"Nigel has become an obsessive masturbator of vitiated constitution. We have induced both hyperesthesia and genital irritability in his physiology, to the extent that, were I to manustuprate him now actively and firmly, an orgasm would result in a very short time. Accordingly I have modified my technique to be one of very gentle and understated stimulation. In the presence of the fetish object, an occasional tug or squeeze is quite sufficient to induce orgasm."

Then Mademoiselle Lange addressed Claire Rollin, Nigel's stepmother. "You will have no difficulty having him declared your ward now. His bearing has been reduced from one of confidence to timidity just as his complexion has been reduced from clarity to a pallor marked with frequent blemishes."

"As his course of training here is complete, who will be masturbating him once he is returned to your household?" Mademoiselle Lange inquired, her perfect eyebrows arching slightly. She had let go of Nigel's penis entirely for a bit and sat casually holding his scrotum instead.

Claire Rollin's eyes rested between Nigel's legs. His penis was erect, foreskin still drawn tightly back, with Mademoiselle Lange's tiny gloved hand grasping him by the scrotum. She answered Mademoiselle Lange's question with an arch smile. "Nikiko will manipulate him while my cousin Nancy Westercroft poses for the masturbation."

"Excellent!" Mademoiselle Lange exclaimed. "It is important that his manustupration training resumes without delay, for too long a lapse might require him to be returned to Chidewell House for a refresher course. It is important to exhibit him in public from time to time, also—at social functions and the like. In that way, people will see that his aspect has changed and his bearing is not one of confident normalcy. Then, just the right word whispered in an attorney's ear—perhaps with a physician's support, which I can also provide—will assure his being declared incompetent."

Claire Rollin nodded, a smile of satisfaction upon her sophisticated face. "And certainly no young lady would deign to be courted by him even if the opportunity arose. Therefore there is no worry about feminine competition, or eventual heirs. His fortune is secure in our hands."

Mademoiselle Lange smiled, still holding Nigel's scrotum. "Quite so!"

Then Mademoiselle Lange asked Nancy Westercroft to join Anna Spence on the dais. Nancy Westercroft had previously been prepared for the occasion and wore sheer silk stockings of a type very similar to those sported by Miss Spence. In a moment, she had removed her shoes, hiked up her skirts a bit to expose her calves almost to the knee, and joined Miss Spence in assuming the tiptoed stance that Rollin found so captivating. His penis lolled once again across Mademoiselle Lange's palm, fat, thick, and indecent. Then Mademoiselle Lange had Nikiko stand opposite her at Nigel's hips. Mademoiselle Lange produced a pair of satin gloves for Nikiko so that she would be equipped to assist Mademoiselle Lange in trying her hand at performing slow genital stimulations on Nigel Rollin. Nikiko was an apt pupil, her pretty lips pursed in concentration as she responded to Mademoiselle Lange's directions as to the modulation of the manual abuse. Nikiko worked his foreskin back and forth between her thumb and forefinger, the motions of her hand covering and uncovering the head of Nigel's penis. Nigel sagged in his bonds, his fevered eyes locked on the teasing tiptoed feet of the posing ladies before him.

"Poor Nigel! He fancies himself in love with Miss Spence! He once attempted an escape from his 'treatment' regimen here at Chidewell House. At the same time, he attempted to 'rescue' Miss Spence, believing her to be an innocent corrupted by our machinations. He believed that, when her duties called her to perform masturbatic manipulations upon him, she did so reluctantly!" All the women laughed at Nigel's incurable romanticism.

Miss Spence acknowledged Nigel's devotion by wiggling her bottom to and fro saucily while still maintaining the fetishistically dominant posture of exaggerated tiptoe. Nikiko's thumb and forefinger slid up and down his penis, sliding the loose skin to and fro while Mademoiselle Lange cupped his scrotum and squeezed gently. Nigel's penis reared, twitching with a compelling delight derived from Nikiko's indecent manipulations. Mademoiselle Lange noted, "He is at crisis! Continue, Nikiko, if you please!" Claire Rollin leaned forward to watch while Anna Spence and Nancy Westercroft peered backward over their shoulders to observe as well. Nigel's eyes were locked upon their feet as he moaned. A moment later, the silver bowl received the frothing jets of his seed!

Scarcely minutes later, the women stood talking while Nigel still sagged limply in his bonds, his penis still drooling a string of excitement into the bowl. Mademoiselle Lange and Nikiko had removed their satin gloves. Nancy Westercroft and Anna Spence had put their shoes back on.

Claire Rollin paid Mademoiselle Lange discreetly with a large sum in a plain envelope. "We will send a carriage for him tomorrow!"

Chapter VI

Frederick Uxbridge was famous for his dinner parties. Famous, at least, within his small circle of devoted friends. An invitation to one of his quiet yet thoroughly elegant functions was much coveted. At the rear of Chudleigh Green, a small formal dining room was situated just inside a great bow window overlooking his small, precisely patterned flower gardens. The upper tier of the bow window was entirely worked in stained glass with scenes from classical mythology. In the center of the gardens below, two marble nymphs cavorted in the small fountain that was the centerpiece of the intricate formal garden.

The round table with its snowy lace tablecloth was

set directly in the arch of the carved balcony rail, which served as one wall of the formal dining room and overlooked the indoor topiary. The great two-story bow window's intricate arches admitted sunlight during the day. The night of Frederick Uxbridge's dinner party, it admitted moonlight instead—as the full moon was just rising over the garden wall, complementing the silhouette of the spire of St. Brigid's Chapel beyond.

Frederick Uxbridge was seated with his back to the balcony rail so that his guests might fully enjoy the moonlit panorama below. Ellen Cromwell was seated directly across from him. Georgie Carstairs, the head of The Ladies' Morals Society, was seated to Frederick's right, while Josie Glade—the head of The Sexual Temperance Union, was seated to Frederick's left. All were in black formal attire of exquisite elegance as befitted the occasion. Illumination was by candlelight.

Frederick Uxbridge was considered a trifle odd by some. He employed fewer servants than some half as wealthy. Phelps, Frederick Uxbridge's trusted butler, was serving them himself.

"I am sorry if I appear preoccupied tonight," Frederick Uxbridge began somewhat reluctantly. "I have had no news from my investigative attorney, Mr. Pemberton. He had communicated to me that he believed he was close to discovering the whereabouts of my nephew Cecil. But somewhere between Blessing Hollow and Cheviot Glen, Mr. Pemberton has vanished from the earth entirely. My clageam to a Stoughton-Rollingsford railway detective of my acquaintance revealed nothing substantial, though the fellow did recall a striking woman with high-heeled boots—the like of which he had never seen for their outlandishness—arrive at the Blessing Hollow station by motorcar. Outside of this, there have been no unusual occurrences. And now I am told that the Pemberton Investigative Practice is closed and about to be sold. I believe Elizabeth to be behind this! No machination of utter wickedness would be beyond her capability. Indeed, I fear the quality that made Mr. Pemberton a very effective investigative attorney—his ability not to be noticed at all—makes the solution of his disappearance all the more unlikely. It is quite possible that Elizabeth paid someone to dispatch him entirely. I am certain that the packet he had prepared for me has been torn to tatters by now!"

Josie Glade's glance was full of concern as her violet eyes played Frederick's face as he spoke. "Were there no clues at all given you in any previous communication from Mr. Pemberton that might in some way mitigate this dreadful news?!" Georgie Carstairs turned to Frederick Uxbridge too, her face mirroring an identical concern to that which Josie Glade exhibited.

Frederick Uxbridge shifted a bit in his chair. "He did mention the possibility of there being a connection to The Ladies' Morals Society in all of this. Of course that seems absurd, for you yourselves know I am a frequent benefactor of your worthy cause. Nonetheless, is it at all possible that there could be one bad apple as it were…?" This last phrase was uttered with a lower tone and a slight flush to Frederick Uxbridge's cheeks, as if he were himself ashamed at the possible insinuation.

Georgie Carstairs replied first. "With all due respect, I believe that such a notion is simply absurd! Did you not say in an earlier conversation, Frederick, that Mr. Pemberton believed that ladies were being used to addict your nephew Cecil to unnatural vice?" Frederick nodded gravely. A slight flush crept across Ellen Cromwell's cheeks at this indelicacy. "Well, I am certain that none of our members could possibly stoop to such depths of wickedness. Such manual abuse is what we fight! Certainly any young woman that would use her charms in such wicked fashion would have been weeded from our ranks long ago!"

An awkward pause followed Georgie Carstairs's reply.

"I am certain that Frederick meant no offense whatever, and his continued support of your organization is in no way jeopardized," Ellen Cromwell said smoothly. "Perhaps this would be a good time for Phelps to appear with the first course." Phelps stepped forward from the shadows, his eyes fixed on Ellen Cromwell as he awaited her final decision on the timing of the meal.

Georgie Carstairs realized that she had perhaps defended her organization a trifle too vehemently. She patted Frederick Uxbridge's arm and gave him a charming smile. "Of course I do not take offense, Frederick. I know that you are just desperately concerned for your nephew's safety."

Josie Glade joined in, ever the diplomat. "We regard even the most trifling possibility of a connection to The Sexual Temperance Union of the Ladies' Morals Society most seriously; have no doubt of that! It is true that such wickedness is what we fight. I believe that Onanism—especially in young men—is the single greatest scourge of our nation today. We will make suitable inquiries throughout our organization, I assure you!" Josie Glade took Frederick Uxbridge's left hand and squeezed it with genuine affection. "Set your mind at ease, Frederick. Righteousness will triumph in the end, and I am certain that your nephew will reappear in due course!"

Josie Glade paused for a moment while continuing to make Frederick Uxbridge the object of her concerned and affectionate gaze. "Frederick," she said at length, "I seem to recall something that may well explain Elithorpe Pemberton's disappearance. Tell me, did he have any interest outside his investigative practice?"

Frederick Uxbridge thought for a moment. "Indeed, yes! Now that you speak of it, he had a passion for Assyriology that bordered on the fanatical. He was always poring over crumbled fragments of cuneiform, trying to decipher their inscriptions!"

"Exactly!" Josie Glade went on, her voice triumphant. "I believe you had mentioned something about his interest in archaeology when you first told us that he had undertaken your nephew's case. This is most interesting!"

"Well, don't stop now! Tell us all!" Ellen Cromwell said gently, smiling and signaling Phelps to bring the first course.

Josie Glade leaned forward and lowered her voice an octave. "I hear that Schliemann has just undertaken an expedition to the Nineveh mound and was placing advertisements in university periodicals for scholars to join him there! Do you suppose he could have forsaken his practice and his publications to fulfill his ultimate dream on the tell of the ancient Assyrian capital itself?"

Frederick Uxbridge was silent for some time, then spoke thoughtfully. "Ordinarily, I would say that it was absolutely out of the question. It is not like Elithorpe to abandon his obligations. One would think he would have at least sent me the packet by post. Yet I suppose Assyriology was his passion. His rooms were so full of fragments and texts that I often wondered where he could even lay his hat, to say nothing of his head.…"

"Well, there! See, Frederick!" Georgie Carstairs intoned. "Perhaps your dark theory of conspiracy is not sound after all. When a man of middle years sees a cherished opportunity, one can never say for certain what he will do!"

As Phelps appeared with the first course, Frederick Uxbridge apologized for the heaviness of his topic, and was soundly forgiven and absolved by his notable guests. He then graciously inquired as to the success of their current ventures.

Georgie Carstairs made a proud announcement. "Thanks to my esteemed colleague, Dr. Josephine L. Glade"—and here she nodded toward her companion, who acknowledged with a blushing smile—"through The Sexual Temperance Union, The Ladies' Morals Society has a booth at the World's Exhibition of Scientific and Medical Curiosa." Both Ellen Cromwell and Frederick graciously congratulated their friends for this significant sign that their work was being recognized, even by the foremost authorities of the day.

Then Ellen Cromwell whispered to Josie Glade. In answer to Frederick's amused inquiry about their secret, Josie Glade asked Ellen Cromwell to ring for Phelps. While they waited, Josie Glade explained, "It seems that you are sitting in a room with three lady conspirators Frederick. Georgie and I wished to procure a gift that would fit your tastes perfectly. You have ever been a gracious host and loyal friend to us and to our worthy cause. Therefore we enlisted Ellen's aid and made her an honorary coconspirator. And without further ado..." Here Josie's *expanise besture* matched perfectly the appearance of Phelps with a wrapped package.

Over the modest protests of their host, the three women insisted that he unwrap it at once. He did so, genuinely moved to find that the package contained a solid silver Steyn-Thorsson cigar service. The pedestal base of the device held a guillotine cutting mechanism for clipping the ends and a lighter secured with a short length of fine silver chain to a niche fashioned precisely to fit it. All three women insisted that Frederick neglect good form and have a smoke while waiting for the main course—just this once. At first he resisted, but they bullied him mercilessly and with great good humor until he acquiesced. Josie Glade clipped the tip of his Havana, and a moment later Georgie Carstairs lit it for him with the silver lighter.

After Frederick had finished his cigar, Phelps bent down to murmur into Ellen Cromwell's ear. She smiled. "Our main course will be a pork pâté served in a light pastry with creme sauce." Her eyes twinkled as she turned to Frederick Uxbridge. "Perhaps our guests would like to choose a claret to complement their meal rather than joining you in your obsessive devotion to Sercial Madeira!"

Frederick Uxbridge laughed and replied graciously, "Of course, my friends, of course. We have an excellent bottle of Chateau Margaux breathing now, a fifty-one, I believe and a pristine bottle of Chateau Huat-Briton—and that is a twenty-six." Both Josie Glade and Georgie Carstairs would not hear of it. They pronounced Frederick's taste for Madeira charming, and nothing would dissuade them from joining him. Ellen Cromwell was the only holdout and asked Phelps for a glass of the Margaux to complement her meal.

"Though I agree with General Booth's pamphlet that the gin houses are a scourge of our cities, still, one must not lump the fine clarets or Madeiras together with such a vile beverage. Why, gin is scarcely a cut above laudanum!" Josie Glade observed somewhat primly. Frederick Uxbridge and Georgie Carstairs nodded in solemn agreement.

Ellen Cromwell observed that many social ills stem from an excessive coddling of the lower classes and that rather than showing a proper gratitude, they lapse into lazy and lawless ways all the more. Georgie and Josie agreed, noting that the Poor Laws coming as they did in rapid succession liberated the poor only to become slaves of idleness and all manner of unnatural vice brought on by the experiencing of their newfound leisure and prosperity. "Imagine, a twelve-hour mill workday, and even that often abbreviated to nine or ten!" Josie Glade breathed, shocked at the scandal of it all. And so the dinner party continued famously. All parties delighted with both the excellent food and the witty, lighthearted social intercourse.

Chapter VII

Dale Armsworthy led Violet Naughton and Francine Glade through the mysterious carpeted upper passages of Chidewell House. Indeed, the edifice at 47 Effingham Court never ceased to delight the two young ladies. Chidewell House brimmed with arcane and experimental goings-on that fascinated the two youngest members of The Ladies' Morals Society no end. And now, as full-fledged apprentices, they were about to experience something that they just knew would be perfectly delicious.

Both young ladies and Dale Armsworthy, their mentor, were clad in similar uniforms. The severe calf-length dresses of gray wool, with their built-in buttoned gloves and high collars, were softened somewhat by lacy aprons. All three pretty women also wore high-heeled oxfords, with heels so high that they would have indeed attracted scandalous attention were they exhibited about Portland Square. Expensive silk stockings graced the ladies' legs, displaying the neat curves of their calves and their well-turned ankles to perfection.

At length, Dale Armsworthy paused before a stout oak-paneled soundproof door and produced a key from her apron pocket. She pressed the key into Francine Glade's hand. She bent toward her eager pupils and spoke softly, her voice rich with soft conspiratorial tones. "Your first real duty lies just beyond that door. I envy you both your discovery of subtle, yet outrageous pleasures. Play and explore as you will. A brief note may explain matters more once you are inside. Remember that, though unobserved, you are to act with the grace and poise of full-fledged members of The Sexual Temperance Union of The Ladies' Morals Society."

With a wink and a toss of her head, Dale Armsworthy disappeared around a bend in the upstairs corridor with a feminine grace that displayed a mastery of walking in her fetishistic high-heeled oxfords. A mastery that Violet Naughton and Francine Glade could only envy. Yet their unfamiliar, ever-so-slightly tottering and tipsy gait in their own high-heeled oxfords was every bit as delicious in its own right.

Violet and Francine lost no time in inserting the key

in the door's sturdy lock and entering the room beyond. They latched the door behind them carefully and looked about the room, perhaps a trifle disappointed at first. The room was a strange mixture of sumptuous decor and scientific contraptions that both young ladies had grown familiar with during their stay at Chidewell House under the tutelage of both Dale Armsworthy and Mademoiselle Lange. There was no sign of a note, though both pairs of eager eyes scanned the room most thoroughly. There was no sign of a potential victim either, and this disappointed the young ladies most poignantly.

Soon there attention of both Violet and Francine was drawn to a large cabinet dominating one end of the room. They approached the cabinet slowly, the light gleaming on the polished heels of their black oxfords and highlighting the affected tiptoed stance that their lovely shoes enforced.

Violet, this time the bolder of the two, grasped the brass knobs of the cabinet doors and pulled them open. Both young ladies started, then gasped at the scene that met their widening eyes. Their surprise soon gave away to delighted giggles at what the cabinet contained.

"It's the Pemberton thing!" Francine breathed between giggles. "Oh, look at him Violet!" Francine's observation was indeed correct. Elithorpe Pemberton was imprisoned in the cabinet. He was suspended in midair, hanging from a complex apparatus that was itself attached to the ceiling of the cabinet. Elithorpe Pemberton's knees were nearly drawn up to his chest, his legs splayed out to each side. He was naked save for a straitjacket that fastened his arms behind him in a helpless posture. His thighs were each bound in heavy laced cuffs of a strong woven fabric that resembled straitjacket material. The cuffs were suspended from the overhead apparatus as well, forcing his contorted and uncomfortable posture within the confines of the cabinet. This infantile contortion demanded of Elithorpe Pemberton by the rigidity of his bondage left his genitals most accessible indeed.

Both Violet and Francine feasted their eyes on the imprisoned investigative attorney's sexual organs most shamelessly. Each pretty young woman delighted in both his helplessness and his discomfiture. "Look, his penis is soft and little!" Violet exclaimed, bending forward to observe more closely in the lamplight.

"That's because Mademoiselle Lange has been subjecting him to prolonged Onanistic experiments, I shouldn't doubt!" Francine chimed in smugly.

Violet looked upward from Elithorpe Pemberton's genitals to his face. His head sagged to one side. His glasses were nowhere to be found. His eyes were open, yet glazed and an almost-idiotic expression was stamped on his features. Both young ladies, well trained in the vernacular of The Sexual Temperance Union of The Ladies' Morals Society, recognized the expression as the signature of a specimen hopelessly addicted to Onanistic manipulation.

Yet they were stumped by his inertia—even accounting for his bonds and the fixedly idiotic expression on his face. "Is he dead? Did they masturbate him to death?" Violet inquired almost hopefully.

Francine stepped forward and caressed his cheek with the palm of her gloved hand. "I don't think so, silly!" Then Francine dropped her eyes and for the first time noticed an envelope on the wide shelf beneath Elithorpe Pemberton's dangling scrotum. She opened it at once and read breathlessly to her companion.

> Dearest Violet and Francine,
>
> Do not trouble yourselves. Elithorpe Pemberton is not dead. Rather he has been injected with a paralytic drug that both deprives him of voluntary motor control and leaves him fully sensate. The effects of this chemical will not wear off for several hours. Until then, consider him your toy. Mademoiselle Lange along with Miss Spence and Miss Bates have been subjecting him to almost continuous genital massages. Mademoiselle Lange wishes you both to continue her experiments as she has been called away by other duties. Delight yourselves!
>
> Fondly,
> Dale Armsworthy

Francine Glade's eyes sparkled. "Do you know what this means, Violet?" she breathed. Then, before giving Violet

Naughton a chance to reply, she rushed on herself. "It is Dale Armsworthy's way of thanking us. It's her thoughtful gift to us that we get to toy with his genitals, in private, and with him in such a helpless pathetic state!"

"He's just our poor little Thingie now!" Violet gasped with delight. "Yes, Francine! Dale is letting us have at him for a bit because she knows that we were instrumental in Thingie's capture. We are the ones who caught him practically drooling over the boots in the shop window off Ladysmith Park. Once Dale and Mademoiselle Lange learned of his fetish for ladies high-heeled boots, the rest was easy. Dale stalked him on the train—an apple for the picking!"

Elithorpe Pemberton was perfectly cognizant of his surroundings. The depth of his despair was nearly bottomless. He knew now that his two youthful tormentors were the very same girls who had sniggered and mocked him as he stood at the ladies' clothing shop window. Indeed, they had been vital players in his capture. In large part, his subsequent subjection to slow and prolonged Onanistic manipulations was their fault.

Elithorpe Pemberton tried to move his bound and paralyzed body for the hundredth time and, as before, found that he could not. That such pretty young ladies, with sweet full lips, expressions of frank honesty, and lovely innocent eyes could delight in his helplessness and nakedness was not lost on Elithorpe Pemberton at all. Despite his misery and the slow manipulations to which he had already been addictively subjected, his penis began to lengthen and rise, pointing increasingly upward from between his legs.

Of course, Thingie's erecting sex organ was not ignored by either Violet Naughton or Francine Glade. The room was soon filled with stifled giggles and mocking references to decency and morality. Violet and Francine both bent succulently at the waist, their faces alive with knowing delight to observe the process from close proximity.

A few moments later, Elithorpe Pemberton hung in his bonds, his penis thick and fully erect, his testicles dangling below in absolute vulnerability. After the curious young ladies feasted their eyes on his most private attributes, they began to explore the secrets of the cabinet which contained their victim.

Violet pointed out the shiny brass plate affixed to the upper portion of the cabinet's base: LADIES' DELIGHT: SIMPLY THE FINEST BRAND OF SCIENTIFIC SPECIMEN CABINETS IN THE WORLD TODAY. The young ladies discovered a recessed drawer just beneath the shelf over which their victim was suspended. To their delight, the drawer contained a precisely weighted scale, some linen clothes, a tiny buckled ring with a lead weight attached, and several little rubber-throated, round-bottomed glass bottles in a walnut rack built especially to accommodate them.

The pretty young ladies—one the niece of the famed research physician Dr. Josephine L. Glade, and the other the niece of Georgina Carstairs, the founder and head of The Sexual Temperance Union of The Ladies' Morals Society—knew immediately what the last two items in the drawer were. The first was a scrotal weight that could be used to increase the duration and intensity of the male orgasm. The second was a set of semen-collection bottles of precisely equal measure that could be used to measure the weight of sperm samples ejaculated in successive male orgasms. Both young ladies determined to put the items to good use.

Francine Glade discovered that doors on the back of the cabinet, identical to those on the front, could be opened to give access to both the front and rear parts of their prisoner. They divided their toys. Francine Glade took the scrotal weights, and Violet Naughton got the specimen bottles. Both young ladies would share the scale and planned to give a detailed report to Mademoiselle Lange on the weight of each consecutive semen sample that they masturbated out of their new toy.

Elithorpe Pemberton was ever so weak. His genitals had been but the playthings of successive teams of lovely young ladies. His initial panic at the injection of the paralytic drug by Mademoiselle Lange soon gave way to a hopeless addiction to the manual pleasures that had been forced upon him. He would have gladly sacrificed his most sacred possession—a cuneiform tablet dating from the reign of Sargon II—for some giggly uncaring trollop to stimulate his genitals once again.

Despite his pleasures, Elithorpe Pemberton was worried. His uncle, the vicar of Whitworth Abbey, had been an avid reader of the works of Tissot, and was not at all remiss at sharing the warnings of the dreadful consequences of Onanistic indulgence. The fact that the women of Chidewell House delighted in performing Onanistic manipulations of him—combined with his knowledge of Onanism's debilitating effects—sparked a part of Elithorpe Pemberton's nature that could accurately be called masochistic. Despite his experience of addictive pleasure, Elithorpe Pemberton was worried that, were he to survive his captivity at all, he would be rendered either an imbecile or a weakling.

Were he able to, Elithorpe Pemberton would have squirmed with helpless delight when Francine Glade reached through beneath his buttocks from behind to fasten the testicular weight-bearing ring to his scrotum. Her gloved fingertips invaded his privacy most willingly, and he found the sensation of the young lady's touch most poignant indeed. Though his testicles were compressed together, causing slightly painful cramps to ripple through his abdomen, the sensation of his scrotum being drawn downward and stretched taut produced a most compellingly pleasurable sensation. Francine was not content to abandon his scrotum once the weights were fastened on, but rather amused herself by placing it on her gloved palm and subjecting it to gentle squeezings and manipulations. Francine raised one pretty leg to rest her knee on the shelf over which her victim was suspended. She licked her lips and savored her secret pleasures.

Violet Naughton reached out her gloved hand to take Thingie by his sexual organ. The contrast between Violet's pristinely starched gloves, buttoned to her immaculate uniform sleeves, and her captive's turgid sex organ, each vein swollen outward in exaggerated three-dimensional relief, was most indecent indeed.

For that matter, the humiliating posture of their bound and suspended naked victim, when contrasted with the pretty young ladies' own proper attire, was poignant as well. The young ladies exhibited no bare skin at all, save for their faces. Their calves and ankles were clothed in the expensive sheen of their silk stockings, which emphasized the feminine curves of their well-formed limbs. The uniform dresses with their proper aprons were fitted tightly enough to the young ladies' feminine forms to show off the inviting curves of hips, breasts, and bottoms. The fact that two such exquisite young ladies could delight themselves addicting a helpless experimentation subject to Onanistic degradation was bizarre in the extreme.

Violet slipped a specimen bottle over the bloated purple tip of Thingie's penis, held it steady with one hand, and with her other hand began to draw his foreskin to and fro. Violet's eyes scanned her paralyzed captive's face closely, searching for any sign of helpless pleasure that she could gloat over as her wicked fingers abused his sex organ. Francine's active fingers were busy as well from behind. She subjected Elithorpe Pemberton's shaved scrotum to furtive twists and squeezes. In his paralyzed state, he could not even writhe!

Violet's avidly searching gaze was rewarded as she found what she sought: expressive evidence that their combined manipulations were inducing vivid sensations of helplessly addictive pleasure that completely conquered their paralyzed victim. A sheen of perspiration glistened on Thingie's forehead. He was breathing heavily. As the manustupration continued, Elithorpe Pemberton began to drool. The specimen bottle bobbed almost comically, imprisoning the tip of his sex organ.

Chapter VIII

Maximillian Phelps lay naked from the waist down, as the morning sunlight spilled through the diamond-shaped panes of his window and laid dappled patterns across the far wall of his room His situation was undignified to the point of ridiculousness. His nightshirt had been tucked up about his chest. He lay rigidly upon his back, his hands at his sides, with a neatly folded towel resting on his stomach. A chair had been pulled up close, and placed directly beside his bed. A small table stood beside the chair. A jar of petrolatum rested on its surface alongside a bowl containing warm water and a bar of floating soap. A second and third small towel were folded neatly beside the bowl.

Maximillian Phelps's penis was very thick and very short. It was surrounded by a dense dark tangle of hair that covered his abdomen. His scrotum hung low, his testicles splayed on the pristine white sheet beneath him. He lay still, concentrating on willing his slowly thickening, lengthening penis to soften. His face was a mask of purposeful concentration.

Outside his window in the gravel drive below, Josie Glade and Georgie Carstairs waited in Frederick Uxbridge's motorcar while he turned the crank. Frederick and Ellen's notable guests had asked to be returned to the headquarters of The Sexual Temperance Union of The Ladies' Morals Society on Primrose Lane so that they could prepare for an award ceremony before the Lord Mayor and the aldermen. The tireless work that they did on behalf of the nation's moral structure was being recognized at last.

The engine of the motorcar caught, then sputtered into life. Frederick Uxbridge climbed into the driver's seat, released the brake, and they were off. The dinner party had ended cordially with a reaffirmation of friendship between the four. Ellen Cromwell enjoyed a light breakfast with Frederick and their guests, but had declined to ride along on the drive back to Primrose Lane. She had other business to tend to.

There was a tap at his door, and Maximillian Phelps swallowed hard. The door opened. Ellen Cromwell stepped into his room without waiting for a reply. She wore a long white apron that covered her from chin to knee. Her hair was up in an impeccable twist without a single strand out of place.

Ellen Cromwell smiled, "Good morning, Phelps! It appears to be a lovely day!" Maximillian Phelps swallowed hard for a second time. Ellen Cromwell moved to sit on the upholstered chair at his bedside.

"Yes, Miss...a lovely day indeed—thank you, Miss." Ellen Cromwell was fond of Maximillian Phelps, and he was dearly devoted to her. In fact, it was said by more than one Chudleigh Green dinner-party guest that he could read her mind, almost divining her wishes and making it unnecessary for her to utter them.

The sight of Ellen Cromwell's supple feminine form in the starched high-collared apron had interfered most significantly with Maximillian Phelps' resolve that his sexual organ remain soft. Already thick and short, it thickened considerably more while lengthening but a trifle. His foreskin remained forward, however, keeping the expanding head of his penis painfully constricted.

Such was the extent of the closeness between the two—fond mistress and devoted servant—that when she saw him apparently in significant pain one afternoon, she badgered him mercilessly until he broke down and told her, blushing furiously, the source of his discomfiture. Rather than being repelled by the intensely private nature of his affliction, Maximillian Phelps found Ellen Cromwell to be at once both sympathetic and concerned.

To his utter surprise, she told him that she should help him with his problem herself, and that she would take great care to minimize the possibility of lewdly pleasurable sensations in so doing. Ellen Cromwell declared that having another assist him with his problem of phimosis would go far in assuring that the necessary manipulations would not lead to addiction to solitary vice.

And so an intensely private little ritual developed between the loyal butler and his trusted mistress. Twice each week, Ellen Cromwell would assist Phelps with therapeutic manipulations designed to ease the symptoms of his condition. Phelps had even once inquired as to whether or not the problem could be corrected surgically. Ellen Cromwell stated that it could most assuredly; however, she strongly advised against a surgical solution. She had lowered her voice and her cheeks had flushed ever so slightly as she stated that the intimate postoperative care that matrons would have to give him following any such circumcision, combined with the pain of the procedure itself, would risk inculcating a masochistic bent in his sexual nature. Indeed, Ellen Cromwell had heard of lewd matrons who were not above taking delight in performing wicked manipulations on their patients who, upon discharge from the hospital, found themselves hopelessly given over to manual self-abuse as a result.

Ellen Cromwell opened the jar of petrolatum and

robbed a bit between her palms and fingertips until they fairly glistened. Maximillian Phelps was at full erection now. He squirmed ever so slightly, a consequence both of deep embarrassment and the pain of his unfortunate condition.

His mistress chided him gently. "I have told you repeatedly, Phelps, that it requires the most diligent exercise of the moral will to subdue the lewd impulses manifested in permitting tumescence. I see that you have failed in this instance to quell that carnal urge." She leaned forward, her eyes liquid with deep concern. She reached out to take his scrotum in one glistening, lubricated hand while his thick penis was grasped by the other. "Have you been performing your breathing exercises when such urges come upon you?"

Maximillian Phelps gasped involuntarily at her touch. She began to apply more lubrication to his foreskin and, ever so slowly, attempted to ease it back with gentle pressure. He collected himself at length to reply. His heart thudded and his voice was thick with a mixture of acute embarrassment and sensual pleasure. "I shall try harder, Miss."

Ellen Cromwell smiled down at Phelps fondly. All the while her hands continued their intimate efforts upon the most private part of his person. "Of course you will, Phelps, of course you will. And I know that you do try gallantly to master your baser urges. If continued diligently, your efforts will bear fruit, I assure you!"

Ellen Cromwell had applied even more petrolatum to her servant's genital, and now both glistening hands gently yet insistently worked his foreskin, easing it back just a trifle. Ellen Cromwell continued, her voice casual and friendly. "When the urge to erect comes upon you, remember the three basic steps. One: Clench your fists. Two: Take a deep breath and hold it. Three: Tighten the muscles just behind your scrotum and grit your teeth. Of course, these methods may not work now, for it is a necessity for me to have to handle you in this manner as part of your therapeutic treatment. Still, the three-step method is tried and true, and will help you in your battle to maintain personal virtue."

Here Maximillian Phelps interrupted his pretty mistress. "Miss…miss…. Please! I—"

Ellen Cromwell snatched her glistening hands away from her servant's engorged privates at once. "Have the lewd sensations come upon you again, Phelps?"

His face was crimson. His chest heaved. He gulped. "Yes, Miss, I had to warn you. Had you continued, I fear I might have—"

"Soiled my hands and your own person no doubt," Ellen Cromwell said crisply. "It was good of you to warn me. I shall pause in my ministrations to give the sensations time to pass."

Ellen Cromwell smiled down at him. "Remember that these are most certainly not indecent manipulations for the purpose of gratifying prurient desires. Rather, these are morally helpful manipulations, however intimate they must, of necessity, be."

And so the slow genital manipulations continued with frequent gasps from Phelps that Ellen Cromwell should stop a moment and wait. But at last her dutiful labors bore the fruit. Phelps's foreskin had worked back completely.

Ellen Cromwell did not yet congratulate herself or consider her proceedings completed. She worked a good amount of petrolatum all about the exposed head of her trusted servant's penis, causing him no doubt the most poignant yet unavoidable sensations. She also applied more lubrication to his foreskin and worked it to and fro, uncovering and covering the glans a good many more times to assure the task was complete. During these procedures Maximillian Phelps lay rigid, slack-jawed, with his eyes glazed. Ellen Cromwell's soft glistening hands most suavely agitated the great thick sex organ they held prisoner—an agitation of kind necessity of course.

On four separate occasions, it was necessary for Ellen Cromwell to wipe away the thin string of arousal that secreted from the engorged purple tip of the butler's penis. Of course, each time it was necessary for her to do so, she chided him fondly yet firmly for his too-quick surrender to lewd sensations.

At last, Ellen Cromwell was finished, and while Maximillian Phelps lay panting and erect, yet much eased of his painful constricture, she washed her hands with the soap and warm water, then wiped them fastidiously on the towel. She stood up and patted Maximillian Phelps's arm warmly. "When you have dressed and put the chair, table and water away, you may continue with your general household duties." With that, his pretty mistress backed away modestly from his room and closed the door softly behind her. Though manifestly proper from the front, her apron left her broad bottom almost bare; and since she had not yet dressed for the day, the apron was her only garment.

As Maximillian Phelps wiped the excess lubricant from his privates and then set about cleaning up the residue of Ellen Cromwell's manipulative treatment, his mistress herself was seated naked on the plush velour cushions of a window seat under a small bow window at the back of her suite of rooms. She drew her legs up beside her and looked down over the formal garden below her window.

Ellen Cromwell was determined to champion the cause of decency whenever and wherever possible. Her tireless work with Maximillian Phelps was but one aspect of her determination. Ellen Cromwell believed that self-abuse was the foundation of many social ills that plagued society. She had recently attended a lecture where it was stated in no uncertain terms that manustupration squandered the best seed, and the seed that remained to impregnate the future wife of a masturbator was inferior seed and resulted in morally and physically weak offspring and, not infrequently, idiocy in the children themselves. The speaker at the lecture had further assured his audience, Ellen Cromwell included, that the more chronic the masturbatory indulgence, the more devastating the effects visited upon the offspring—all caused from their fertilization of the egg by inferior male seed. The speaker went on to say that empires fell when they slipped into moral decadence, not necessarily from the decadence itself, or any Heavenly judgment upon it, but rather from the best of the nation's seed being spilled through lewd self-manipulations. The speaker also hinted darkly that performing genital manipulation on another was akin to murdering the subject's best and brightest offspring.

At the reception following the Morals Crusade meeting, Ellen Cromwell determined to begin atoning for past wickednesses. She adjusted her position on the velour cushions of her window seat, kneeling now, sitting on her bare heels, her buttocks pouting cheekily above the arched soles of her trim bare feet. She rested her chin on her forearms and looked down over the garden below. Ellen Cromwell could feel that her nipples were erect. Her nipples were always erect after she assisted Phelps with the intimacy of his private affliction.

Ten years before, during an extended stay at the Hotel Alcazar, Ellen Cromwell had performed just such lewd manipulations on a member of the opposite sex. It did not matter that the manipulations were performed at the urging of her sophisticated cousin Juliana. It also did not matter that Juliana had stated a most logical reason for their necessity.

Juliana Hand's fiancé was a famed operatic tenor named Montague Wyvern. Ellen Cromwell, then barely eighteen years of age, was delighted when her wealthy cousin Juliana offered to share her hotel suite with her. Their suite was on the same floor as that occupied by Montague Wyvern and his operatic mentor, an elderly Neapolitan who had achieved great fame at the summit of his own career years before.

As the older and wealthier of the two, Juliana Hand was more than a trifle jaded and almost impossible to shock. However, Ellen Cromwell was stunned when one evening just before one of Monty's performances, Juliana produced a narrow volume bound in burgundy leather that depicted scenes of sensual acts—scandalous in the extreme!

Ellen Cromwell gaped as her cousin flipped through the pages of explicit text, interspersed with more exquisite line drawings, all depicting the same type of sexual act: women manipulating the aroused genitals of bound and contorted men. The women were all fully dressed and their facial expressions were placid and complacent, in stark contrast to the anguished longing stamped on the faces of their unfortunate subjects.

Later that same evening, all through the opera, Ellen

found that the lurid images still burned in her mind and distracted her from an elaborately staged performance of Ernest Reyer's *Fervaal*. The performance was generally well received, though Monty's tenor solos were not quite up to par—certainly adequate, but not outstanding. Ever the perfectionist, Montague Wyvern fell into a rather unseemly despair following their performance. Ellen was supportive. Ever the cool head, Juliana appeared in deep thought.

Then, Ellen Cromwell's cousin Juliana combined her powers of persuasion with her ability to make the most outrageous schemes seem not only practical but sensible as well. She suggested that if her fiancé Montague Wyvern were subjected to genital manipulations to the point of seminal emission before each operatic performance, the range and power of his voice would be enhanced, especially toward the highest end of the tenor scale. Further, it would lead to weakness of character were Monty to perform the manipulations upon himself, and it would be a compromise to the chaste relationship they enjoyed until marriage, were Juliana to manipulate her fiancé.

Ellen Cromwell gasped when Juliana suggested that she was the only logical candidate to perform the genital manipulations. Before she could regain her composure and voice her objections, Juliana's smooth voice was saying, "Of course this act would not be for the generation of prurient pleasure, but rather to enhance the tonal range, and tenacity of a God-given gift."

Such were her cousin's powers of persuasion that scarcely a day later, Ellen Cromwell found herself performing the intimate service that was but an outrageous concept when the idea was first broached.

The ritual developed simply and unfolded quite the same way before each performance. Ellen Cromwell and her cousin Juliana Hand sat side by side on a comfortable scroll-armed settee in their Hotel Alcazar suite. Montague Wyvern would present himself, naked from the waist down. After he assumed the knee-chest position on the rich carpet at the feet of his fully dressed fiancée and her cousin, the manipulations would begin. Ellen Cromwell would first draw on white kidskin gloves, as it would be highly improper for her to actually touch Monty's genitals with her bare hands. The uniquely humiliating position that Juliana had Monty assume left his genitals perfectly vulnerable to the hands of his young manipulator. Indeed, his scrotal sac dangled in full view of both young women while his slender, though thickening penis was near at hand as well. Juliana always supervised the manipulative proceedings. It took but a very few minutes before Monty contorted at their feet and his sperm spilled up across his stomach.

Ellen Cromwell attained proficiency in this manipulative act almost at once. Looking back on those events of years ago, Ellen regarded her quickly attained expertise to be a manifestation of some inherent tendency to vice, hidden in her nature. That Montague Wyvern suffered the most compelling sensations while contorted at their feet, there could be no doubt whatever. Despite the operatic tenor's own naked vulnerability, Juliana Hand made certain that Ellen Cromwell was always attired in the most modest fashion when she performed the masturbation.

Soon Ellen Cromwell began to secretly enjoy performing this debasing act upon her cousin's fiancé and derived a furtive guilty pleasure from the exercise of her newfound duties. Strangely enough, the quality of Monty's tenor solos did seem to improve, and his voice was clear and pristine on even the very highest notes. At the same time, it seemed to both Ellen and Juliana that Monty was weakened ever so slightly due to the manipulations before each performance. He appeared to lack a bit in willpower and was cowed more easily both in disagreements of an artistic nature with his operatic peers, and in minor disputes with his fiancée. Ellen Cromwell continued to tell herself that she was performing a vital service, and helping Montague attain the fame that he had always strived for—with every part of his being— and certainly deserved.

Ellen Cromwell secretly had adored the helpless look of naked passion on Monty's face as his penis reared in her daintily little kid-gloved hand—helpless to escape her firm manipulations. She was covertly amused at the low dangle of his scrotum as it bounced against his bare bottom in time to each stroke of her hand on his penis. When the sensations mastered him and he ejaculated, more often than not, Ellen Cromwell's eyes were on the slack-jawed, glassy-eyed expression of his face than on the strangled purple tip of his penis as it disgorged its jets of seed up across his stomach and abdomen. All the while Monty remained rigid in the infantile posture of the knee-chest position at their feet, obedient to the last detail.

Ellen Cromwell smiled, her attention momentarily wavering from her reverie by the sight of a lovely songbird scarcely two yards from her window. She shifted position to watch it more closely. The broad pallor of the cheeks of her bare bottom contrasted exquisitely with the shadowed cleft that separated them. Ellen Cromwell's nipples were still erect. At length she returned to her shameful memories.

All in all, she had masturbated Montague Wyvern dozens of times. He became addicted to the "pleasures of the hand" in a very real sense. Years later, Ellen realized that her cousin Juliana had thoroughly despised Monty, and though they married later, Juliana bore him scant real affection. Juliana referred laughingly to the manipulations Ellen performed on Monty as "making him a temporary castrato." Juliana had attached herself to Monty, not out of genuine regard, but rather to ride the coattails of his fame and thus increase her own social standing. In this she was successful. Monty achieved a great deal of fame, and Juliana's receptions were legendary.

Ellen sat up and stretched languidly. Her pear-shaped breasts culminating in very large nipples. She had last seen Juliana and Monty at one of Juliana's receptions two years before. Juliana laughed at the way Monty kissed Ellen's hand in greeting, as if renewing a pleasurable memory. Ellen Cromwell's cheeks flushed from the very recollection. She had also glimpsed Juliana and Monty's pimple-faced boy, peering over an upstairs banister at the dazzling throng below, of which she was a part.

The sight of the boy filled Ellen Cromwell with pangs of guilt. Perhaps the morals lecturer was right in his assertion that performing genital manipulation on another was akin to murdering the subject's best and brightest offspring. Had she not succumbed to her cousin's depraved logic and become a fiendish exponent of moral wickedness, perhaps this poor pale, awkward boy, gawking over the banister, then blushing crimson, would have been a strong, confident lad instead. From then on, Ellen Cromwell was committed to a course of moral decency.

Chapter IX

Twenty-four hours after the dinner party that Frederick Uxbridge and Ellen Cromwell held for Josie Glade, the noted physician specializing in sexual neurosis, and Georgie Carstairs, the nationally recognized head of The Sexual Temperance Union of The Ladies' Morals Society, Frederick's nephew, Cecil Uxbridge, found himself in a most disquieting predicament.

He lay naked on a cold table in a clinical room that fairly bristled with arcane medical contraptions and instruments of scientific curiosity, trussed in the implacable and pitiless embrace of a heavy woven straitjacket, and acutely uncomfortable as the device wrapped both of his arms about him with such tightness that he could barely breathe. He was terribly conscious of his bare genitals as they dangled vulnerably due to his forced assumption of the ridiculously infantile knee-chest position. His assumption of the knee-chest position was involuntary; specialized straps sewn firmly to the shoulder portion of his straitjacket had been buckled to matching loops, themselves attached to strong fabric belts that encompassed Cecil's upper thighs.

Despite his nakedness below the waist, Cecil's main concern was that he might topple from the experimentation table—the surface was barely smaller than the area of his back—and hurt himself, bound and contorted, on the hard cold tiles of the floor below.

He need not have concerned himself. To his right, arms folded primly, stood Mademoiselle Lange. She was clad in her signature uniform of a stylish black dress with a high collar of intricately worked lace. An immaculately starched white apron covered her from her breasts to her calves. Her hair was twisted up impeccably in a swirl without a single strand out of place. Her wrists and hands were clothed nearly to the elbow in gleaming black examination gloves of India rubber. Her ensemble was completed by elegant stockings and black patent leather oxfords with immodestly high heels.

Mademoiselle Lange arched her pencil thin, precisely arched eyebrows and pursed her perfect lips. Cecil Uxbridge had begun to voice his concern at the prospect of falling from the examination table. Mademoiselle

Lange stepped closer to him, her dress clinging to the curves of her hips and buttocks. She delivered a stinging slap to his right cheek with her India rubber-gloved hand. "I told you to be silent!" she said matter-of-factly, her voice low.

Across the examination table from Mademoiselle Lange, Anika Bates, standing on Cecil's left, nodded approvingly. Anika Bates was a striking young woman. She was clad in the uniform of the Chidewell House matron: a severe calf-length dress of gray wool with a high collar and built-in buttoned gloves, accessorized with a lace apron, elegant stockings, and patent leather oxfords with outrageously high heels. Anika Bates had a very fair complexion, and this, combined with her jet black hair that hung almost to her bottom when let down, accounted, at least in part, for her striking appearance. Her aspect was also noteworthy in that her eyebrows were very dark and quite thick, lending to her face a quality of severity that its inherent sweetness would otherwise have negated. Mademoiselle Lange found Anika Bates, along with Anna Spence, who was not present, to be her indispensable assistants in the bizarre duties constituting the Chidewell House regimen. Indeed, Mademoiselle Lange was known to refer to the pretty young matrons, Miss Bates and Miss Spence, as "my two Annas."

Anika Bates looked down at Cecil's reddening cheek approvingly and then walked to a side cabinet. She undid the cuff buttons that secured her gray uniform gloves to her sleeves, removed them one at a time, and replaced them with gleaming gloves of India rubber, identical to those worn by Mademoiselle Lange. Cecil fought down the urge to squirm in his bonds. He knew that any attempt to free himself would be in vain. He was bound and watched over by two lovely, severe women. Still he did not like the look of the gleaming gloves—not in the least! He was becoming more and more aware of his bare genitals.

He swallowed hard.

At the direction of Mademoiselle Lange, Anika Bates moved back to the examination table on which Cecil Uxbridge was bound, pushing a small cart that moved easily on silent wheels. On its surface was an unfolded immaculate white cloth containing instruments of medical examination and experimentation. Cecil did not like the look of the instruments, but he did notice the way the light in the room reflected from the high heels of Miss Bates's oxfords and the way her stylish shoes emphasized the curves of her calves and the fine turn of her ankles.

Then the door opened. Dr. Josephine L. Glade stepped into the room! She was clad in a black calf-length skirt, a gray tweed vest, a white blouse with a round collar, and a black tie. Sheer silk stockings graced her legs, and her feet were attired in black lace-up shoes with heels of outrageous height. The shoes were cut low on her feet in an exaggerated version of the rage then sweeping

Paris. Josie Glade's left hand and arm were both clad beyond the elbow in a single shining India rubber examination glove. Her right hand was bare. In it, she held a battered leather-bound notebook and an expensive fountain pen. However, the most striking feature of Josie Glade's costume was the black mask that concealed the upper portion of her face and the black velvet cloth that draped down from the mask and concealed the lower portion as well.

Josie Glade and Mademoiselle Lange exchanged the easy greetings of familiar friends. In fact, there was a secret association between certain members of The Ladies' Morals Society on Primrose Lane and Mademoiselle Lange, Dale Armsworthy, and the matrons of Chidewell House at 47 Effingham Court, just off Portland Square. The Ladies' Morals Society camp, best represented by Josie Glade, were well aware that Mademoiselle Lange was employed by stepmothers and jealous half-sisters to addict young male heirs aged eighteen to twenty-one to the vice of manual abuse through constant manipulations by designated maids or matrons, and the inculcation of fetishism as a reinforcement.

Once totally addicted to the unnatural vice of forced manipulations performed on them by the wicked female accomplices of their spiteful relatives, the young males' pallid complexions and weakening constitutions, combined with their downcast, indecisive demeanors were all that was necessary—once the proper insinuations were interjected—to have them declared the wards of the very female relatives who had engineered their downfalls. The stepmothers and half-sisters, now with unrestricted access to their victims' very fortunes, found themselves most generous in repaying Mademoiselle Lange and her matrons for their invaluable services.

The Ladies' Morals Society, while not approving of the callous defilement of the moral purity of myriad young men, found the victims of Chidewell House invaluable research subjects in the effects of prolonged Onanistic manipulations and pathologically induced fetishism. Suffice it to say The Sexual Temperance Union believed that the wickedness that transpired in the cellars and attic rooms of Chidewell House would at least bear a bit of good fruit were the accurately observed results documented in pamphlet form and used in the oral reinforcement of the entire nation. In truth, as Josie Glade often said, "Onanism is the scourge of our Sceptered Isle!" And how better to document its effects than by close observation of them firsthand.

Josie Glade customarily observed the specimens collected for the purpose of being subjected to manustupratic manipulations before and after their regimen began. In this way, she would have a baseline of comparison for scientific documentation of the ill effects. Through warnings in public morals meetings of The Sexual Temperance Union, the sacrifice of but one specimen could save many an unfortunate from the debaucheries of manual abuse that ominously threatened the nation's genetic pool. Josie Glade was a woman of science and had often steeled herself and set her resolve against her natural urge to uncover and expose this wicked trade in the moral uprightness of a few young men—and all for the greater good!

Despite his desperate wishes to the contrary, Cecil Uxbridge's penis responded rather obviously to the sight of Dr. Josephine L. Glade. It rose and lurched to erection in a matter of two or three seconds in direct contradiction of his conscious will. His two female captors noticed it at once, as did Josie Glade—the object of his prurient affection.

Josie Glade bent forward to observe his erection more closely. Her voice was clinical, though beneath her mask, a smile teased about the corners of her pretty lips. "His erectile response has all the urgency of satyriasis."

Mademoiselle Lange nodded. "We have not yet embarked upon his full regimen of manual abuse. We wished to give him a few days to become more acclimated to his new surroundings, and we wished you to have a chance to subject him to a thorough examination before we had induced any taint to his character."

Josie Glade did not approve of Mademoiselle Lange's direct admission of deliberate debauchery. However, her disciplined mind overcame her natural repugnance and progressed logically. "I cannot subject him to either an adequate or a thorough examination with the straitjacket on him. Perhaps you have another harness that could be used to ensure his confinement, yet that would allow me more access to his person?"

Mademoiselle Lange stepped to a large medical cupboard and returned to Cecil's examination table with a complete harness bristling with heavy buckles and fashioned of wide straps of supple new leather. While Josie Glade watched, arms folded, Mademoiselle Lange and Miss Bates divested Cecil of his straitjacket. Any illusions he may have had about leaping down from the examination table once the straitjacket was undone, and running naked—with an erection—down the corridors of Chidewell House, then bolting through the front doors and dashing down the steps onto the bustle of Portland Square—were shattered by the firm efficiency of his two captors. Once the straitjacket was unfastened, Cecil found his arms too numb to be of much use at all in effecting an escape. Nonetheless, Miss Bates held his wrists in an iron grip while Mademoiselle Lange placed him in the harness.

As Mademoiselle Lange buckled the straps of the harness about his person—with no more thought of his dignity than a nursemaid would give a child or an asylum matron would give an inmate—Cecil's entire consciousness became one vast realization of intense shame. He willed his erection to subside over and over again, but it did not. His scrotum lolled against his thighs as Mademoiselle Lange pulled him this way and that, raising him and prodding him as necessary, just to subject him to a new form of humiliating bondage. His hard penis pointed toward the gaslights suspended from the ceiling as a smiling Anika Bates, seeming to take delight in his every indignity, held him firmly and supported him from falling off the narrow experimentation table.

Mademoiselle Lange fastened a thick leather belt about his waist. It was attached to two straps that ran up over both his shoulders and came down across his chest to rejoin the belt in the front. Another strap was passed about the hollow of his knees so that he could again be placed in the naked shame of the knee-chest position, as the strap about his knees was fastened to his chest harness. Finally, his wrists were secured by two smaller straps that buckled to the harness at his shoulders so that he was trussed firmly and absolutely helpless.

Cecil's erection had not subsided in the least. Something about the stern and mysterious aspect lent to the masked woman affected Cecil's sensibilities most dramatically. The contrast between the tasteful propriety of the women's costumes, combined with the outrageous immodesty of their high-heeled shoes, heated Cecil's desires and increased the effect of the mask. To Cecil, Josie Glade was an enigma, and the mask lent her qualities that made her appearance all the more mysterious and sadistic. Cecil struggled futilely against his bonds, making the supple new leather creak a bit. Mademoiselle

Lange and Miss Bates laughed at his efforts. Josie Glade busied herself writing in the leather-bound notebook with her fountain pen.

As Miss Bates watched over him with the gleeful eyes of an uncaring jailer, Mademoiselle Lange assisted Dr. Josephine Glade in subjecting Cecil to a very slow and detailed physical examination—an examination that gave no consideration whatever to its subject's dignity or sensibilities, an examination that violated his person repeatedly and most invasively.

Josie Glade listened to Cecil's heartbeat, felt and prodded the lymph glands under his jaw, inserted her gloved fingers into his mouth to grasp his tongue and draw it out for closer inspection. She pummeled and prodded his chest, sides and abdomen, felt his legs and the joints and muscles of his arms. She had him breathe deeply in and out until he grew quite faint and told her so. All the while, she made notations in her leather-bound book. All the while, Cecil's penis remained shamefully erect.

After measuring his head with wide metal calipers and passing her palms repeatedly over and about his skull, searching for protuberances, Josie Glade pronounced him apparently free of cerebral anomalies. She said his head showed no inclination of rhombic distortion, and that both his parietal and frontal lobes appeared normal in every way.

After Cecil responded to certain probing questions, Josie Glade told Mademoiselle Lange that he seemed to be in very good health altogether. She pronounced his skeleton entirely masculine, noted that there was little hair on his trunk, but that his pelvis was narrow and masculine and his shoulders average. Josie Glade saw no evidence of either hereditary taint or congestion of the head. In response to a second wave of questions, she was able to determine that Cecil was not tabetic, nervous, incontinent, or melancholic. He had no symptoms of neuralgia or manifestations of psychical degeneration. Returning to his skull once again—Josie Glade was also an enthusiastic student of phrenology—she noted that Cecil's occiput exhibited no abnormalities. Close inspection of his eyes and ears revealed no ocular or auditory irregularities.

Then, to Cecil's intense shame and horror, the examination focused on his private parts. As he lay tense, blushing, but still hugely erect, Mademoiselle Lange assisted Josie Glade in applying generous dollops of petrolatum to the gleaming fingertips of her black rubber-gloved hand. Anika Bates smiled smugly down at Cecil all the while, gloating over what was in store for him, her gloved hands pressing him firmly down at the shoulders.

As Josie Glade approached, the glistening fingers of her gleaming glove raised almost fastidiously in the air, Cecil squirmed unavailingly and pleaded for mercy. Mademoiselle Lange delivered a second stinging slap to his cheek and told him to be silent. Anika Bates's facial expression had become a hypocritical mask of mock pity.

Miss Bates continued to hold Cecil down against the experimentation table by pressing his shoulders down firmly. Mademoiselle Lange moved to the foot of the table and spread Cecil's bare buttocks. Josie Glade stepped forward daintily in her lace-up shoes with their outrageously high heels, her lubricated glove at the ready.

A moment later, Cecil jerked and grunted as Dr. Josie Glade slowly inserted first one lubricated finger, then two, then three, into the clenching resistance of his most intimate orifice. To his intense discomfort and amplified shame, Josie Glade was not content to hold her fingers still in his rectum, but rather probed him most firmly, searching thoroughly for any signs of abnormality, even in that most private place.

Cecil's penis twitched and jerked, its head swelling purple to even greater dimensions. A small bead of moisture oozed from the gasping slit in the tip of Cecil's penis and dribbled down the tip. "I have stimulated a reproductive gland found adjacent to the rectum in males," Josie Glade noted clinically. Despite her clinical tone, a crimson flush was creeping across Josie Glade's cheeks beneath her mask.

Josie Glade would never admit it even to herself, but she took a secret guilty pleasure in what she was doing to the helpless young man who lay squirming on the table. She enjoyed being fully, properly, even stylishly clad herself while subjecting her naked victim to the utmost indignities. Had she even admitted her secret feelings to herself, Josie Glade would simply have dismissed them as irrelevant and not allowed them to impede the progress of her deliberate and exhaustive scientific studies. After all, she did such things solely to ensure the moral health of her nation.

Cecil lay erect, drenched with perspiration. As the rectal examination continued, he was seized with an almost overwhelming urge to void his bowels. Of course he did not actually need to do what his urge seemed to demand. Rather it was his body's instinct to repel this most intimate of invasions.

At last Josie Glade considered her probing to be complete. She had detected no sign of ill health, no abnormalities of any kind. "Now, Cecil," she said calmly. "I want you to expel my fingers from your person by tensing your sphincter, as if your body was completing a normal function of waste elimination." His vivid discomfort made Cecil only too willing to obey. In fact, the sensations he was experiencing compelled him to comply. His entire body tensed as he grunted and contorted. Mademoiselle Lange and Miss Bates both stifled their laughter as he freed himself at last in this most undignified way.

Josie Glade removed the used glove and put on another, wiggling her fingers primly and drawing it up past her elbow once again. She was smiling beneath her mask. Cecil lay gasping with relief. The sexual sensations he had experienced as Josie Glade's fingers plopped free of his bottom were so powerful that he had been in imminent danger of spilling his seed then and there before his three tormentors. Cecil Uxbridge shuddered at the thought.

Yet still baser indignities were in store for Cecil Uxbridge before the long-sought end of his naked exam would come. Josie Glade next turned her attention to his sexual organs. She instructed Mademoiselle Lange to gather both his scrotum and his erect penis in her gloved hand and hold them for her, exhibiting and turning them about as necessary. Cecil lay rigid in his bonds, gasping at the unfamiliar sensation of someone else handling his private parts. Cecil was desperately afraid that before this most unbearable portion of his exam drew to a close, he would shame himself and spill his seed while his gloating captors watched.

His secret fear soon proved well-founded indeed.

Cecil's prepuce had retracted well when he first erected, and Josie had Mademoiselle Lange draw it to and fro once or twice. This act made Cecil squirm ineffectually against the straps that held him, in a mixture of shame and pleasure. Josie Glade noticed that there was no sign whatever of phimosis; Cecil's prepuce was loose and pliable.

Josie also noted that his erectile center was free of inhibition and fully functional in every way. Josie also stated that as he grew older, Cecil might become subject to irritable weakness of the genitals and should avoid manustupratic manipulations at all costs. At this, Mademoiselle Lange and Miss Bates smiled. Josie ignored their smiles and exchange of meaningful glances and made notes in her leather-bound journal with her fountain pen.

Josie Glade stated that Cecil Uxbridge was absolutely free of anesthesia of the sexual organs. She asked Mademoiselle Lange if Cecil exhibited constant erections even when harnessed alone to his bed at night. When Mademoiselle Lange said no, Josie Glade determined that Cecil bore no sign of priapistic tendencies. Dr. Josie Glade asked Cecil if he soiled himself in his sleep with nocturnal pollutions, but Cecil blushed more and fell silent. Mademoiselle Lange interjected that she had detected no telltale traces of nocturnal pollutions when she had examined Cecil's sheets closely. Cecil's dismay was boundless!

Dr. Josie Glade noted that Cecil's genitals bore no signs of laxity, then said that due to the limited time she had to perform the examination, it would be impossible to detect any periodicity in the rate of his sexual excitement, but suggested that Mademoiselle Lange should have one of her matrons make a simple chart from which it could be determined later by tabulation.

Josie Glade observed that Cecil Uxbridge's penis was of average size as it reared in Mademoiselle Lange's

India rubber-clad fist. Josie Glade expressed concern over the visible signs of a peculiar sensuality about Cecil's character. She diagnosed him as exhibiting all the key characteristics of both satyriasis with paresthetic tendencies and hyperesthesia. Josie Glade stated clinically that she expected both to worsen markedly under his regimen of "treatment" at Chidewell House, until he finally became subject to irritable genital weakness and perhaps even impotence.

Next, Josie Glade had Mademoiselle Lange release her purchase on Cecil Uxbridge's scrotum and hold only his penis. To Cecil's ever-increasing shame, Josie Glade reached down between his legs and held his scrotum with her gleaming black-gloved hand. Cecil cried out in alarm as the masked physician squeezed his scrotum in her fingers, rolling his testicles about and examining them most judiciously for irregularities. Jose Glade managed to write in her leather-bound journal with her right hand while she examined Cecil's scrotum with her left.

Mademoiselle Lange and Miss Bates listened with interest to Josie Glade's clinical observations as she wrote carefully in her journal, almost as if dictating to herself. "The descent of Cecil's right testicle is imperfect, though the left hangs lower than the right, as is customary—the deviation between them suggests an imperfect descent of the right. His testicles are firm, exhibiting no evidence of atrophy, though both are a trifle small."

Cecil lay gritting his teeth in a mixed agony of sexual pleasure and extreme humiliation. His penis twitched in Mademoiselle Lange's gloved hand and the lovely masked doctor, who had inserted her fingers deep into his rectum, was now holding his scrotum and feeling carefully for the duct on the back portion of each of his testicles where the vas deferens attached. Whenever Cecil looked directly upward, he would see the rise and fall of Miss Bates's pear-shaped breasts beneath her apron as she watched the proceedings intently and held him down with a gloved hand pressing on each of his shoulders.

The women did not realize how near the end of his tether Cecil Uxbridge had become. It was then that Mademoiselle Lange adjusted her position, pulling his penis back to hold it more closely against his abdomen with her gloved hand. At the same moment, Josie Glade took a more firm purchase on his scrotum and noted aloud to Mademoiselle Lange and Miss Bates that Cecil was exhibiting an active erectile reflex and that perhaps he had been overstimulated—especially because of his sexual excitability.

Josie Glade was about to suggest that Mademoiselle Lange should release Cecil's penis for a moment—though she herself continued her thorough scrotal examination—when the inevitable occurred. Cecil let out a whimper of pleasure and intense shame as his penis began to rear rhythmically in Mademoiselle Lange's gleaming fist. Then, as Cecil lay rigid as an iron bar, the head of his tormented sexual organ expanded and disgorged a torrent of thick seed over the gloved hands of his captors. Mademoiselle Lange and Miss Bates watched smiling as Cecil's penis jerked spasmodically, soiling the women's gloves and his own thighs and abdomen liberally. At last, when Cecil's orgasm ended and he lay limp and transfixed with utter shame, Dr. Josephine L. Glade raised her gloved hand and rubbed a bit of his semen between her gleaming thumb and index finger. "The amount of spermatic discharge, the fluidity and consistency seem entirely normal. Though, were he under my regimen, I would have him undergo male continence training at once."

For Cecil Uxbridge, the next few minutes in the cold examination room were like a long, slow nightmare. Mademoiselle Lange and Josie Glade removed their gloves while Miss Bates washed his genitals, thighs, and abdomen clean with a warm, wet cloth. The smug, superior way Miss Bates smiled down at Cecil as she did so made him feel like an incontinent infant. And when she squeezed his penis to milk out the last few drops, he plumbed the absolute depths of shame!

Josie Glade suggested that due to his hyperesthesia and overly active erectile reflex, Mademoiselle Lange should add a testicular restraint to his harness. Mademoiselle Lange agreed and she and Miss Bates helped him rise stiffly from the table, after unfastening the knee-chest portion of his harness. As he sat up, still naked, and wrists bound at his shoulders, his limp penis lolled against his thigh and dribbled a last bit of fluid. Miss Bates took firm purchase on his arms and marched him to a corner medical cupboard where Mademoiselle Lange, waited holding the testicular restraint.

Under Josie Glade's direction, with help from Miss Bates, Mademoiselle Lange fastened him in the restraint. Two narrow leather straps were buckled tightly about the base of Cecil's scrotum. Then two other straps were fastened about his legs, one just above each knee. A third set of straps connected the straps about his scrotum to those about his lower thighs. Cecil started and grunted with pain and surprise as Miss Bates pulled his scrotum downward and cinched the straps tight, then buckled them in place.

Josie Glade made Cecil walk about a bit, and he did as she commanded. He walked gingerly, still in full harness. The sensations that the testicular restraint gave him were at once mildly painful and stimulating. Each step gave Cecil slight cramps up through his lower abdomen, combined with an acute consciousness of his bare, bound genitals. Mademoiselle Lange and Miss Bates stood, hands on hips, noting his peculiar, awkward bound gait with complacent satisfaction. Josie Glade pronounced the harness a most effective tool indeed.

Josie Glade and Mademoiselle Lange were soon conversing in low voices in a corner of the room. Mademoiselle Lange interrupted their confidences for a moment to tell Miss Bates to escort Cecil Uxbridge from the basement examination room to his own room on the third floor. Miss Bates did so with a cool institutional efficiency. She took a firm purchase on the straps of Cecil's testicular restraint, reaching through beneath his bare buttocks from behind. Using this humiliating hold as an ingenious bridle, Miss Bates frog-marched Cecil from the room and through the soundlessly carpeted lower passages of the Chidewell House cellars to the back stairs.

Cecil hoped desperately that they would not be seen and that they would finish his forced and humiliating transit through the house in anonymity. His luck held out until they reached the landing between the first and second floors. Miss Bates still had Cecil by his testicular punishment straps and was cajoling him to make haste—for she did not have all night to fasten him down to his bed—when she looked up and smiled a greeting. Cecil's eyes followed her glance. To his shame and horror, he saw two pretty young ladies—perhaps barely younger than himself—descending from the second-floor staircase. The light was abundant, so there was no hope that his nakedness would not be seen in all possible clarity.

Cecil was not too overcome with abject humiliation to appreciate the beauty of the approaching young women. Both were smiling with ill-disguised amusement at the sight of him. The young women were clad almost identically to Miss Bates in Chidewell House's severe calf-length gray uniforms with crisp starched aprons. The young women sported identical high-heeled oxfords on their dainty feet. Cecil could not help thinking that such shoes—with their high, gleaming heels forcing a hips-and-buttock-wiggling tiptoed strut—were somehow wicked. The young women's frank gazes looked Cecil up and down as they paused to chat with Miss Bates.

Cecil all but felt their gazes linger on his bare sexual organs. In shame he tried to swivel his hips to salvage the merest shred of modesty, but Miss Bates thwarted his pathetic design by firming her purchase on his scrotal straps. The young ladies took in every detail of Cecil's genital harness with delighted fascination. Before they took their leave of Cecil Uxbridge and Miss Bates to continue descending the stairs, one of the young ladies giggled and purred, "Mademoiselle Lange says we may get to wheel him out to Brimley Heath and use the pneumatic jacket and suction pump!"

Scarcely five minutes after the humiliating encounter on the landing, Cecil Uxbridge lay in his third-floor room, helplessly strapped down to his bed and still in harness. After giving him a self-satisfied gloating smile, Miss Bates put out the lights and abandoned him to the darkness. Cecil lay still. The despair of ever being free of his predicament lay heavy upon him. His full-length window could be opened to give access to a chin-high masonry balcony. The French doors were ajar. A light summer breeze ruffled the sheer curtains and transmitted to the room the bustling sounds of Portland Square three stories below. To Cecil, the clop of horses' hooves, the sound of hansom cabs in the street, and the rare occasional motorcar were the sounds of freedom, and a life he had known and lost.

Cecil was awakened when a key turned in the sturdy lock of his door. It opened to admit two more of his jailers. Cecil had never laid his eyes on the two young women who entered his room. They each wore the severe gray uniform of Chidewell House matrons: the high collars, starched aprons, silk stockings, and scandalously high-heeled oxfords. To his surprise, the women introduced themselves to him in an almost-mocking fashion. The tall woman with dark hair, high cheekbones, and a dazzling smile was Miss Armsworthy. The matron with the curvaceous hips and impudent upturned nose was Miss Spence. Both wished him good morning.

As the women stood above him, their nimble fingers undoing the straps that held him fast to his bed, Cecil began to realize that the piercing shame of having his genitals almost constantly exposed to ladies never seemed to grow dull. It just wasn't something one could become accustomed to. To distract himself, Cecil watched their gloved hands unbuckle the straps that had held him down. They meant to free him of those anyway, though he was still in body and genital harness. Cecil found the dainty gray gloves that buttoned to the cuffs of the matron's uniforms and matched them exactly to be quite captivating.

In a trice, he was free. With firm hands about his waist and at his shoulders, Miss Armsworthy and Miss Spence sat him up, helped him get stiffly to his feet, and marched him from his room to another chamber just across the bright sunlit upstairs corridor. This new room had a rather grim businesslike look about it that Cecil did not like at all.

The furnishings of the room were dominated by a heavy oak table topped with gleaming black padded leather. Three large glass-fronted medical cupboards stood against the walls. Every spare corner was jammed with complex medical or scientific contraptions that were too intricate for Cecil to comprehend.

Cecil was propelled to climb up onto the table by his two new tormentors, acutely aware that as Miss Spence steadied him with a gloved hand to his thigh, her fingers brushed the side of his penis briefly. Cecil felt himself flush a hot crimson. Miss Spence laughed, her tones musical. She looked mischievously at her companion. "This one has dignity and puts on airs," she cooed.

Miss Armsworthy's reply made Cecil Uxbridge's color only deepen. "He thinks he's saving himself for a chaste young lady, no doubt," she observed with a dazzling smile beamed Cecil's way. "Instead, he's only saved himself for our hands!"

Cecil gathered their meaning at once though his outrage was futile. That they meant to addict him to manual abuse was obvious. Perhaps they were going to subject him to it now!

Chapter X

Crosby Westercroft had the grim persistence of a bulldog hidden in the body of a frail invalid. His shoulders were stooped, his complexion was pallid, and his bearing one of delicate ill health. He walked with a cane that minimized his tendency toward a severe limp because one leg was a trifle shorter than the other. For the lack in his physique, Crosby Westercroft compensated by carrying a small German automatic pistol of advanced—though considerably miniaturized—design. Nature itself compensated for Crosby Westercroft's physical shortcomings by giving him memory and a razor-sharp intellect.

Crosby Westercroft was a longtime associate of

Elithorpe Pemberton. Though not partners in a strictly business sense, Elithorpe Pemberton turned to Crosby Westercroft when he required expertise in various scientific disciplines that were lately proving invaluable aids to the properly equipped investigative attorney.

Crosby Westercroft was concerned about his associate's abrupt disappearance. His concern was not based on an emotional reaction—at least, not in the usual sense. Crosby Westercroft had consciously suppressed all emotion until he was not sure that any existed at all —even deep below the surface of his consciousness. His school fellows had made his life a dismal torment, and his lack of success later with the fairer sex was so spectacular that he disengaged his emotions altogether. This emotionless detachment made him a formidable adversary. The search for his associate's whereabouts became an intellectual exercise to which he devoted his Olympian mental faculties with the single-minded concentration of a predatory animal.

Despite his unflagging attempts to obtain a warrant to search Elithorpe Pemberton's business, he was restrained repeatedly by magistrate's order until he was informed curtly by a constable stationed at the door that the property within had already been auctioned by Sotheby's. Crosby Westercroft made several unsuccessful attempts to trace the buyers of the auctioned items, but had sadly reached an impasse with each probing inquiry.

Then, through a tedious bit of investigation on his part, Crosby Westercroft uncovered the whereabouts of the secretive Elithorpe Pemberton's flat on Pomfret Road. Hours later, he stood on the doorstep of 53 Pomfret Road with a magistrate's warrant in hand and accompanied by an armed private constable. Pomfret Road's being in a different district had resulted in Crosby Westercroft's finding a magistrate altogether more sympathetic to his cause.

Crosby Westercroft produced a key that was very versatile indeed. A moment later, he and the armed constable entered Elithorpe Pemberton's private flat. The flat was a complete shambles. Books and periodicals lay scattered about the floor, many of them looking deliberately torn to pieces before being flung about in haphazard abandon. Nearly every item of furniture that wasn't fastened down had been turned topsy-turvy. Gilt-framed etchings had been torn from the wall and cast about to add yet another dimension to the atmosphere of deliberate destruction.

Crosby Westercroft knew his associate well enough to be certain that the usual state of his flat—or anything else he owned—would be impeccable. Mr. Westercroft and the armed constable retreated from the flat just long enough to ask the neighbors whether they had seen or heard anything unusual. Both men met a wall of stolid protestations of complete ignorance to the extent that the armed constable muttered, "None of this lot would see anything out of the way in the corridors and wards of Bedlam itself."

Both men returned the scope of their exacting attentions to Elithorpe Pemberton's flat and made an exhaustive search. Though the carnage in the flat bespoke a great deal of malicious contempt, there appeared to have been a rather thorough search made as well—so the entire purpose of the prior invaders wasn't wanton destruction. Both men proceeded to search the entire flat bit by bit, room by room, overturned drawer by overturned drawer. They missed nothing.

In Elithorpe Pemberton's study, Crosby Westercroft found what was to him the saddest of all results of the wanton destruction. Priceless cuneiform tablets lay scattered about the floor. All were broken, as if the perpetrators took great care to see that all were shattered. Crosby Westercroft stooped down to examine the fragments and noted that they appeared to have been tossed to the floor and then broken by either the metal tip of a cane or the spike heel of a woman's shoe. Upon closer examination and comparisons with the brass tip of his own cane, Crosby Westercroft determined that the perpetrators included at least two women. Once being flung to the floor, the tablets were smashed by at least two different types of ladies' high spike heels.

At first glance, a large statue of an Assyrian winged man-bull on a pedestal in the center of the study floor appeared to have been left unmolested. Upon closer examination, however, Crosby Westercroft noticed that the carved tip of the bull's male part had been chipped off. After a brief search, Crosby Westercroft found the missing piece of the bull's anatomy at the black marble feet of a small, delicately carved statue of Semiramis.

Crosby Westercroft then turned his attentions to the large desk that dominated one corner of Elithorpe Pemberton's study and now had some of its side panels smashed in. The desk was a ponderous piece of furniture, and Mr. Westercroft examined it thoroughly for signs of secret compartments or hidden drawers.

With some difficulty, he got down on his hands and knees to peer under the desk and feel for any protuberance that might activate a hidden mechanism. After nearly five minutes, a tiny knot down near the floor gave way when pressed—with an almost-inaudible click—and a small compartment was revealed about an inch above the floor. From this compartment, Crosby Westercroft retrieved two small bound packets. One appeared to contain documents relating to a case—perhaps the one that resulted in Elithorpe Pemberton's disappearance.

Crosby Westercroft did not bother to give the packets more than a cursory examination there in Elithorpe Pemberton's flat. But scarcely an hour later, after dismissing the armed private constable and returning to the privacy and comfort of his own room, Mr. Westercroft spread the contents of both packets on his desk and examined them closely.

He was pleased to note one packet contained some findings from the case that Elithorpe Pemberton was working on when he disappeared. The case of Cecil Uxbridge, who had been abducted from his stepmother Elizabeth Uxbridge's home—perhaps with her complicity. Crosby Westercroft noted that Elithorpe Pemberton's client was one Lord Frederick Uxbridge—of whom he had heard—the uncle of the abducted young man.

Crosby Westercroft read the contents of the first packet carefully. References were made to a woman named Anika Bates and an unnamed woman. Both women seemed to have been employed previously by The Clackton Sanitarium. There were no photographs of the unnamed woman, but here was a photograph of Anika Bates. She was a striking woman with jet black hair, thick, dark eyebrows and porcelain skin. Crosby Westercroft could not say whether the observer would be more struck with Anika Bates's loveliness or the severity of her demeanor.

He determined to pay a visit to the Clackton Sanitarium and then take his findings to Lord Uxbridge himself. Meanwhile he turned his attention to the second packet. He was more than a trifle surprised to find the second packet contained photographs of a more private nature, that had obviously been hoarded secretively and carefully by Elithorpe Pemberton.

The first photograph showed an old man, completely naked and on all fours like a dog. Seated smugly upon his back was a laughing young woman wearing tight riding trousers, a buttoned vest, leather gloves, round-collared white blouse, and tie. Her legs were clad in bewitching high boots with outrageously high heels.

The outlandish boots gave the woman's trim little feet an arousing, yet somehow prim and dainty tiptoed pose. Wickedly gleaming Spanish spurs graced the heels of the woman's boots. The old man was stark naked, and his sexual organ was swollen with arousal, rearing up from between his legs as he crawled along, bearing his lovely burden.

The second photograph depicted the same old man lying upon his back. The same woman and a lovely companion—both similarly accoutered—stood above him, each with a foot on his body. The original young woman's booted foot was on the old man' chest while the second young woman's booted foot rested on his erect penis, pressing it against his abdomen.

In the third photograph, the first young woman was standing with her full weight on the old man's chest. Somehow he was bearing it as he lay beneath her. Her companion stood on the floor beside her and helped her balance by resting her gloved hands on the broad curves of her hips. Both young women were laughing.

The fourth photograph depicted the same young woman still standing placidly on the old man's chest, while her companion knelt down beside him and had taken his sexual organ in her hand. Crosby Westercroft studied the photograph closely and without emotion. The old man had had a discharge and had soiled his own abdomen with this seed as a result of the women's intensely shameful games with him.

So here was a secret weakness in Elithorpe Pemberton's nature—one that could have abetted those who were intent on his undoing. Perhaps he was lured by someone who well understood his predilections—someone who led him to his destruction.

Crosby Westercroft was content with his success. After his visit to the Clackton Sanitarium, he would visit Lord Uxbridge at Chudleigh Green. He would have more than one interesting nugget to convey—of that he was certain.

Cecil Fothergill's Matron

Agnes was delighted with the change in her father-in-law, Cecil. He had gone from lion to lamb in such a short time! Even Edgar—who rarely noticed anything but his morning paper and his stock reports—had pronounced his father's quavering bellow at all hours of the day or night to perform an exhausting assortment of personal hygiene tasks, and other, more trite functions less frequent.

"Agnes! Agnes! See to my pee bottle!"
"Agnes! I've spilled my soup!"
"Agnes! I need anther pillow!"
"Agnes! More tea!"
All such clamors were now silenced delightfully.

Neither of the maids Agnes and Edgar employed in their large town house had the stomach for Cecil's temper or his disposition. Both had declared that they would seek positions elsewhere rather than deal with Cecil's crotchets, so the lot had fallen to Agnes for quite some time. Then a close friend of hers—in a similar predicament with an aging father-in-law, but at least one who was considerate—told her of the Primrose Matron Agency, which specialized in just such services. Agnes's friend had mentioned that the Primrose Agency rejected her request for their services—something about thinking Agnes's friend was too close to her father-in-law to allow a matron a free hand with him. Somehow it seemed odd, Agnes's friend had said, almost as if they treated old men like children—a firm hand, discipline, and all. Agnes could only hope that her Primrose matron would take a good firm hand with Cecil.

She rang the agency right away. The woman on the other end of the line did seem rather oddly interested in finding out how Agnes got along with her father-in-law, and almost pleased to hear that he was a tyrant and that she quite loathed him. The arrangements were made quickly. The Primrose Agency was rather expensive, but they came well recommended, and Agnes's sanity hung in the balance.

At first, Agnes had thought the young matron who arrived on her doorstep would not do at all. But the opulent black motorcar that delivered her did not wait; it sped away with an understated roar of power. Ellen was a brunette of medium height with frank, yet pretty features. Agnes was mildly annoyed to catch Edgar eyeing Matron's curves now and again through the introductions. Ellen had curves which even her sensibly heeled oxfords, plain black skirt, and full-cut white blouse could not hide. Matron's uniform was accessorized by a proper black tie, crisply starched white gloves, harmony point stockings, and a white straw hat with a black band angled over her brow. Later, on the telephone, the head of the Primrose Agency grew testy when Agnes commented about the quaintness of the matron's uniform. "The white gloves are symbols of fastidious cleanliness and would give evidence of any slatternly tendency in our matrons at once! The hat is a symbol of the Primrose Agency and has been so since our founding in 1914. Our matrons have been tending to old men for forty years!" Agnes could hear the woman's voice, tight-lipped with anger on the other end of the line. She never questioned the uniform again!

At first Agnes thought her young matron would not do because she seemed so quiet and agreeable. Agnes feared that Cecil would be impossible with her. And Cecil did resent his matron at first. But within a fortnight he had changed, and changed dramatically. The change amazed Agnes! Cecil grew quiet and passive, perhaps almost submissive. His requests were few and made in low tones. Somehow he seemed smaller and perhaps weaker, too.

Agnes quite liked the change. She took a secret guilty pleasure in seeing Cecil somehow humbled, though she had no idea what magic Matron worked behind closed doors to make him so. And the doors were most often closed. By Primrose Agency policy, Matron stayed with Cecil in his own small suite of rooms on the third floor. Matron explained that, for the first two months, she would see to him entirely. Only after the initial "training" phase would she take her usual alternate weekend holidays. Perhaps this young matron from the Primrose Agency would be Cecil's comeuppance!

Already the glow had returned to Agnes's cheeks. She moved with more confidence and sureness. There had been two bleak periods in Agnes' life. The first when she and Edgar were newlyweds and Cecil—as the titled head of a prestigious London law firm, and her father-in-law—had made her feel inferior and inadequate at every turn. She and Edgar had moved away from Cecil's shadow when Edgar became full partner in a brokerage house. Then came twenty-five good years as Agnes and Edgar raised two sons and a daughter and business thrived.

Then, at age forty-eight, Agnes's second bleak period began. Cecil returned to her life, this time as an invalid. She had hoped that he would see her in a new light, or at least respect her as his benefactor and caregiver. But despite the indignities of his present situation, and his dependence on her for matters of personal care, he had still made her feel small and stupid. Agnes's respect and awe had turned slowly to hatred. And with her emancipation, brought about by the procurement of services from the Primrose Agency, she determined never to feel that yoke again!

Agnes was attractive for her age. There was a new spring in her step. For the first time in a long time, she began receiving compliments at social functions and parties as to the smartness of her wardrobe and her elegant looks. Men noticed her again, and even though Agnes was always faithful to Edgar, she drank in their looks like tonic. Women asked Agnes if she had changed hairdressers and if she had, could they please have a referral.

Something about Cecil's bearing in the presence of Matron told Agnes that he feared her, and that she had some sort of unnatural or improper hold on him. Had Cecil been the sort of father-in-law to inspire love and devotion, she would have spied on Matron to see exactly what she was doing to him in order to obtain evidence for her dismissal. But as it was, Agnes began spying on them with the guilty hope that she could discover and gloat over whatever cruelties or irregularities Matron was subjecting him to! Agnes was a quiet, soft-spoken woman and far more intelligent than her diffidence let on. She was firm and fast in her affections and implacable in her hatreds! And Agnes hated Cecil and hated him heartily.

So Agnes found excuses to linger about outside the

door to Cecil's rooms. But as his bed was located in the farthest chamber back, she heard nothing of interest. As time passed, she made frequent fruitless attempts to uncover the secret of Matron's hold over him.

Finally it came time for Matron's first weekend holiday. Agnes was finally readmitted to Cecil's rooms to take care of him for the weekend. She noticed only three odd things. First was the marked change in how Cecil treated her. He was very submissive and seemed rather afraid of her as well. Gone were his demanding tirades and his derogatory cruel humor. He seemed a shadow of his old self.

But this was not enough to stem the tide of Agnes's cold hatred; it was too long-standing and deep-rooted. She ruled over her humbled tormentor with a calculating coldness, and took a gloating delight in the intimate embarrassing services she performed for him.

Second, all Cecil's pubic hair had been shaved away. He was as bald as an infant. His scrotum was shaved bare as well.

Agnes liked the change. It made Cecil seem infantile, and more naked than nakedness itself. She was sure that if she asked Matron why she had shaved Cecil, the answer would be for reasons of hygiene. So she did not ask. She just savored yet another indignity. Slowly the old accounts were being balanced in her favor.

Third was the battered portmanteau, part of Matron's property—that was in a corner of Cecil's dayroom. It was secured with a heavy lock. Agnes had the brief bizarre notion that this bag contained the "instruments of discipline" (or torture) with which Matron had enslaved and humbled Cecil.

When Matron returned, she herself mentioned having to shave Cecil's genitals. She smiled and explained that it was for reasons of hygiene and part of the Primrose Agency policy. Agnes was not satisfied. One warm afternoon, when Matron had taken Cecil down into the garden in his wheelchair in the old service elevator, Agnes slipped down into Edgar's basement workshop to get a hand auger. She ran lightly up the steps to the third floor and bored a small hole carefully through the stairwell wall. Just as she hoped! The tiny hole let Agnes see into Cecil's bedroom, lending her a vantage point view from over the foot of his bed. Agnes was determined to discover the source of Matron's power over her father-in-law. She looked forward to gloating over any cruelties that Matron might be inflicting on her old nemesis. Her suspicions were pleasantly aroused. Surely Matron was doing something highly improper to Cecil!

Agnes waited with baited breath throughout the evening. She wanted to be at her newly made peephole when Matron put Cecil to bed and tended to him. Surely if any wickedness were to occur, it would happen then!

That evening found Agnes sitting at her peephole as quiet as a mouse. The door to Cecil's bedroom opened. In came the wheelchair with Cecil in it, pushed by Matron. Matron had kicked her shoes off, but still wore her white gloves and white hat, symbols of the Primrose Agency. She helped Cecil into bed and moved the wheelchair aside. Then she went into the other room for a moment and returned with her portmanteau. She drew up a stool beside Cecil's bed and sat down, placing her case on a low table beside her. She had Cecil spread his legs. The she drew up his nightshirt to expose his genitals!

Matron took Cecil's shaved scrotum in one white-gloved hand while she opened her portmanteau with the other. The portmanteau contained rows of tiny round-bottomed glass bottles—all neatly labeled, rolled lengths of thin white cord, several long, narrow pincushions bristling with rows of needles, small bottles of antiseptic, several syringes, various harness-type fastenings, and neatly rolled leather straps.

Matron deftly bound a length of white cord in a figure eight around Cecil's penis and scrotum. She kept crossing and twisting the cord until his genitals were bound tight. Agnes' heart thudded as she watched Cecil's penis enlarge and stiffen to full excitement. Matron sat comfortably in her chair by Cecil's bed, her stockinged feet arched daintily on the carpet.

Matron began to pull the loose end of the cord that bound Cecil's genitals gently and rhythmically to stimulate him for a bit. Then she poured antiseptic into a tiny tray that had been fitted precisely to cup the bottom of a bottle of antiseptic. Agnes held her breath as Matron removed five needles from a pincushion to soak them in the antiseptic.

Then Matron spoke. "Have you been a good boy Cecil?"

Cecil squirmed and nodded, somewhat distracted by the genital stimulation he was undergoing. "Yes, Miss."

"Have you been sweet to Agnes?"

Cecil's penis bobbed up and down in time to the motions of Matron's white-gloved fingers gently pulling the cord. "Yes, Miss." The head of his swollen penis was turning a bloated purple.

"You will still have the needles Cecil. It's part of your masturbation training now!"

With that, Matron released her hold on the cord and took a tiny pinch of the skin of Cecil's scrotum between her fingertips. Then her deft fingers slipped a long, wicked needle through the pinch of skin! As Matron prepared another, the first needle lay securely across the front-center of Cecil's scrotum, held neatly in place by the pinch of skin that it had penetrated. Matron slipped the second needle through another pinch of skin just above the first. Between insertions, she pulled the cord a little to keep Cecil addicted to the genital stimulation. In a few moments, all five were inserted. They made a neat horizontal column down the front of the old man's scrotum.

"Are you ready for your masturbation training, Cecil?" Matron purred, her voice soft and innocent. Agnes was amazed. Matron took another length of cord from her portmanteau and stood up. To Agnes's profound surprise she made Cecil lift his head up off his pillow as she wrapped a loop of cord about his neck!

Matron was now standing primly on tiptoe, her hat still in place at the proper angle, her white gloves still crisply starched. She kept one white gloved hand on the loop of cord around Cecil's neck while her free hand recaptured the cord that had been wrapped so carefully around his genitals earlier. In another moment, Matron began again the rhythmic pull on the cord that stimulated Cecil's genitals while her other hand twisted and tightened the cord about his neck! Agnes gasped in surprise. Some of her more wicked friends had showed her a book with just such an illustration in school. It was an engraving that depicted two Japanese women doing something similar to a shogun.

Agnes knew that a constriction of blood flow and oxygen to the brain often increased the level of sexual pleasure as orgasm approached. Agnes clutched her knees and stared, her mouth open, her blood pumping with a curious and not entirely unwelcome mixture of sensations. Matron smiled down at Cecil and continued to masturbate and half-strangle him simultaneously. Cecil had only tensed himself and held his breath at the painful insertion of the needles. Now he began to thrash about on the bed, his spindly old legs spread wide apart, his nightshirt flopped up quite to his belly now.

"Do you enjoy your restricted-breathing masturbation training Cecil? Hmmmmm...do you?" Matron's voice was a soft coo.

Of course Cecil could not answer. His mouth was gaped open in an instinctive attempt to draw more air into his lungs.

"Of course you need this training, don't you?" Matron went on, her voice prim and self-righteous in its tones. "Your masturbation training keeps you sweet and submissive, doesn't it? There, now...don't fight it, just submit to the sensations like a good, sweet little man!"

Agnes swallowed hard as she watched each vein along the shaft of Cecil's abused penis stand out in bloated relief at the intensity of the carnal abuse to which he was being subjected. The white cord that subjected him to genital bondage was also the instrument of his enslaving masturbatory pleasure. His testicles were sharply defined due to the tight binding of the thin white cord. Matron kept tightening the cord about his neck also, not to the point of complete strangulation, though Cecil's face and scalp were beet red and his lips perhaps the slightest trifle blue. His breathing was constricted to enhance the addictive sensations of helpless delight that were now mastering him.

Agnes stared, her mind transfixed as the drama through the peephole before her played slowly to its inevitable conclusion. Cecil squirmed less and seemed more rigid, as the sensations of slow strangulation-masturbation mastered him more completely. Matron paused in her ministrations but once—and that to take a round-bottomed bottle from her portmanteau and fit it over the bloated, tormented tip of the old fellow's sex organ.

Matron regarded him with a sort of clinical fondness with which an experimenter might regard a laboratory subject. Both her hands kept busying themselves. One with his slow half-strangulation, and one with his slow masturbation. The needles that she had placed through his scrotum glinted in the subdued light of the room as the rhythmically pulled cord caused his testicles to bounce up and down. The old fellow began to claw futilely at the sheets below his withered straining buttocks. A strange snorting noise sounded from deep within his throat. Agnes watched as his penis began the slow series of convulsive twitches of impending orgasm. With Cecil's body absolutely rigid, his mouth gaping open and his eyes wild, his penis began the ignominy of its messy surrender. Agnes could see each desperate hot squirt of sperm as it was fired from the strangled imprisoned tip of Cecil's penis into the bottle. Agnes was even certain that she could hear each squirt. Matron smiled and maintained both motions without pause while she observed Cecil's desperate release clinically.

After the shuddering spasms of Cecil's orgasm had subsided, Matron loosened the cords from about his neck and genitals. He lay limp and helpless as an infant as Matron carefully removed the bottle from the tip of his sex organ, making very sure not to spill a drop of his sperm. Matron was very interested in the quantity and consistency of Cecil's sperm and expressed a future determination to weigh his ejaculate and observe it closely under a magnification lens. She also expressed interest in a possible correlation between the tightness of the cord about his neck and the volume of fluid that he emitted during orgasm. As Cecil lay gasping and recovering himself, Matron crossed her legs prettily and made some entries in a small leather-bound journal. Agnes then gathered that all the Primrose matrons used similar techniques to subjugate their charges and kept each other informed of the various best results.

Agnes was flushed and weak-kneed when she descended the attic stairwell and shut the upstairs hallway door, as quiet as a mouse. Later in the evening, she lay awake beside a snoring Edgar as she relived the scene she had observed from her secret vantage point. She relived it with a relish that shocked and surprised her. Still vivid in her mind was the sight of Matron smiling as she prepared a syringe after completing her journal entries.

Cecil had begged her not to give him the injection, but she laughed and ignored his pleas. "Don't be silly Cecil. How can you hope to recover from your masturbation training without the complete relaxation that this paralytic affords!" Matron swabbed his inner thigh with antiseptic—his nightshirt was still tucked up on his abdomen—and injected him with obvious delight. In a few moments and after a few brief convulsive twitches, Cecil lay still, imprisoned by chemical paralysis for the night. Matron covered him, after first pulling his foreskin down to cover his glans and tucking his nightshirt back down around his thighs.

The following morning dawned sunny and warm. After a relaxing breakfast with Edgar, Agnes took a walk in the garden. Matron was there pushing Cecil in his wheelchair. She smiled when she saw Agnes and came over, treading carefully across the dewy grass in her polished high-heeled oxfords. Matron patted Agnes's arm and walked with her, leaving Cecil alone for a moment.

Agnes's heart thudded at what Matron said.

"I know about the peephole that you drilled with Edgar's hand auger. It's directly below the dried rose bouquet and quite invisible. I do not take offense to such things, and I find your curiosity rather charming." She regarded the blushing Agnes closely and went on. "I have heard tell that a bit more pressure than that which I used last night can produce asphyxia in a masturbation subject and that his asphyxia is so gradual as to be undetectable later since there is no discoloration of the victim's neck. Further, it has been said that such asphyxia—when combined with the physiological stress of slow masturbation—is always pronounced as a heart attack or fit of apoplexy by the subsequent attending physician."

Matron smiled sweetly. "Cecil may live and require a matron's care for five more years. With a lump sum half of what would be required to provide a matron's care for such a length of time, such an asphyxiation could be quietly accomplished."

Matron smiled again. "Something to consider perhaps?"

A Dose of Chadwick's Sleeping Tonic

Dominance is asserted abruptly only in warfare and in the baser aspects of primitive physical struggle, Edwin Upton reflected as the mantel clock chimed the hour. He sat alone in his darkened study, the leather-bound companions of his life stretching away to his right into the shadowed corners of the room.

More often, dominance and submission are matters of delicate balance, resolved slowly at the subconscious level with the passage of time, and the manifestation of consistent determination by the one party, and consistent weakness by the other—and this in trifling matters at first. In household affairs, a relative imbalance of wills is registered on the scale by countless little acquiescences until the preponderance of evidence shifts inexorably and absolutely to reveal the master and the vanquished.

Edwin Upton leaned forward to stub out the glowing stump of his Havana cigar in the intricate little jade-trimmed ashtray by his side. As he did so, the cushions of the deep leather wing chair in which he sat creaked comfortably beneath him. His clothing was ill-matched to his surroundings, and as he got to his feet to walk to the heavy curtained window to his left, his steps were slow and weary. Edwin Upton pulled the curtains open just a bit and stood at the glass, gazing thoughtfully down at the carriages and pedestrians in the street below. A hansom cab turned the corner onto Brompton Road, then a rare motorcar flashed past, its running lamps trimmed for the early twilight. He noticed that a knot of well dressed ladies had collected below the gas standard on the corner—waiting for the omnibus.

Edwin Upton wore but a single item of clothing—a long-sleeved nightshirt that fell to his thin knees. A pair of delicate wire-rimmed spectacles were his only accessory. Edwin Upton, the fourth Earl of Plimsoll, and master of Basilby House at the corner of Drayton Gardens and Brompton Road, was, in truth, master of nothing and earl of thin air.

He stepped back from the window and walked to his bookshelves, running his hand gently along the spines of the thick volumes that were so dear to him. At least she had left him this single fragment of his once-spectacular domain, he thought ruefully. At least here he was still master—for the moment.

Edwin Upton sat down wearily at his study table and opened one of the volumes that lay pleasantly scattered there in enticing disarray. "Milton!" he said wryly to himself. And—appropriately enough—Milton's *Samson Agonistes!* How very like his own fate was Samson's, Edwin realized. Physique notwithstanding, both men had been neutralized and enslaved by a temptress. Both, in their end, but pathetic pawns of her power.

Edwin heartily regretted his marriage to the lovely Sophie Payne, but he gravely doubted were she to exercise her exquisite charms on him all over again he would be better able to gainsay her or extricate himself from her machinations. That Sophie could exercise a phenomenal amount of charm and persuasion was an understatement. She had fallen like a meteorite into his dull life and set him ablaze with a passion he thought had abandoned him long before. To a man of Edwin's years, the fire of aroused passion is at once a rare and sublime pleasure, and a poignant echo of lost youth, rendering its subject all the more vulnerable to and dependent upon its object. Even though Edwin knew his friends' dire warnings—that Sophie loved naught but his fortune—rang true, he was captivated and enslaved by her bewitching beauty nonetheless—and that overcame all else.

Sophie Payne was a bewitching little beauty, and even Edwin's friends had made no mistake about that—at least judging from their sidelong glances when she was in the room—and this fact alone caused him a furtive, secret satisfaction that he, a man past middle years, could attract an extravagant young woman. In this respect, he was the envy of his friends, even though they were all properly scandalized by the wedding announcement, discreet though it was.

And Sophie Payne was indeed a bewitching beauty. There was no flaw in her from the dainty soles of her perfect little feet to the crown of her golden hair. Her eyes could be so wide, innocent, and full of sympathy that they would easily have captivated a man far more jaded and worldly than Edwin Upton was upon their first meeting. And Sophie's full-lipped, pouty little mouth, so firm and determined that it was a delight to succumb to her whims—at least in the beginning, before the extent of her lust for power was revealed, and her remorseless cruelty unmasked.

And so it was that Edwin was conquered before he knew the battle had been joined, and was enslaved long before he felt the figurative cold clasp of the iron collar about his neck.

And now, tonight, Edwin was confined to his study as Sophie and the servants—whom she had finally subverted to her will and control—prepared for a dinner party—to which he was not invited. The extent of the indignities to which she subjected him knew no bounds.

In his mind, Edwin Upton briefly and painfully reviewed the list of abnegations and surrenders that Sophie had demanded of him to reduce him to his present state. In the very beginning, Sophie had displayed a protective, almost-obsessive regard for his age and health that he found flattering at first, and reassuring in that he considered it indicative of her true warmth and feeling. After a while, he realized that this was simply a ploy, a lever Sophie used to separate him from longtime friends and associates.

At first he missed the social intercourse of old very little—after all, Sophie substituted herself for his associates. Indeed, though perhaps Sophie Payne feigned the extent of her interest in art and in his extensive library she was by no means ignorant. She was well read and had obviously benefited from an extensive education. She proved nearly his equal in knowledge of literature, art, and science. Often, however, he could not help feeling that while such things—to his mind—were objects to be desired in their own right—to her they were simply means to an end. The only books that seemed to genuinely interest her were obscure little volumes by S. A. D. Tissot, Albert Moll, Richard von Krafft-Ebing, John Humphrey Noyes, John Harvey Kellogg, and Ellen White.

The second phase of Sophie's plan to sever his connections with the entire outside world was the elimination of his longtime trusted solicitor. She had exhibited extreme patience in this regard, undermining Edwin's confidence in his associate ever so slowly until finally, he grew more receptive to her casually phrased objections to the man's continued employ. In the end, Edwin had proved fainthearted and could not bring himself to formally sever their longtime professional relationship. Here Sophie was most willing to represent "his wishes" by proxy, and she dismissed the astonished and dismayed gentleman herself while Edwin stood by silently—patently uncomfortable—too cowardly to intervene or reassert his own wishes.

Of course, the resulting vacuum in his affairs needed to be filled at once, and here Sophie just happened to have her own trusted firm of solicitors who would be willing and most capable in the handling of these matters. Due to the easy rapport between Sophie Payne and the young men of Rutgers, Preston, and Fulgate, Edwin soon found himself uncomfortable in their periodic meetings. His own words seemed to ring hollow in the room, so that after a bit, he informed Sophie of all his affairs and appointed her informally as his agent in all correspondence and meetings with his new team of legal representatives.

In the coming months, Edwin was given an occasional document to sign, which Sophie explained was but a formality of little consequence. It would not be necessary for him to trouble himself with reading the details on the tedious pages. Ever so slowly, piece by piece, Edwin signed away the control of his entire fortune—and even the right to govern his own affairs—to Sophie Payne.

The third phase of Sophie Payne's takeover of every aspect of Edwin's life was her slow gaining first of influence, then of control over his longtime trusted servants. In countless little ways, he was made ever so subtly to appear indecisive. His decisions, when made, were often cast with the merest hint that might indicate he was losing his faculties. Sophie did not rush this process, but rather paused frequently between the various phases of its implementation for good measure. But at last she succeeded here—as in all other aspects of his life—until now, were he to issue a rare order to his own servants, they would look questioningly to Sophie for a signal whether to comply. Finally, her control over his servants was applied to the point where the household staff obeyed Edwin with a grudging reluctance that sometimes bordered on outright impertinence.

And now that Sophie ran the household and controlled Edwin's business affairs, and now that Edwin was deprived of his solicitor, his old friends, and his associates, Sophie dictated that he should stay in his nightshirt as he was not well, required much rest, and he needed to "conserve the acuity of his faculties."

Edwin had the run of Basilby House part of the

time, but were Sophie to give a reception for one of her many friends or a dinner party, she would first suggest that he might be more comfortable if he remained in his study and bedchamber while the party carried on downstairs. She would then suggest that he looked tired and a trifle pale, and that she would send his evening meal up to his rooms so that he might retire early for some much-needed rest. The lock for his elegant wardrobe was changed and Sophie Payne kept the key "until he was again strong enough to take up his former role in society."

The intelligent reader must be inquiring what would possess a brilliant man of keen mental faculties to be degraded and treated in so wretched a fashion. I must confess that this is a cautionary tale with a moral which will soon become evident. By now the intelligent reader would find it absurd to believe that even the vibrant charms of a winsome beauty like Sophie Payne would be sufficient to enslave the fourth Earl of Plimsoll in every aspect of his life.

And this would be true, save for the fact that Sophie Payne had—throughout the unfolding of her plan—been engaged simultaneously in addicting Edwin fiendishly to a degrading and unspeakable vice. And the more his addiction progressed, the more weak and helpless he became to confront her, or to gainsay her machinations.

This addiction to unnatural vice was inflicted by proxy through the expertise of Chadwick, Sophie

Payne's own personal maid. Here the progression of the story must take a brief aside so that the reader will understand how these vile acts came to be practiced upon Edwin.

It would be wrong to assume that Edwin experienced no pleasure in his state of virtual slavery. Despite his new role as de facto prisoner in Basilby House, his life was not devoid of pleasure. Chadwick the maid was the sole administrator of these most powerful inflictions of unwholesome pleasure upon his person.

Scarcely a week after Edwin's marriage to Sophie Payne, Chadwick was summoned to Basilby House to look after her mistress. The closeness and familiarity between maid and mistress was obviously of long standing and included genuine affection.

Edwin took an almost immediate dislike to Chadwick's manner. Chadwick's mode of dress was strict and unvarying: black high-heeled oxfords, silk stockings, a severe black skirt, a long-sleeved, round-collared white blouse, black tie, crisp white cotton gloves, and often, a low-crowned white straw hat with a black band worn at a jaunty angle that somehow added to the impertinence of her demeanor. Chadwick's dark hair was always worn up behind in a tight swirl, and Edwin thought her rather thick dark eyebrows were indicative of habitual sensuality. In this he was more correct than he knew. Chadwick was an attractive young woman, in her twenties, perhaps more handsome than lovely. Edwin thought her uniform a trifle too snug and too revealing of the generous—though not excessive—curves of her hips, bottom, and pert breasts than propriety would dictate.

At first, Chadwick was not openly impertinent to Edwin. However, something about her countenance, the set of her lips—ever so slightly upturned at the corners as they were even when she was not smiling—signified a mixture of complacent contempt and impudent amusement, veiled just enough by an outward assumption of politeness and compliance that was all the more insulting due to its lack of genuineness.

That Sophie chose Chadwick as the instrument of the vile pleasures to which she had Edwin subjected added insult to injury. That Sophie made him submit himself to such indignities at Chadwick's hands was an unending source of gall.

The lure that kept him as helpless as a pinned butterfly during the vile proceedings was the sight of Sophie Payne in her outlandish tightly laced patent leather boots with their outrageously high heels that forced her trim little feet into an almost-indecent tiptoed pose. For while Chadwick's hands caressed him wickedly beneath his nightshirt, Sophie always stood or sat above him, holding her skirts up to exhibit herself to the thighs—resplendent in her high-heeled boots. Even as a youth, Edwin had frequent pollutions to lewd visions of mocking, laughing women in high-heeled boots. How and where Sophie had obtained the boots Edwin did not know, though they were reserved solely for the occasions of his shame. By some vicious intuition, Sophie had divined and exploited his weakness.

Such was his addiction to this captivating close-up view of Sophie Payne in her wicked boots that the sight held him a virtual prisoner. Chadwick could thus practice her carnal handiwork beneath his nightshirt and deplete his virility. During these debauching episodes, the expression on Sophie Payne's wide-eyed face was so sweet, innocent, and sympathetic as she gazed down at the proceedings with parted lips and flushed cheeks, as to render the surpassingly lovely vision of her all the more corrupt and wicked.

Edwin surveyed the chamber bell, suspended from the ceiling in the corner of his study. Another one of Sophie's infernal little alterations, he thought wearily. Rather than a braided bellpull in both his bedchamber and study connected to a system of numbered bells in the kitchen—"belowstairs"—that would summon servants at his whim, the pull in his bedchamber now rang only in his study.

Sophie and Chadwick were even now likely to be across the hall, profaning the sanctity of his private domain in preparation for the indignities soon to come. They referred to what they did to him as "A Dose of Chadwick's Sleeping Tonic," and rang for him when their preparations were complete.

Even as Edwin's thoughts were thus occupied, the bell jangled. Edwin sighed and stood up. Already the evidence of his addiction to the enslaving caresses which Sophie had Chadwick inflict on him was tenting the front of his nightshirt most indecently. As Edwin crossed the hall obediently, the state of his nightshirt remained mute testimony to the extent of his degeneration. Even the prospect of such fulfillment could induce it.

Edwin rapped softly on his own bedchamber door and Chadwick opened it from within. Her smile of greeting was as self-satisfied and smug as always. Across the room, Sophie Payne awaited him, seated primly upon a stool. Her dress was the epitome of propriety with its high collar and long, full sleeves. Sophie's hair was worn long and loose. Her face seemed radiantly sweet. "Come, Edwin, the dinner party will commence directly, so we will soon have other, more pressing matters to occupy us. Assume the usual position, if you please!" Though her words bespoke petulance, her tones were sweet and soft. Sophie's booted feet rested on a plush ottoman. Beside it, an unfolded handkerchief lay carefully placed upon the intricate pattern of the Moorish carpet. Beyond the handkerchief was an upholstered chair for Chadwick's comfort.

Chadwick escorted Edwin condescendingly to his station over the handkerchief and, still smiling, assisted him as he knelt to assume an undignified, even ridiculous posture. Edwin now knelt astride the handkerchief, his elbows resting on the ottoman, his eyes nearly touching Sophie's lovely bewitching boots. Sophie drew the hem of her skirt upward gently until her fashionable boots were revealed to his enraptured gaze from highly arched, dainty little soles, to the tops of her thighs. Dozens of delicate little gleaming eyelets assured a snug fit and made the boots conform exactly to every supple curve of Sophie's ankles, calves, and thighs. Edwin's eyes lingered on the wicked heels, whose height thrust Sophie's delicate weight forward, lending to her posture a strong element of affectation and forcing her on tiptoe. His eyes caressed the gleaming pointed toes of Sophie's boots, while his nostrils inhaled the scent of the shining black leather. Sophie turned her booted feet this way and that, rotating her ankles to enthrall his gaze.

Behind him, Chadwick had seated herself comfortably on the upholstered armchair, and tucked her skirt immodestly up about her knees. Her own patent leather oxfords sported heels far higher than what could be found even in a fashionable cobbler's shop. Chadwick looked to her mistress for the usual sign to commence and received the nod she sought. Then her pristine white-gloved hands stole beneath the hem of Edwin's nighshirt from behind to have their carnal, intimate way with him.

Edwin gasped, jaw hanging a trifle slack, as his eyes drank in their fill of the booted goddess at whose feet he knelt, while his nerves were agitated suavely and his most private parts violated soundly.

Despite Edwin's contempt for Chadwick, each time her gloved hands exercised his private parts, the certainty that Sophie's perversity engineered his release to come at the hand of she whom he so despised turned topsy-turvy in his head. During those very moments of vile pleasure, this realization heightened the intensity of the lewdly addictive sensations.

Chadwick bent forward at the waist, her face a mask of self-righteous detachment if not censure while her knowing hands played his nerves like a Stradivarius, drawing him against his will toward an intense rhapsody of shameful delights.

It was during these moments before his discharge, as Chadwick's skilled hands postponed his release again and again, that fluttering sensations in his chest often alarmed Edwin. It was as if this surfeit of illicit pleasure which Chadwick's hands forced upon him as they worked gently and deftly beneath his nighshirt had overtaxed his heart to the point of affecting its rhythm adversely.

At long last, with a low, gasping sigh, Edwin succumbed to the inevitable. As Chadwick drained his strength from him, his eyes remained riveted on the gleaming pointed toes of Sophie's stylish high-heeled boots.

After the desperately intense, shuddering moments

had subsided, Edwin found that his shame always peaked as Chadwick grasped his arm and helped him rise on unsteady legs. Edwin's eyes always avoided the spread handkerchief upon the floor and its feeble contents that spoke so eloquently of his abject state and his carelessly squandered manhood.

Sophie and Chadwick then led Edwin to his bed. As they tucked him in with their careless hands and their self-satisfied smiles, he realized that he was but a ghost in his own house, rendered all the more insubstantial each time he surrendered to Chadwick's clever, violating hands. They left him alone in the darkness and went out.

It wasn't long before Edwin Upton fell into a leaden sleep, even as the voices and joyous clamor from below signified that Sophie's elegant guests had arrived and her dinner party had commenced

The Playthings

Nurse Slade walked primly down the gleaming white-tiled corridor, past the rows of numbered drawer-doors, each with its own status gauges and security keypad. Nurse Slade was sadistic enough to enjoy her work thoroughly! Despite her proper demeanor and her crisp, primly starched white uniform, Nurse Slade allowed herself the slightest mincing wiggle of her hips to punctuate each stride. The medical cart she was pushing rolled forward on silent rubberized wheels. The only sound in the long corridor was the measured feminine click of Nurse Slade's dainty white shoes with their fashionable bows and exaggerated high heels. Nurse Slade's posture was thrown forward by the high spike heels of her shoes in such a way that the curves of her calves, hips, buttocks, and breasts were accentuated. In addition to her unusual shoes—which were actually regulation in the facility-nine building—her ensemble consisted of a modestly long, white uniform with a long-sleeved, high-collared top, and an equally crisply starched white cap. Her flesh-tone stockings had seams and big flirty toe and heel reinforcements. Nurse Slade's hair was up in a tight bun, styled perfectly not a single strand out of place. Nurse Slade's full-lipped mouth was set in a firm, determined line. When it came to tending the pleasure-units, Nurse Slade went strictly by the consortium's facility-nine guidebook, and she enjoyed it!

The cart that Nurse Slade pushed contained medical equipment and its own pressurized distilled water cylinder connected to a tiny faucet and sink, a pile of neatly folded sterile cloths, a box of gleaming black rubber elbow-length gloves, and a drain-away suction device with a whole assortment of disposable rubber tips of various sizes. The drain-away's suction hose was connected to a small reservoir tank, hidden in the closed lower portion of the cart's metal cabinet. There was also a small control panel with a built-in chronograph-stopwatch.

Nurse Slade loved her work in the facility-nine building. The building was situated outside a medium-sized town where it was least likely to attract unwanted attention. Nurse Slade—a fully qualified and trained medical professional earned four times the salary she could command in a local hospital—or even in the city hospital of the largest metropolis not too far away. Every day Nurse Slade and over ninety other pretty nurses, reported to an office building at the start of their rotating shifts.

From the small parking garage in the basement level of the office building, the nurses were chauffeured, in curtained vans, to the facility-nine building where they began their shifts. When the vans arrived at the facility-nine building, they drove into one of several large freight entrances, each secured by an automatic overhead door that the drivers controlled with dashboard buttons.

The huge facility-nine building, situated down a long country road, attracted little attention. It had few windows. The locals who entered the small immaculate lobby seeking employment were informed politely that the facility functioned as a storage terminal and was not hiring at the present time. Facility-nine was actually a fully equipped surgical hospital with the most advanced medical equipment. Several of the worlds' best surgeons —all female—worked in facility-nine under the utmost secrecy. The consortium that employed their skills paid them astronomical salaries—far greater than what they could have commanded in the finest private hospitals.

The corridor down which Nurse Slade walked was

lined on each side by a single row of numbered drawer-doors. Nurse Slade and her cart stopped by a door designated L246. Above the security keypad, a small green light blinked on and off rhythmically. The pleasure-unit in L246 needed milking! Nurse Slade smiled.

And it was expecting her, too! The status gauges indicated a rapid pulse and a rather high blood pressure, as if the poor creature inside knew what she was going to do to it—and knew it to be imminent. The penile plethysmograph gauge indicated a surgically enhanced erect phallic circumference of just over eight inches— certainly more than respectable!

Nurse Slade entered her master access code on the security keypad just above the drawer-door of L246. As she waited for the door to open, she snapped on a pair of the black rubber gloves. The facility-nine guidebooks all rigidly prohibited nurses from handling the pleasure-units directly.

The door to the L246 pod retracted silently upward into the wall and the drawer upon which the pleasure-unit lay slid outward into the corridor with a soft hiss of compressed air. Nurse Slade smiled with anticipation, relishing her power as the giver of both pain and pleasure.

The sterilized pleasure-unit was a male, approximately twenty-five years of age! It was limbless. What would have been its arms and legs terminated in short, perfectly rounded, featureless stumps. It reclined upon its back on a black cushion of rubberized pneumatic foam. A thick webbed strap about its middle held it firmly in place. Its body was nearly hairless. All hair from its head, face, armpits, genitals, and chest had been removed by electrolysis when it was first acquired. Only its eyebrows remained. The pleasure-unit was naked—there was no need of clothing as the acclimatization pods were all conditioned rigidly for both temperature and humidity. A hydrating nutrient feeding tube protruded from one corner of its mouth. A thick black solid-waste elimination tube disappeared up between its buttocks. Its erect penis was capped with a black rubber external catheter whose tube plugged into an especially designed wall socket on one side of the acclimatization pod. There were electrodes on its chest, and scalp, and the plethysmographic sensor was a narrow band fastened rather tightly about the base of its hugely thick penis. From back inside the acclimatization pod came a dim pink glow from the daytime band lights and the soft whirring of ventilation fans.

Nurse Slade checked its chart. This one was acquired eight months ago and had its surgery one week after its acquisition. It had gone through its sensory-deprivation regimen, its nurture therapy, and was now in the first week of its sexual-prowess training. If all went well, it would bring a very handsome price in another month or so.

There was great demand for customized pleasure-units on the world market these days. With the worldwide emancipation and equality of women came a whole new industry. Wealthy women the world over could pay a vast sum and have a fully trained pleasure-unit and its life-support pod delivered to their palatial homes. The consortium guaranteed a four-day turn-around for every worldwide order—or a full refund. Setup was also included. A maid or a private nurse could be trained by a helpful consortium representative to care for a pleasure-unit in just a few days.

Nurse Slade noticed that the pleasure-unit still had its scrotum. This one had been sterilized by vasectomy rather than testicular reabdominalization or castration. Some women, when ordering customized options, specified that their pleasure-unit's scrotums should be removed surgically—they regarded them as unsightly. The testicles were still viable and were placed back up into the abdomen —from where they had descended in the first place. The fact the testicles could not escape the higher body temperature of the abdomen guaranteed sterility as well as a vasectomy. However, suppose a client or some of her friends had a sadistic urge—testicles left vulnerable within the scrotum added another delightful option. Of course, the wealthy women who ordered pleasure-units solely to play out their sadistic tendencies nearly always insisted that the scrotum and testicles remain intact. An intact scrotum made the facility-nine nurse's own duty of occasionally punishing recalcitrant pleasure-unit trainees easier too. Nurse Slade enjoyed punishment duty most of all!

Nurse Slade bent prettily at the waist, her smug face now scant inches from the pleasure-unit's own beseeching one. "Its time for me to empty your testicles for you!" Nurse Slade cooed. "Hold out as long as you can, because if you come too soon, I'm going to have to punish you. We can't sell pleasure-units that are premature ejaculators now, can we?"

The poor thing couldn't even answer Nurse Slade. It just gurgled pathetically. She could see the fresh scar across the front of its throat where its vocal cords had been removed. The ability to talk was not considered desirable by most of the bored young women who purchased their pleasure-units from the consortium. Nurse Slade set the stopwatch built into the small control panel of her medical cart.

Nurse Slade reached down and held the pleasure-unit by its hard penis to remove its external catheter and made a mental note to replace the catheter's nozzle tip when she was finished masturbating it. Nurse Slade always thought of the pleasure-unit as things, never as people. The operative pronoun was "it," never "he." Nurse Slade found her duties in the facility-nine building to be deliciously cathartic. Were she to have a rare argument with her husband, or occasional difficulty with her teenaged children, or become annoyed with one of her many girlfriends who shared the pleasant tree-lined neighborhood where they all lived, she would just secretly take it out on the helpless pleasure-units at work, and be paid scrumptiously in the bargain! Not to mention how great sex with her husband was after her shift was over!

Nurse Slade stood prettily, her legs together, the perfect seams of her stockings on display, and remained bent slightly at the waist as she took the pleasure-unit's scrotum in one rubber-gloved hand and its thick, rigid penis in the other. In another moment she was masturbating it, skinning its big penis up and down with firm clinical strokes. The pleasure-unit squirmed helplessly in its bonds and grunted, its eyes locked on the swelling curves of Nurse Slade's breasts beneath her tight high-collared uniform blouse—the delights of its nurture therapy were still recent in its mind.

It looked up at her worshipfully. Nurse Slade and her colleagues were uniformed goddesses to it, so crisp and white and clean. They even smelled nice. The sensory overload when a nurse unlocked the absolute quiet of the acclimatization pod and released a pleasure-unit—even if only for a brief time—took on the intensity of a religious experience. That the nurses expertly administered intense pain and intense pleasure simply added to the unpredictability of their divine nature. The pleasure-unit writhed in its bonds. After many hours of near-total sensory deprivation, the sensations of slow masturbation were almost agonizing in their intensity. Still, it was pathetically desperate to please Nurse Slade. It was determined not to ejaculate before the proper time—and not only for fear of genital punishment either—but also in an almost-comical desire to make her proud, to please the lovely creature before whom it was as helpless as an infant.

Somewhat prudishly, Nurse Slade ignored the private physical signs of her own sexual arousal, though she did wish she had a stool to sit on so she could cross her lovely legs together—tightly! She pressed her thighs together and tensed her buttocks. Her lips were parted and her cheeks flushed prettily as she gently abused the pleasure-unit's hugely engorged sexual organ. Nurse Slade savored the feel of absolute power. She delighted in having the helpless "man-things" under her thumb. She loved both masturbating them and punishing their vulnerable genitals.

"Am I making you feel good between your legs?" Nurse Slade inquired coyly. Then she giggled. "Ooh, you poor wittle thing! You don't have any legs, do you? Just stumps—that's all!" Her eyes sparkled with amusement. "Well, anyway... Am I making your genitals feel good? Do you like what I'm doing to you? Hmmm?" Like most consortium nurses, Nurse Slade had acquired the habit of talking baby-talk to the pleasure units as she tended them, sometimes even when she administered their genital punishments sadistically.

The pleasure-unit squirmed and panted, now drenched with perspiration, its mouth gaping as its chest heaved, desperately trying to suck in enough air. The bloated purple tip of its thick swollen penis oozed a steady stream of precome, that lubricated Nurse Slade's rubber gloves and gave soft squishy sound effects to the masturbation. The pleasure-unit struggled silently, soundlessly mouthing pathetic pleas for sexual release and an end to the refined torment of the slow masturbation-training that Nurse Slade inflicted gloatingly.

Nurse Slade's own secret sexual arousal assured that she had no pity. The masturbation was so very slow, clinical, and thorough that she had to back off ever so slightly when the status panel indicated that the pleasure-unit's blood pressure and heart rate were nearing the red zone. Nurse Slade loved the big, floppy, helpless drooling thing that she worked in her hands. Her black rubber-gloved hands looked so little and bossy as they pulled on it and abused it. She also secretly gloated over the fact that her victim, now limbless and voiceless, could never divulge what she did to it in the secret consortium facility. And soon it would disappear forever, simply a commodity on the international pleasure market.

At last, even Nurse Slade's latent sadism could prolong its torment no longer. She gave its penis a few firm pulls and tugs to push it past the point of no return. It was time to finish it off. The pleasure-unit went limp, its gaping mouth emitting a series of pathetic gurgles. It was drooling, too. Its penis began to spasm in Nurse Slade's hand. She reached quickly for the nozzle of the drain-away suction device and slipped it over the tip of the pleasure-unit's sex organ to catch its seminal fluid. She laughed softly as she watched its contortions as it climaxed, its body thrashing with abandon against its bonds. All throughout the pleasure-unit's orgasm, one of Nurse Slade's hands was occupied holding the drain-away's suction nozzle securely over the tip of its twitching sex organ. Nurse Slade's other hand was employed by firmly gripping its scrotum and kneading its helpless testicles to empty it out.

"Poor thing, you have more than exceeded your punishment deadline," Nurse Slade said with grudging approval and perhaps just a trace of disappointment. "Let it happen. Squirt your sperm for me and let me make you nice and sleepy!" she purred smugly, goading her victim.

Finally it lay limp, drenched with its own sweat and apparently senseless. Nurse Slade removed the drain-away nozzle and changed it, to prepare for the next pleasure-unit. Nurse Slade remembered to catheterize it with a new external catheter. (She loved using the internal catheters, but they were to be used only as a follow-up to a punishment session). Nurse Slade entered the close-code on the keypad, and the acclimatization pod retracted back into the wall. As the door slid silently down to seal it in its prison once again, Nurse Slade snapped off her rubber gloves and observed the status panel with smug satisfaction. The pleasure-unit's heart rate, blood pressure, and erectile circumference had all decreased drastically, and the blinking green light indicating that a pleasure-unit was due for masturbation had gone out.

Nurse Slade took the elevator down into one of the lower levels, where her next duty zone was specified. The facility-nine building had two aboveground levels and nine belowground. Each level was composed of a grid of twenty-five east-west running hallways and twenty-five north-south running corridors. The status panels on the outer face of each acclimatization pod alerted constantly patrolling nurses as to which pleasure-units needed punishment and which needed milking. The elevator was spacious, and Nurse Slade shared the ride with two other nurses—all with their fully equipped medical carts. All three women chatted pleasantly. One would never dream from hearing them giggle and chat about mundane things that their duties involved such heartless and sadistic treatment of their utterly helpless charges.

Nurse Slade stepped off the elevator onto sublevel eight. Before she resumed her duties and again patrolled the white-tiled corridors looking for active punishment and masturbation status-panel lights, she took a breather in the nurse's break room. There was a break room on every level.

Nurse Slade was also scheduled to meet a junior nurse in the break room and take her along for the remainder of her shift to train her. The break room was well equipped both for comfort and convenience, and was nearly full, but Nurse Slade spotted the junior nurse right away.

She smiled and the junior nurse came over to her table. The junior nurse was young, probably about twenty-two, and very cute. She looked friendly and walked in her extremely high heels with that unfamiliar ever-so-slight awkwardness that was charming in its own way. She introduced herself as Junior Nurse Masters. Nurse Slade took to her at once and decided to take her under her wing right from the start.

After break, Nurse Slade and Junior Nurse Masters began patrolling the hallways and corridors of sublevel eight looking for status-panel lights indicating that a pleasure-unit needed either milking or punishment. They spotted one almost at once. It was blinking red just ahead up the corridor! A punishment light! Nurse Slade carried herself with a detached professionalism that gave no indication of her delight.

Junior Nurse Masters looked a little eager and admitted she had never performed a proper punishment before. Nurse Slade told her that there was really nothing to it. Nurse Slade had already trained several other junior nurses and was an expert at teaching them their duties. Nurse Slade also explained to Junior Nurse Masters that she had once worked in the postoperative blocks, tending pleasure units after their testicular reabdominalization surgery. They had to be masturbated eight to ten times per day to help their testicles adjust more quickly to the shock of their new abdominal placement.

Nurse Slade pushed their medical cart right up beside the acclimatization pod with the blinking red punishment light. The gauges on its status panel indicated that the pleasure-unit inside was extremely nervous. Its blood pressure and its pulse rate were both elevated. Understandably, the plethysmographic penile circumference reading showed no trace of an erection.

"It knows its testicles are going to be subjected to a punishment session any minute now!" Nurse Slade told Junior Nurse Masters as she reviewed the status-gauge readings with her. The drawer-door to this acclimatization pod was labeled L891. Nurse Slade asked Nurse Masters to enter the eighth-level access code on the keypad. Then both women snapped on their black rubber gloves.

A second later, the door to L891 retracted up into the wall silently. The drawer with its acclimatization pod slid outward into the corridor with a hiss of compressed air.

This pleasure-unit seemed to be in a state of extreme apprehension. It lay gulping and squirming on its rubberized wipe-clean cushion of black pneumatic foam. The web strap that held it down creaked with its futile efforts to escape. It had almost dislodged its feeding tube from the corner of its mouth with its exertions, and a gob of hydrating nutrient solution oozed down its chin. Its solid-waste elimination tube was in place up between its tightly clenched buttocks, and its external catheter was secure. Nurse Slade pointed out the scar where its vocal cords had been removed so they wouldn't have to hear it scream when they punished it.

Its penis was limp and soft while its scrotum dangled low, its big, vulnerable testicles splayed loosely between its smooth leg stumps. it looked up at both nurses, its eyes darting between them while it gurgled its futile pleas for mercy.

Nurse Slade smiled. She had just noticed that Junior Nurse Masters was looking down at the pleasure-unit, her face alive with knowing delight. A fellow sadist made a most enjoyable partner!

Nurse Slade took a minute to review some of the testicular-punishment techniques that she employed in the course of her duties. Junior Nurse Masters paid close attention, licking her pouty lips from time to time. Her cheeks were flushed prettily with anticipation. Nurse Slade always enjoyed explaining the finer points of genital punishment to the junior nurses. It increased their eagerness to participate in the process, and it added to the apprehension of the pleasure-unit victim, as it lay naked and limbless, with two pretty nurses standing over it, matter-of-factly discussing techniques that would soon have it contorting in agony.

It seemed like forever to Junior Nurse Masters, but finally Nurse Slade was finished with the preliminary portion of the lesson. Now it was time for some hands-on training. Nurse Slade reached down and took the pleasure-unit by its scrotum and squeezed—abruptly and hard. The pleasure-unit trembled, gritting its teeth in a valiant effort not to give in to the intense cramping pain that tortured its abdomen.

"While this initial method may appear to lack finesse," Nurse Slade explained, while maintaining her pressure on its testicles, "it is a valuable technique to begin with as it sensitizes the pleasure-unit's testicles almost immediately, so it can truly experience the agony of the more advanced punishment phases which I employ later. Now I will simply move into the second phase of punishment."

Nurse Slade delighted in inflicting intense pain on the pleasure-units. However, she was a professional and did not neglect her training responsibilities—especially with so potentially apt a student as Junior Nurse Masters. She changed her grip and the pleasure-unit began to gurgle and thrash, now in even more intense pain. "I call this the 'twist-and-slap method.' It is an excellent way to quickly bring the pleasure-units to a crescendo of agony."

Nurse Slade began twisting and slapping the pleasure-unit's vulnerable scrotum. Its mouth opened and shut as it spasmed on its pneumatic cushion and gurgled its mute screams of agony. "Oh, please!" Junior Nurse Masters begged, her soft, sweet voice dripping with sadistic eagerness. "May I please have a turn, Nurse Slade?"

Nurse Slade smiled and complied generously, despite

her own enjoyment of the task at hand. "Of course you may!" Nurse Slade showed Junior Nurse Masters the proper grip to employ. In another second, the pleasure-unit was subjected to a second round of agonizing punishment. Junior Nurse Master's face was ecstatic as she twisted and slapped the pleasure-unit's big, vulnerable testicles.

"Is it normal to enjoy doing it to them this much, Nurse Slade?" she inquired breathlessly, her cheeks flushed and her lips parted.

Nurse Slade smiled as she noticed that Junior Nurse Masters's thighs were pressed tightly together as she stood prettily and inflicted the sadistic punishment. The pleasure-unit was trembling and drenched with its own perspiration as it writhed desperately against its bonds. "If a nurse does her duty and employs her skills according to her instructions, then however she feels is irrelevant!" Nurse Slade said somewhat primly—though with a gleam in her eye. "Though why shouldn't a highly trained medical professional not derive pleasure and satisfaction from her duties?"

Nurse Slade let Junior Nurse Masters enjoy herself abusing the pleasure-unit's helpless testicles with the twist-and-slap technique for quite some time. Then she noted that it was time to demonstrate her favorite testicular punishment technique, which she called "punitive milking."

Junior Nurse Masters watched wide-eyed as Nurse Slade took one of the pleasure-unit's testicles in each hand, holding them between her index fingers and her thumbs. Then she began a series of very severe and rhythmically alternating squeezing motions, almost as though she were milking a cow. The effects were immediate and dramatic. With this third phase of sadistic punishment to which his already-agonized testicles were being subjected, the pleasure-unit contorted and thrashed about, half-crazed with pain. His mouth gaped in silent shrieks of intense agony.

Junior Nurse Masters couldn't take her eyes off the pleasure-unit's big penis which, despite its surgically enhanced size, remained flaccid. It looked so helpless as it flopped back and forth in time to its owner's agonized contortions. At long last, Nurse Slade let Junior Nurse Masters have her turn.

Junior Nurse Masters employed the "punitive-milking" technique and delighted in the torment she was inflicting. Nurse Slade had begun to monitor the status panel's blood-pressure and heart-rate gauges just to be safe. If the pleasure-unit's vocal cords had not been removed, the corridors and hallways of sublevel eight would have resounded with piercing shrieks of agony as the pretty junior nurse took to her duties eagerly.

Nurse Slade didn't neglect her duties in any aspect of the training. Several times she showed Junior Nurse Masters how to alter her grip slightly in order to inflict more intense pain.

Nurse Slade directly addressed the pleasure-unit only once while Junior Nurse Masters was punishing it. "You poor wittle thing!" she cooed, her voice full of mock sympathy. "We wouldn't have to make you suffer so if you hadn't had a messy accident when the advanced-sexual-prowess trainers were stimulating you. We can't sell pleasure-units that squirt their sperm before their women owners have been fully satisfied, can we?"

Scarcely five minutes later, Nurse Slade and Junior Nurse Masters resumed their patrol of the white tiled halls and corridors of the facility-nine building as they searched for more pleasure-units that needed milking or punishment. Their cheeks remained prettily flushed for the rest of their shift.

The hapless pleasure-unit they had just punished still writhed, again sealed in its acclimatization pod, and catheterized as additional punishment. The solid-waste elimination system in its acclimatization pod was on a punitive setting that alternated forceful enemas with suction evacuation. But its intense sufferings were all worthwhile. In a few short days, it would delight a female buyer!

The Research Institute

D aphne Blaine crossed her legs prettily and looked down at Edgar Wrightwell, who squatted miserably before her on the lushly carpeted floor of the limousine. Edgar was naked below the waist. A heavy straitjacket pinned his arms behind him, its straps cinched tight.

Daphne Blaine's ivory sling-back pumps with their wicked high heels and ultrafeminine bows had been kicked off and had ended up on the floor where Edgar squatted. Daphne wore sheer glossy stockings that flattered every curve of her legs. Daphne's stockings sported flirty toe and heel reinforcements, and the seams that ran up the back of her shapely calves were arrow straight.

Daphne wore a tight ivory suit with a short fitted skirt and a fashionably flared blazer. Her white high-collared blouse was starched stiffly. Daphne's dark hair was twisted up in a tight bun that was impeccability itself. Daphne's alluringly petite figure and sweetly innocent face belied a heart that delighted in the humiliation and discomfort of the helpless.

Daphne Blaine's size five feet had the highest arches that Edgar Wrightwell had ever seen, and her toes looked exquisite, ensconced in the daintiness of their sheer nylon embrace. Daphne swung her left foot on the carpeted floor of the big automobile and wriggled the pert little toes of her coyly arched right foot scant inches from Edgar's nose!

"What's the matter, Edgar, sweetie?" Her voice dripped sweetness and mock sympathy. "Did you expect your ride to tour The Research Institute to be different?"

Edgar Wrightwell couldn't answer. A black rubber ballgag filled his mouth and was fastened about the back of his head far too tightly for him to reply. Edgar was a wealthy tabloid publisher well past middle age. He was used to being treated with deference and respect —at least by his underlings in the multimillion-dollar publishing enterprise.

Edgar Wrightwell was shocked at the particularly nasty turn events had taken in the last several hours. There he squatted "bottomless" and totally helpless. The utter indignity of his predicament was not lost on him at all. His straitjacket pinioned his arms so tightly, he could barely breathe. The straitjacket's bottom was fastened with leather straps to two steel rings. One steel ring was built into the limousine's floor, the other protruded from a recessed fixture in its ceiling. When Edgar struggled in his bonds, the creaking of the leather straps was an audible testimony to the futility of his efforts. To add insult to injury, he was acutely aware of his nakedness. His knees had begun to ache.

"Is his penis hard, Daphne?" inquired a smug conceited voice from behind Edgar Wrightwell. Anna Masters, the director of The Research Institute, was seated immediately behind him on the plush tooled-leather elegance of the limousine's forward-facing rear seat. Daphne Blaine sat in front of Edgar on an equally luxurious rear-facing jump seat. Edgar was naked below the waist, absurdly helpless and surrounded. The dark-tinted windows of the big automobile assured the complete privacy of its passengers. Communication with the driver in his forward compartment was by phone only. There was no window between them at all.

Edgar's heart sank. Every mile that fell away beneath the tires of the big limousine was taking him farther from the world he controlled and the circles in which he moved—toward the unknown.

"His penis is soft and limp!" Daphne replied, more than a trace of scorn in her voice.

"Perhaps he is nervous and needs time to be acclimatized to his new surroundings. Rumor has it that he has sampled several of the pretty young underpaid female employees who slave away in the offices of his tabloid. Of course, he's the one calling all the shots there, isn't he?"

"I'm sure you are correct, Daphne," Anna Masters observed. Her voice was clinical, indicative of her advanced education. "Indeed, his lack of control in this situation is responsible for his temporary lapse in sexual vigor. Of this I have no doubt!"

Dr. Anna Masters wore black-leather patent slingback pumps with pointed closed toes and very high heels. Her flesh-tone stockings were seamed and complemented her red floral-print dress. She wore a black velvet blazer. A pair of dark-rimmed glasses completed her authoritative ensemble. Her blond hair was worn in a short bob which added sensuality to her look without in any way diminishing the severity of her demeanor. Dr. Masters personified the scientific curiosity of a stern and dedicated researcher.

"Perhaps if you manipulated his sexual organs just a bit, Daphne," Anna Masters suggested maliciously. "It might help him relax, and we could see what he is made of—in a manner of speaking. I think we both might forgive him if he developed an erection under the encouragement of a little genital stimulation."

Daphne Blaine was happy to comply with Dr. Masters's suggestion. She uncrossed her pretty legs and sat forward on her jump seat, both ankles together, her stockinged feet deliciously arched on the carpet. She bent seductively at the waist and took Edgar Wrightwell's soft penis gently between the thumb and forefinger of her left hand. Daphne smiled knowingly and began stroking Edgar's penis lewdly. Her strokes were skillful, light, and rapid and the motions of her fingers on his penis made his low, dangling scrotum flop and bounce in rhythm. Edgar gulped behind his gag and began breathing heavily through his nose. Daphne giggled. "Oh, he likes it when I do naughty things to him between his legs!"

Dr. Anna Masters took the opportunity to give Edgar Wrightwell a lecture as Daphne Blaine continued her gentle manual stimulation of his sexual organs. "Tabloid publishers can be so irresponsible." Her voice was smug and matter-of-fact. "The stories about The Research Institute that you published are not only shocking and libelous, but lacking in depth and vision. They are based solely on hearsay from two disgruntled nurses who left my employ some time ago. Of course, we were obliged to set you straight sooner or later!"

Edgar's penis was now erect. His balls swung to and fro between his legs as Daphne Blaine fisted him, his penis sliding through the warm, compelling clutch of her palm with each stroke. Despite his helplessness and the abject humiliation of his predicament, Edgar found the pleasures of the masturbation—inflicted on him against his will—to be most intense indeed!

"That's right, Dr. Masters!" Daphne said firmly, nodding her head in emphasis while maintaining the unrelenting rhythm of Edgar's masturbation all the while. "The terrible things that he published about us! And I simply can't imagine who would ever believe it all!"

Dr. Anna Masters thanked her pretty associate for her support while retrieving a rolled copy of Edgar Wrightwell's tabloid from her leather attaché case. "I have the article here and I'm going to read just a bit to refresh your memory."

"A female doctor and her nurses at a plush institute—secreted deep in the countryside—subject wealthy old men to degrading experiments that involve bondage, foot fetishism and hours of prolonged masturbation. The wealthy old men are told that they can sign away their fortunes and live out their lives carefree in surroundings of the utmost luxury. The brochures that promote The Research Institute also imply that there are lovely young women on staff who will see to their every sexual need as well. When they arrive at the institute, they find things to be very different and often not to their liking at all. They are sexually relieved, all right, but the nurses subject them to a very degrading form of slow masturbation that utterly robs them of dignity. The legal documents in which they signed over their entire fortunes are all ironclad, so there is no means of escape. Even if they succeeded, they would be destitute."

Dr. Anna Masters's smug, conceited voice paused from her reading. "And then, Mr. Wrightwell, you go on to quote the spurious allegations of my fired ex-employees—Nurse Inga and Nurse Sally. Despite my many loyal employees, there are always one or two in any large group who try to spoil everything. Well, we simply won't allow it!"

"Yeah, we have other plans, don't we?" Daphne Blaine giggled. Edgar was at the end of his tether, and she had found it necessary to stop stimulating his penis for a bit. Instead, she contented herself with holding his scrotum and kneading his testicles lightly. Daphne snickered. "We would never masturbate old men at The Research Institute. Would we, Dr. Masters? Of all the ridiculous ideas!"

"Precisely!" Dr. Masters exclaimed. "And that's where our little friend here comes in. After an abbreviated treatment of reeducational therapy at our Institute we will have him so addicted to both masturbation and fetishism that he will be totally under our control. Our plaything and pawn, if you will. Then we will release him, and he will write a retraction to his offensive article. He will say he went undercover and penetrated to the source of the story at the institute itself. And of course he found that both nurses were lying through their teeth. He will go on to write such a glowing review of our efforts that our enrollment prospects will increase tenfold. So you see, Daphne, even the most difficult individuals can be retrained and made useful with a little honest scientific effort on our part."

Daphne agreed wholeheartedly. "And I think your idea was brilliant, too, Dr. Masters! Imagine offering him a nice limousine ride to our facility and plying him with drinks and appetizers the night before at a reception held in his honor. And of course he was thinking all the time that we were just bribing him and that it would do no good. And then you had me slip that little surprise into his drink and presto! He wakes up naked and straitjacketed. And before he knows it, he's getting his limousine ride to The Research Institute, all right, but it's not going exactly how he expected." Daphne giggled. "Not what he expected at all!"

Daphne had now resumed Edgar Wrightwell's slow masturbation. His hard penis had drooled a string of precome into her palm, and its swollen head was turning a bloated, strangled purple from her expert manipulations. Daphne Blaine considered herself to be an artist when it came to the manipulation of the male sexual organ. And she considered her expertise to be an art form in itself that could be made either punitive or pleasurable depending on the whim of the masturbator.

"Don't you think that a man's scrotum is both disgusting and silly at the same time?" Daphne Blaine asked Dr. Anna Masters as she continued Edwin's genital stimulation. "I mean, the testicles—the source of their manhood—are just vulnerably dangling there in that ridiculous little wrinkled bag, almost out in plain sight, but ever so easy for women to use in controlling a man and giving him either pain or pleasure, whatever they feel like doing!"

"The scrotal sac is one of many silly things about men in general," Dr. Masters observed, a scornful note in her professionally modulated voice. "I find it absurdly simple to twist a man about my finger in a very short period of time. The ridiculous equipment that hangs between a mans leg's is every woman's aid in this respect. And I do find it advantageous to keep the males in our institute shaved around their penises and scrotums. It helps make them more docile and ashamed. Of course, slow masturbation training is best in this respect," she continued. "I find prolonged masturbation the best tool to make men obedient and weak-willed—just as they should be at all times!"

Edgar's body tensed abruptly in his straitjacket. Daphne smiled to see his Adam's apple bob up and down convulsively. Dr. Anna Masters had reached through between his legs and beneath his bare bottom from behind to grab his scrotum. She squeezed his testicles gently for a bit and then pulled downward on his scrotal sac—not enough to cause real pain, but it increased the intensely shameful pleasure of the masturbation that Daphne subjected him to gleefully.

Edgar Wrightwell realized instinctively that he was in the hands of a master in the art of manipulating a male's private parts. Daphne herself was a consummate expert in this, but now he was experiencing the handiwork of her mentor and teacher. His heart thudded and his brow glistened with perspiration as both women manipulated his sexual organs.

"Be ready with the penis-squeeze technique, Daphne," Dr. Masters warned a trifle bossily. "I'm not prepared to put him out of his misery and let you finish him off—not just yet! To really addict a man to masturbation, women need to play with his sexual organs for an extended period of time before permitting a climax. That way, when he is allowed to climax, the intensity will be such that he will find it addictive."

Daphne knew all the signs of an impending orgasm in male masturbation subjects. As a nurse at the institute, she had participated in hundreds of sessions of slow masturbation training. She and a partner had once kept one old fellow on the verge of sexual release for three continuous hours. She loved to watch their penises twitch after the few final pulls and tugs that were designed to bring them over the edge. Their penises would twitch spastically and then erupt in gooey cascades of thick white semen.

Daphne Blaine felt Edgar's penis spasm in her hand. She changed her grip immediately to cease the stimulation and squeezed the base of his penis firmly. Edgar's penis reared between her fingers. For a moment, she thought she had gone too far and had swept him over the brink. But then Edgar's penis reared again and only a single gob of sperm appeared, as if by magic, at the vent of the gasping slit in its tip. Just one single gob. Daphne giggled. She loved stopping their climaxes in midstream. Edgar Wrightwell moaned pathetically. He tried to speak, too, but the ballgag muffled his words beyond comprehension.

Anna Masters had handled Edgar's scrotum until his climax was narrowly averted. Then, as Daphne continued his masturbation—after waiting a few moments for the danger of full ejaculation to subside—Dr. Masters recrossed her legs and raised the pointed patent leather toe of her right high-heeled shoe up under Edgar's buttocks to prod his scrotum. She wiggled her foot, dangling his big testicles gently on the fastidiously polished pointed toe of her pump. Edgar moaned again at the humiliating intensity of these new sensations.

Poor Edgar! His slow masturbation was continued for the duration of his ride to The Research Institute in the limousine. Daphne had to employ the penis-squeeze technique to avert his orgasm over a dozen more times.

Finally Edgar heard Dr. Masters's smug voice ask Daphne to let go of his penis for a bit and let her have a turn. As Daphne did so, his momentarily abandoned penis throbbed noticeably with every beat of his pulse. The bloated tip of his sex organ oozed a quivering string of precome down onto the carpeted floor of the limousine. But then he felt Dr. Masters's warm knowing hand steal between his legs from behind and reach through under his buttocks. She pulled his penis back at an unnatural angle until its swollen gasping glans pointed toward the toes of her fashionable high-heeled shoes.

Dr. Masters twisted his foreskin a bit to give him maximum friction and sensation while holding his penis between the ball of her thumb and her index finger. Then she worked him lightly and rapidly with short strokes, masturbating him in a way that he had never experienced before. The poor fellow was panting through his nose now and drooling from the agonizing pleasure of the sensations that were mastering him. The cramping pain of his knotting thighs—a side effect of his uncomfortable squatting posture—and the tight misery of his straitjacket were all forgotten. His penis moistened Dr. Masters's palm liberally with gooey drops of precome that formed with increasing regularity at its gasping, tormented tip.

Then Dr. Masters changed her grip and took his penis in her fist, still holding it pulled back under his bare bottom at an unnatural and uncomfortable angle. "Make love to her fist! C'mon, Edgar, be a good boy and fuck her fist! Wiggle your bottom and fuck her fist like a good little man!" Daphne's voice dripped with scorn as she ordered Edgar to participate in his own masturbation. Dr. Masters even laughed herself as he complied. The straitjacket and the leather straps that connected it to its steel rings allowed him just enough slack to wiggle by raising and lowering his buttocks over and over again. Of course, this added to the cramping pain in his thighs but Edgar Wrightwell no longer cared.

He was simply desperate not to have the lewd sensations that he experienced as his bare excited penis thrust through Dr. Masters's warm skillful palm ever end—not until he achieved his humiliating sexual gratification and had his messy climax. Dr. Masters held her hand still and Edgar fucked it, his drooling penis with its strangled, bloated head sliding in and out of her fist as he bounced his bound, squatting body up and down absurdly. He hoped desperately that she would not take her hand away before allowing him his sexual release.

But Dr. Anna Masters had no such plans. She smiled as she spoke to her assistant. "We'll have no trouble making this one eat out of our hands now, Daphne. Look how easily he debases himself in order to experience a little fleeting pleasure—intense as it may be!"

Daphne was laughing openly at Edgar, abandoning all pretext of sparing his wounded pride. "He's drooling, Dr. Masters, and his face is turning all red! Let's finish him off and drain him dry!"

Dr. Anna Masters cupped her free hand just under where the sliding tip of Edgar's tool came thrusting out of her grip at the downward termination of each plunge. Daphne raised her delicious little tiptoed feet and rubbed their stockinged soles all over Edgar's sweating, straining face to inflame him. Edgar kept thrusting madly, fucking Dr. Masters's fist like an animal, mindless in its helplessness and its desperation for whatever form of release it was allowed.

A second later Edgar's penis reared and spasmed in Dr. Masters's fist as his eyes closed in response to an agonizing crescendo of pleasure. His breath fairly whistled out about the edges of his ballgag as his orgasm began. The powerful searing squirts as the jets of Edgar's sperm spurted into Dr. Anna Masters's palm—over and over again—were actually audible in their intensity.

Edgar's climax was prolonged beyond all endurance as Dr. Masters intensified it skillfully as she squeezed his penis rhythmically, milking him in time to the spasms of his sex organ.

At last he sagged in his bonds, drenched in perspiration, exhausted beyond belief, drained of his manhood and nearly senseless. Suddenly shame overcame his pleasure. The totality of his degradation knew no bounds. He knew then that this smug young woman whose hand was full of his carelessly wasted sperm had defeated him utterly.

Fifteen minutes later, the limousine was admitted through a wrought-iron gate and purred up the long private drive to The Research Institute. Daphne Blaine and Anna Masters left the limousine, smirking. Edgar was placed in the charge of two sternly pretty nurses in tight uniform dresses, high heels, and black rubber aprons.

Fifteen days later, Edgar Wrightwell's tabloid printed the only retraction in its history, and The Research Institute's clientele surged accordingly. Dr. Anna Masters became very wealthy indeed!

The Secret Police Nurses

The Changjin Experimental Prison was a vast facility that included huge sealed, windowless buildings with elaborate rooftop ventilation systems, high guard towers equipped with the latest night-vision equipment, electric gates, sunken exercise yards, underground cell-blocks, soundproof interrogation rooms, its own fully equipped research hospital, and luxurious quarters for the guards and Secret Police nurses that made up the staff. Staff quarters on the upper levels of the administration wing were graced with a lovely rooftop garden—with its own swimming pool surrounded by a perfectly manicured lawn—and actual trees.

Secret Police Nurse Cho-Lak wiggled as she walked down the spotless white-tiled corridor of the experimentation wing. She couldn't help the slight flexing twist of her hips and buttocks as she walked, any more than she could help her mincing steps that were accentuated by the measured feminine click of her high heels on the polished floor. Nurse Cho-Lak wore the regulation uniform of Changjin Experimental Prison. All Secret Police nurses were required to wear People's Army uniform—brown pointed-toe pumps with heels of such exaggerated height that they thrust their wearers' weight forward—forcing a wiggling baby-stepped walk and seductively emphasizing the curves of the Secret Policewomen's buttocks, calves, hips, thighs and breasts.

The rest of Cho-Lak's Secret Policewomen's uniform enhanced her feminine curves. She wore a brown skirt so short and so tight that if she were even to bend over in the slightest, the hem would slide up deliciously—almost to her hips. The curves of Nurse Cho-Lak's pretty legs were shown off exquisitely—even without the luxury of nylons—a rarity in Cho-Lak's stringently secure and almost totally sealed country. A matching brown uniform blouse was tucked primly into the skirt. Despite its proper long sleeves and high collar, its tight fit emphasized the firm points of her pert breasts. A peaked dress cap matched the skirt and blouse, and Nurse Cho-Lak's People's Army red epaulets and collar insignias, along with a black tie, completed her strict yet fetishistic ensemble. Nurse Cho-Lak's jet black hair was twisted up in a tight, perfect swirl. Not a single strand was out of place!

Nurse Cho-Lak pushed a gurney. Though its handles were of normal height for her, they extended downward so low that the cushioned bed portion—with its thick leather straps to hold down unwilling experimentation subjects—was barely six inches above the floor. The gurney was also odd because the cushion that would soon hold her prisoner-patient—though of normal width—was barely four feet long!

As Nurse Cho-Lak pushed her gurney down the spotless corridor, she glanced down frequently at her feet clad in the dainty little brown pointed-toe pumps with their bizarre high heels. Without the smooth slide of nylon and due to the cut of her stylish shoes Nurse Cho-Lak's toe cleavage was delightfully exposed. The flirty little clefts between all of her nestling toes were very much on display! The sexy cut of Nurse Cho-Lak's shoes also emphasized the high, wrinkled underswell of her arches.

Nurse Cho-Lak loved her work in the experimental prison. She was so fortunate to have written that essay praising the central government while still a schoolgirl! After that, she prospered mysteriously no matter what befell her peers. So now, instead of bending over, planting rice shoots in a terraced paddy with her pretty feet planted firmly in thick black mud, she was making a hundred times the salary of most of her peers and got to wear such lovely stylish uniforms as well! Not only that, she got to take out her aggressions on the patient-prisoners nearly every day. And now, to add to her sadistic delight, just three days ago she had been appointed to work with the most special prisoner of all—the specimen! The state had no mercy on its enemies, and neither did Secret Police Nurse Cho-Lak. She loved her work!

Nurse Cho-Lak turned a corner and started down another corridor. This one was busier. She passed several other Secret Police nurses dressed identically to herself who nodded and smiled as they minced by in their high heels. The other nurses were pushing gurneys, too—these were of normal size and contained prisoners fresh from the masturbation rooms. The prisoners had been injected with a paralytic drug that left them fully sensate, yet totally helpless, and then were wheeled to the masturbation rooms before being taken to the experimentation wing. The prison's female doctors believed that masturbation robbed the prisoners of their endorphins and left them more "suggestible" in the interrogation/experimentation phase.

Nurse Cho-Lak smiled as she saw the prisoners wheeled by, naked and helpless, their stomachs and abdomens gooey with the sperm that had been drained from them by pretty women in white lab coats in the masturbation rooms. Their penises were limp. Nurse

Cho-Lak paused by the open door to one of the rooms to watch a prisoner in the final stages of his masturbation. While his Secret Police nurse stood by smiling, ready to wheel him away to the experimentation wing after the masturbation, a pretty masturbation nurse was working him over. She looked so studious, prim and proper with her jet black hair up in a tight bun. She wore glasses and a spotless white lab coat.

She had kicked off her high heels, and her petite bare feet were arched prettily on the rungs of her stool as she sat above her prisoner's gurney and masturbated him. Her legs were crossed. Her uniform skirt rode high on her thighs. The masturbation nurse held the prisoner's scrotum in one hand and was flogging his penis with the other. Due to his paralyzed state, he couldn't move or even cry out. He just lay there, drenched in sweat, naked and panting out his desperation for release in his cruel little masturbator's hands.

Nurse Cho-Lak watched as the patient's abused penis twitched and jerked in the little hands that held it prisoner—worked it and pulled on it. Then she watched the semen erupt in a thick gooey spray and the masturbation nurse direct it—as she laughed and kept pumping—so that her prisoner was drenched in his own seed to add to his shame. After the prisoner's gooey penis went limp in her hand, the masturbation nurse looked up and smiled at Cho-Lak. The sadistic pleasure she took in her work was obvious on her sweetly pretty face.

Nurse Cho-Lak smiled back at her colleague and continued pushing her bizarre gurney down the corridors. At the next junction, she turned left and came to the highest security wing. It was reserved for the most secret state-sanctioned experiments. She applied her hand to the palmprint recognition pad and the door opened silently.

The corridors beyond the door were painted baby pink and illuminated with softer, more muted recessed lighting. Nurse Cho-Lak pushed her gurney into a room labeled with the sign EXPERIMENTAL PROTOTYPE PRISONER STORAGE ROOM 1-A. The center of the room was dominated by a large pale blue unit that looked like an incredibly complex and oversized one-drawer file cabinet. Hoses, gauges, and dials were attached to it everywhere. Status lights flickered on and off across its control panel. There were three other such units in the room—all arranged in a precise geometric pattern. But the control panels on the other three were blank, and there was no soft hiss of air-regulation pumps from inside them. The other three units were empty—for now.

Nurse Cho-Lak punched her security clearance code on the access pad of the unit's keyboard. Then she stood prettily, her eyes fixed on the drawer door as she waited for it to open, her face alive with anticipatory delight. There was a soft hiss of compressed air. Then the drawer slid out into the room at Cho-Lak's feet. There on a black pneumatic foam cushion lay her plaything, the prototype prisoner! The specimen! He lay before her naked. No clothing was needed due to the rigidly climate-controlled interior of the unit that served as his cell between experimentation sessions. The specimen was helpless. His big, hard penis was more thick than long. It jutted up from just below his shaved hairless abdomen. His big testicles were clearly defined in his low, dangling scrotum that splayed loosely on the cushion as it hung vulnerably down past his bare buttocks.

But the most unusual thing about this specimen was not the fact that he was naked. Naked prisoners were commonplace in Changjin Experimental Prison. What was unusual was the fact that this prisoner had neither arms or legs! All four of his limbs terminated in smoothly rounded, featureless stumps!

Secret Police Nurse Cho-Lak squatted down by her prey, her face alive with knowing, sadistic delight. "Want to come out and play?" she purred, her voice dripping with mocking sweetness. "Dr. Ling-Yap has another little session in mind for you if you would be kind enough to accompany me to her experimentation room. And Nurse Song-Ni will be there, too. Remember how hard she made your penis get last time?"

The specimen gulped and nodded. He well knew that it was utterly forbidden for prisoners to speak in Changjin Experimental Prison. He swallowed hard as he stared at Nurse Cho-Lak, noting the drum-tight stretch of her uniform skirt across her splayed thighs as she squatted above him. He gulped as he saw the delicious display of her toe cleavage, and the lovely arches of her bare feet—highlighted by the low, flirty cut of her fetishistic pumps, and even the trim pretty shape of her bare thighs.

In what now seemed to him like his past life, he had been a powerful minister of state and a district commissar before he fell out of favor with the People's Revolutionary Council and was taken at night, without a trial—and in a closed van—to Changjin Experimental Prison. And now he existed, utterly without dignity, yet not utterly without a degrading form of pleasure—one that he now found headily addictive. To be the helpless prisoner, pet, and plaything of the pretty Secret Police doctors and nurses was his only fulfillment now. He well knew that Nurse Cho-Lak delighted in sexually teasing him and making fun of his helplessness, but he did not care. In his suddenly and drastically narrowed world, she loomed like a goddess promising delight as well as shame and degradation.

Nurse Cho-Lak saw his penis increase in hardness and circumference in response to her proximity and the sight which she presented to his starved senses. She giggled, a sweetly feminine, yet gloating sound. She stood up and pushed the low gurney right up beside the drawer cell on which the specimen lay. Then she squatted down above him again to half-lift, half-roll him onto her gurney so that she could wheel him into the grueling discomfort and indignity of Dr. Ling-Yap's experimentation room.

Of course, Nurse Cho-Lak always managed to touch the prisoner's sexual organs "accidentally" when she moved him from his drawer cell onto her gurney. As she lifted him, one of her hands supported the side of his chest just beneath the armpit of his right arm stump. The palm of her other hand lifted him from between his legs, cupping both his scrotum and his penis! Her armless and legless prisoner grunted in helpless delight and squirmed, trying vainly to wiggle against her teasing hand to prolong the delicious sensation of her touch on his private parts.

His pathetic attempt just made her giggle again. In a moment, he found himself strapped down and helpless on her gurney.

Once again Nurse Cho-Lak minced in her high heels down the corridors of the top-secret wing of Changjin Experimental Prison. This time she was bound for Dr. Ling-Yap's well-equipped suite of highly classified experimentation rooms. This time the low custom-made gurney that she pushed contained the specimen—armless, legless, utterly helpless, and hugely erect. The specimen was so placed that he could look up at her and see her lovely amused face—above and beyond the bloated purple tip of his own tormented sex organ. He could also watch her thighs tense and flex as she walked in her high heels, the strutting wiggle of her hips. The specimen could only imagine what Nurse Cho-Lak would look like from behind, with her bottom wiggling deliciously in the skintight snugness of her Secret Policewomen's uniform skirt.

As they reached the electric door that led into Dr. Ling-Yap's experimentation suite, a knot of Secret Police nurses and masturbation nurse specialists passed them on their way to the elevators that would take them up to the garden lunchroom. They nodded and smiled at their colleague Cho-Lak but pointed and laughed mockingly at the specimen that lay strapped down on her gurney, naked and helpless. Nurse Cho-Lak giggled to see that the teasing only made her prisoner's penis swell even larger. A second later, the door swished open to admit them into Dr. Ling-Yap's experimentation suite.

Dr. Ling-Yap was delighted to see the specimen again, and she had her experiments all prepared. Dr. Ling-Yap was a young, pretty, spectacled woman in a tight uniform skirt and a white lab coat. She wore high-heeled pumps with low-cut sides identical to Nurse Cho-Lak's. Her black hair was pulled up in a smooth, perfect bun. Her only insignia was an armband on her sleeve that attested to her status as a senior prison physician and major in the State Security Force. The specimen's penis stiffened even more because Dr. Ling-Yap displayed toe cleavage as well.

Dr. Ling-Yap asked nurse Cho-lak to raise the gurney

to the level of a wheeled pedestal table that stood in the center of the experimentation room. Nurse Cho-Lak pressed a button on the gurney's handle, and the cushion on which the specimen lay was lifted hydraulically. Dr. Ling-Yap helped nurse Cho-Lak unstrap the specimen. Then Dr. Ling-Yap went to a wall cabinet to get a special harness—designed just for their armless and legless prisoner.

Nurse Cho-Lak lifted the specimen to a vertical position with one arm around his torso and her other hand teasingly supporting his crotch with a firm grip on his private parts! Dr. Ling-Yap fastened the naked specimen in the harness—a thick leather belt connected by straps to a leather collar that she buckled about his neck.

As Nurse Cho-Lak supported the excited prisoner and held him by his scrotum, Dr. Ling-Yap fastened another strap between the specimen's harness and a hanging overhead cable. She checked the cable connection and then stepped to a wall switch and activated the cable's tension, slowly raising the specimen up and out of Nurse Cho-Lak's violating hands to hang in the air— secured only by his harness. Nurse Cho-lak lowered the cushion of the hydraulic gurney while Dr. Ling-Yap moved the wheeled pedestal table until it was directly in front of the suspended prisoner.

Then Dr. Ling-Yap carefully fastened electrodes to the prisoner's scalp, chest, and genitals—handling his excited private parts perhaps more than was necessary in the process. The electrodes would help her measure his sexual arousal in the experiment to come. The wires from the electrodes ran to a small control console beside the prisoner from which Dr. Ling-Yap would control the experiment and make notes in her logbooks as it progressed.

Nurse Cho-Lak was delighted. She would be masturbating the armless and legless specimen during the experiments, mainly because the few masturbation nurses with a high enough security clearance to participate in Dr. Ling-Yap's experiments were already scheduled elsewhere.

Nurse Cho-Lak oiled her hands and stood smugly beside the suspended specimen while Dr. Ling-Yap summoned Nurse Song-Ni. Song-Ni was an interrogation specialist well known throughout Changjin prison, for her sadism. But she sometimes did extra duty as a teaser (or a masturbator) in the experimentation rooms.

The specimen gasped as Nurse Song-Ni strutted into the room. She was even tinier than Dr. Ling-Yap and Nurse Cho-Lak. She was clad in a baby pink, skintight, rubber, long-sleeved micro-mini dress with a high collar and built-in gloves. The pink rubber dress was stretched tight across the curves of Nurse Song-Ni's hips and bottom. She looked so cruel and dainty with her hair up in a tight authoritative bun and her pretty little bare feet displayed wickedly in matching baby pink slides with seven-inch heels. Nurse Song-Ni's walk was halfway between a prance and a wiggle, and she smiled wickedly. She turned about and bent over seductively to display her shiny rubber-clad bottom to the armless and legless specimen as he hung helplessly, suspended in his harness. A tiny portion of the bare curves of Nurse Song-Ni's bottomcheeks were just barely visible below the tight pink hem of her rubber dress. Nurse Cho-Lak knew that the baby pink rubber dress had to be shipped into their country from thousands of miles away and was incredibly expensive in the land of blue green quilted shapeless jackets and baggy pants. But to the elite and well-connected administrators of Changjin Experimental Prison, nothing was impossible.

Dr. Ling-Yap explained that the purpose of the experiment was to turn their prisoner into a hopelessly degenerate specimen—so addicted to having pretty women handle his sexual organs, and so subjected to induced fetishistic impulses, that he would be nothing but putty in the hands of a skilled female experimenter. The ramifications of these experimentation methods were almost limitless, and Dr. Ling-Yap was excited by them. She explained to Nurse Cho-Lak and Nurse Song-Ni that political prisoners could be incarcerated, enslaved to masturbation by prison nurses, and then released back into society now totally spineless and unable to bring about political change. These experimental methods could have wide-ranging applications for interrogation and punishment, too!

It was time to begin the experiment. Dr. Ling-Yap stepped to her control console to monitor the dials connected to the specimen's electrodes. Nurse Song-Ni climbed up onto the pedestal table directly in front of the suspended specimen. Her tight proper bun contrasted starkly with the lasciviousness of her pink rubber clothing. Her pink rubber dress had ridden so high on the smooth curves of her bare thighs that she grasped its hem with both her rubber glove—clad fists to tug it down. The only result was an ineffectual squeak of rubber against rubber and Nurse Song-Ni's low giggle as she noticed the specimen watching her efforts and the increased swell of his bare penis because of them.

Nurse Cho-Lak reached down under the suspended specimen's bare bottom from behind to grab his scrotum in her right hand and—still standing sexily tiptoed in her brown high-heeled pumps with her toe cleavage on display—she took the specimen's hard penis in her left fist and began abusing it gently, sliding its loose skin to and fro and up and down. Nurse Cho-Lak savored the expression of helpless delight and humiliation that crossed the specimen's face as she handled his genitals.

As Nurse Cho-Lak smiled and masturbated him, the armless and legless specimen squirmed in his harness as he hung helplessly and watched Nurse Song-Ni cross her legs and giggle. Dr. Ling-Yap and Nurse Song-Ni watched the tip of the specimen's tormented penis expand and turn a bloated purple under the slow teasing of his sexual organs, administered by Nurse Cho-Lak. All three cruel Secret Policewomen delighted in his shame and degradation.

Nurse Song-Ni crossed her legs and kicked off her high-heeled slides to point her dainty little bare toes, thus giving the specimen a penis-stiffening show to add to the intensity of the slow masturbation that he was experiencing. As Nurse Cho-Lak continued her expert stimulation of the specimen's genitals and Dr. Ling-Yap observed the progression of her experiment clinically, Nurse Song-Ni raised one pretty leg in the air, all the while keeping her perfectly formed toes pointed rigidly. The specimen's haggard eyes followed the motion of her foot and watched her as she laughed and reached up to stroke the curves of her thigh and calf with her pink-rubber-gloved fingers—almost as if she were inspecting her own flawless legs conceitedly, more to exhibit their beauty than anything else.

By now the specimen's penis was freely drooling the evidence of his helpless arousal in Nurse Cho-Lak's hands. Her palms and fingers were slick with his pre-come. Nurse Cho-Lak loved stimulating a prisoner's bare genitals and making them lose control slowly. The specimen's gooey arousal just proved that she was an expert manipulator. Nurse Cho-Lak rolled the specimen's testicles about in her right hand as she kept pulling on his stiff, bloated tool with her left.

Dr. Ling-Yap monitored the specimen's blood pressure and pulse rate as well as the electrical conductivity of his skin that indicated how much he was perspiring while undergoing his ordeal of shame and arousal. Dr. Ling-Yap said that it was now time to enter the enticement-and-mockery phase of the experiment.

Nurse Song-Ni got up on the pedestal table, kneeling lusciously on all fours with her pink rubber-clad bottom presented almost in the specimen's face and her exquisitely high-arched bare feet on display. She looked back over her shoulder at the specimen who was now practically drooling both from the sight of her and from the skillful way that Nurse Cho-Lak abused his genitals in her cruel, knowing hands. Nurse Song-Ni wiggled her bottom to and fro to entice the specimen all the more.

"Oooh you poor thing!" Nurse Cho-Lak exclaimed, her voice soft and dripping with mock sympathy. "Imagine if you were a real man...a whole man.... Then the lovely young woman before you would undoubtedly let you possess her and ravish her." Nurse Cho-Lak giggled, kept masturbating the specimen, and resumed. "But you are just our plaything, our toy, our specimen, aren't you?..." Nurse Song-Ni kept wiggling her bottom alluringly, exaggerating her swelling feminine curves wickedly.

"Imagine as my hands stimulate you—that you are fucking Song-Ni!" Cho-Lak went on, her voice soft, sweet, sympathetic. "Imagine you are thrusting your penis deep inside her. Just think how good it would feel if she was wiggling her bottom while you did it—just like she is now...." The specimen was drenched in sweat and panting, squirming in his harness and wiggling as he tried to increase the intensity of the already unbearably addictive sensations he experienced from Nurse Cho-Lak's masturbation.

Nurse Song-Ni kept wiggling as Nurse Cho-Lak began skinning the specimen's penis back and forth furiously. "Imagine your penis up under Song-Ni's pink rubber dress...thrusting into her...thrusting into her for all you're worth!" A high whimpering moan of agonizingly intense sensation erupted from the specimen's throat as his penis twitched and spasmed in his masturbator's busy hand.

Nurse Cho-Lak cupped her left hand over the tip of the specimen's penis to catch his seed while she squeezed his scrotum hard with her right hand, still gripping him under his bare bottom. Nurse Song-Ni laughed mockingly as the specimen's semen squirted into Nurse Cho-Lak's hand with such force that it oozed out from between her fingers to spatter the tiled floor, far short of its desperate goal of reaching the cruel scornful object of its desire.

The specimen contorted and writhed, panting and gulping as he fired salvo after salvo of his worthless seed into his tormentor's hand, his bleary pleasure-crazed eyes fixed on the teasing pink rubber-clad curves of the luscious temptress before him. At last his penis went limp as he sagged weakly in his bonds, acutely ashamed—now that his pleasure had subsided—of what had just been done to him. Nurse Cho-Lak kept hold of his limp penis in her gooey hand and pulled on it a time or two to milk out the last pathetic drops, the motions of her hand mocking his postorgasmic weakness.

The specimen thought that they were done with him, but they were not. During the course of the next several hours, he was subjected to many more indignities and had his seed drained from him four more times in a variety of imaginative ways.

At last Nurse Cho-Lak wheeled him back to his drawer cell and lifted him from her gurney to its pneumatic foam cushion. He was so weak and tired after his ordeal! Before sealing him in the confines of his high-tech prison, Nurse Cho-Lak smiled as she stood above him. His penis was drained and limp. She kicked off her left high-heeled pump, arched her pretty bare foot, and brought her toes to his mouth. She rubbed her arched bare foot all over his lips and nose and then ordered him to suck her toes. Nurse Cho-Lak sighed with delight as the specimen's obedient tongue probed slavishly between her bare toes.

A relaxing end to a day of enjoyment for a Secret Police nurse!

The Rubber Sanitarium

Chapter I

The two pretty women minced down the corridor in their seven-inch high-heeled patent leather pumps. Their heels clicked precisely on the tiles below their feet as they walked. Both were very regal, and both wore their hair pulled up in a perfect blond swirl. Their high heels forced their steps to be short and dainty, and their walk was halfway between a prance and a hip-wiggling strut. Both women were clad in scandalously short dresses fashioned from gleaming black rubber. The rubber dresses clung smoothly to the generous feminine curves of their hips, bottoms, and breasts. The seamless rubber dresses had high proper collars as if to offset the boldness of their indecent hemlines and both dresses sported built-in rubber gloves—also of the same gleaming black. The women's shapely legs were bare, and their naturally fair complexions enhanced the smooth curves of their calves and flexing thighs. The effect of their entire ensembles was at once both domineering and provocative.

The Gräfin was escorting Dr. Gerda Harm on a tour of her facility, of which she was rightfully proud. Dr. Harm was impressed and had every expectation of obtaining lucrative and fulfilling employ at the Gräfin's Rubber Sanitarium. And even though the lovely young doctor was unused to the bizarre uniform required of the sanitarium's all-female staff, she rather enjoyed the sexual power that it gave her—not to mention nearly seven inches of extra height! The prospect of being staff physician—with generous backing from the fabulously wealthy Gräfin's nearly unlimited research budget for medical and scientific equipment—lured her as well.

The Gräfin had just finished explaining to Dr. Gerda Harm some of the unusual treatments to benefit her patients. Some of them were at once so innovative—yet so bizarre—that the fascinated young doctor could hardly wait to see them exhibited. And that is where they were heading now—to the experimental treatments research wing of The Rubber Sanitarium! The Gräfin had explained that the stress of hectic modern life had taken a terrible toll on the health of her patients and that desperate and sometimes strange methods were necessarily employed to relieve them of their negative effects. Soon Dr. Harm would be deeply involved with the implementation of these treatment regimens herself—and the Gräfin hoped that she too would be innovative in the design of her own new treatments as well.

They paused briefly in the corridor outside Treatment Room A and then stepped inside. A male patient stood on tiptoe, naked below the waist, clad only in a shining black rubber straitjacket! A hook dangling from an overhead wire engaged a metal ring on the shoulders of his straitjacket, forcing him helplessly into his unnatural posture. The only furniture in the brightly illuminated room was a high stool. On the stool sat one of the Gräfin's most experienced sanitarium nurses, a young woman named Prudence. Prudence was clad in a head-to-toe full bodysuit of featureless—and ever so smooth—gleaming black rubber. It resembled a wet suit because it covered her completely. Yet, unlike a wet suit, the suit that Prudence wore was so snug that it both emphasized and enhanced the curves of her femininity, adding perfection of form without a trace of bulk or thickness. She appeared as a smooth, flawless being from a bizarre and beautiful planet. The only gaps in the suit were two rounded eyeholes and a narrow mouth opening that went from the base of Prudence's nose to her chin.

Dr. Gerda Harm was both fascinated and repulsed by the helpless patient's large, slowly thickening sexual organ. The Gräfin explained that Prudence was going to relieve this patient's stress by relieving his sexual tension and that, in the draining of his sexual fluids, his tension would be released as well. The Gräfin went on to say that Prudence was an expert in a unique and novel method of relieving patients sexually. Dr. Gerda Harm stood leggily—yet still somehow primly—in her indecent rubber dress and her high heels to watch the process, her curiosity at its peak. The Gräfin told Prudence to begin.

Prudence raised her smooth rubber-clad legs in the air, bending her pretty knees and supporting herself with her rubber-clad hands on the rear of the stool's seat cushion. She crossed her lush rubber-clad thighs and swiveled toward the patient with a smug smile on her full lips. In a moment, his thick, excited penis was nestled indecently between Prudence's crossed rubber-clad thighs. Prudence was a very strong and healthy young woman. As she began wiggling her legs, shifting her weight to and fro, she was virtually masturbating the straitjacketed patient with her thighs.

"My dear, see the poor fellow's drawn face and all the tension that his expression exhibits!" the Gräfin cooed. "I am sure Prudence will have him feeling much less constrained in a very short while."

"Prudence does seem to take pleasure in her duties as a nurse in your Rubber Sanitarium," Dr. Gerda Harm observed. "I shall look forward to working with her!"

As the women watched, Prudence continued milking

the patient's trapped penis between her athletic rubber-clad thighs. The patient's excitement mounted quickly. He began breathing heavily almost at once, although his face was flushed crimson at the humiliation of what was being done to him and the fact that it was being done in front of two lovely, scantily clad young women who had strict institutional authority over him. However, Prudence was an expert. She prolonged the patient's arousal by slowing the tempo of her milking motions whenever his crisis seemed imminent.

"We find that the tension release from a male orgasm is more beneficial and pronounced if the treatment is continued for quite some time and a premature climax is prohibited," the Gräfin explained. "And that is what Prudence is doing now, moderating the extent of his arousal and using her thighs to control him as well as to stimulate him."

Dr. Harm found her fascination with the entire process mount as she watched the nurse's rubber-clad thighs exercise the patient's now hugely excited sexual organ.

The straitjacketed patient's ordeal was drawn out expertly for nearly twenty minutes until at last he was allowed his climax. Prudence's athletic rubber-clad thighs wrung an intense orgasm from him, and he jiggled his hips forward and backward shamelessly to intensify the addictive sensations as he ejaculated. His entrapped sex organ spasmed between Prudence's thighs for a very long time indeed. He produced an enviable quantity of seed that drooled and spurted all over the tiled floor at Dr. Gerda Harm's feet.

As the patient sagged weakly in his bonds and Prudence dabbed her thighs clean with a soft cloth, the Gräfin and Dr. Gerda Harm were already on their way to the next treatment room. The Gräfin explained that her research budget was enormous and that one of her scientists had invented a drug called Orgasm gas. This was a specialized central nervous system stimulant that induced tremendous feelings of sensual excitement. Dr. Harm was delighted to hear that Treatment Room B was used to subject patients to Orgasm gas therapy and that a demonstration was just now being prepared for her to observe.

Dr. Harm gasped in anticipation as she and the Gräfin stepped into Treatment Room B. It was a much larger room than Treatment Room A. The Orgasm gas chamber itself dominated the center of the room. It consisted of a plexiform semicircle that reached from floor to ceiling and was attached to the walls behind it by airtight rubber seals. Admittance to the chamber was through an airtight door from another room behind the wall at the rear of the chamber itself. The door sealed tight when it was shut. A large reversible rubber glove protruded from a sealed rubber gasket in one side of the plexiform chamber wall. The reversible glove was similar to those used in airtight laboratory glove boxes and was constructed such that someone standing outside the chamber could reach into it without being exposed at all to the gas inside.

A nearly naked woman stood at a small control panel outside of the chamber at one side. A rubber hood covered her face and obscured her identity. The only openings in the hood were the two small eyeholes and a tiny round hole at her mouth. Her only other garment was a pair of black rubber elbow-length gloves. She stood on tiptoe barefoot, bent at the waist, her bare buttocks emphasized by her indecent posture. The nipples of her large breasts were held in suction nozzles with hoses attached to a pumping device on the floor at her feet. The pump was running on low with a muted rhythmic hum. The Gräfin introduced the nearly naked woman as Liesl and said she was an expert at controlling the precise flow of gas to the Orgasm gas chamber. The Gräfin also said that Liesl was lactating—hence the breast-milking device that was attached to her nipples. Liesl's rubber-clad fingertips were poised over the dials that would soon control the gas flow and its proper mixture with oxygen. Several gauges on the control panel would allow her to calibrate the modulation exactly. Dr. Gerda Harm's fascination with the bizarre regimens of The Rubber Sanitarium only deepened.

As the Gräfin and Dr. Gerda Harm watched, the door into the Orgasm gas chamber swung open to admit three people. The first was another sanitarium patient, naked like the one in Treatment Room A had been, save for a black rubber straitjacket. Two female nurses accompanied him, one grasping his elbows and one turning to shut the door of the chamber behind them. The nurses were clad exactly as Prudence had been, in rubber bodysuits that covered them alluringly—and ever so smoothly—from head to toe. Each sported a gas mask! Only the straitjacketed patient would be breathing the Orgasm gas. This patient showed no sign whatever of an erection. His testicles were drawn up tight beneath his flaccid penis.

The Gräfin introduced the two gas-chamber nurses to Dr. Gerda Harm as Eva and Justine. Then she turned to the pretty young doctor and whispered, "My dear, you will simply adore this particular experiment!" Eva and Justine nodded to Liesl, who looked expectantly at the Gräfin and received the go-ahead. Liesl's rubber-clad fingers fluttered expertly over the dials. Dr. Harm could hear a low, soft hiss as Orgasm gas was introduced into the chamber. The Gräfin smiled. "Liesl is so mischievous when she is lactating! She will probably slow the flow on purpose to make the patient's anticipation level rise before he feels the full effects."

Dr. Gerda Harm stared at the patient expectantly, observing his face and genitals for the first signs that the gas was taking effect. The chamber nurses, now one on each side of him, held him fast. Dr. Harm had not noticed before, but this particular patient was a very small man and the chamber nurses were tall, shapely, powerful women who towered over him.

Soon Dr. Harm could see the patient's chest rise and fall more as he began to breathe more heavily and his face began to flush just a bit. Liesl continued to adjust the dials, standing lewdly on tiptoe as the suction pumps drew rhythmically on her lactating breasts. The Gräfin licked her lips with barely constrained glee. Of all the inventions at The Rubber Sanitarium, this was one of her proudest. She turned to Dr. Harm as both women stood fetchingly in their tight rubber dresses and watched the experiment proceed. "Orgasm gas has practically limitless applications!" she boasted. "Imagine its application for crowd control. Imagine an entire army contorting on the battlefield, helpless from the intensity of their orgasmic release. You will see in a moment how dramatic its effects are.... Look!"

The chamber nurses were holding the patient tightly now. He was exhibiting all the signs of intense sexual arousal. His chest rose and fell rapidly with each excited breath. His face was flushed with both shame and excitement. Even as Dr. Harm and the Gräfin watched, his penis thickened and stiffened convulsively. Soon every vein along its length was standing out in rigid relief.

As the women watched, a small string of clear arousal dribbled from the bloated purple tip of the patient's sexual organ and hung swaying as it slowly lengthened— almost to the chamber floor. The patient's arms moved futilely beneath the tight embrace of his rubber straitjacket. The Gräfin explained that he was desperate to masturbate to alleviate the intensity of his sexual arousal. The Gräfin motioned for the nurses to let go of him so they all could see what he would do. And as Liesl controlled the gas/oxygen mixture, the nurses did so!

Even in his state of tremendous sexual excitement, the patient realized that he would never be able to free his arms and masturbate, so he dropped to his knees and crawled to the feet of the chamber nurses, who stood over him with their hands on their hips, complacently secure in their gas masks. The patient was panting and gasping as he knelt and began desperately trying to rub his sexual organ on the rubber-clad legs of the chamber nurses. They laughed behind their masks and kicked him away, but he always crawled back and tried desperately to release his pent-up passions against the smooth rubber that covered their lovely legs.

Finally he staggered to his feet and Eva decided to help him out—just a bit. She bent her leg and raised her thigh just enough to brush it a time or two across his sexual organ. The patient panted like a rutting bull and ejaculated his copious seed all over Eva's thigh. He would have fallen to the floor had not Justine stood behind him and held his hips to steady him. Then she turned him a bit to better exhibit his continuing climax to the Gräfin and Dr. Harm, who stood enthralled outside the chamber.

The patient's mouth hung open as the gasping hole in the strangled purple tip of his bloated penis expanded to emit jet after jet of his thick seed. Some of it hit the plexiform wall of the chamber itself and dribbled down to form a gooey puddle on the floor. It took nearly a full minute for his orgasm to subside. Then the patient sagged weakly back into Justine's arms.

The Gräfin told Dr. Harm to watch closely. Eva stepped forward and took the patient's still-erect penis in her hand as Justine held him, his head lolling upon her ample rubber-clad breasts. Just the touch of Eva's rubber-clad hand was enough to send him into another intense climax again under the influence of Orgasm gas. This climax was even more intense that the first, and longer-lasting, too—though substantially less semen was produced.

The Gräfin nodded to the chamber nurses when the patient was exhausted and seemed spent after his second orgasm. Half-carrying him, they pushed him gently up against the plexiform wall of the chamber where the reversible rubber glove protruded from its gasket at waist level. "Make him have another climax, Dr. Harm. You must observe the effects of our therapy at close range!"

Dr. Gerda Harm reached into the chamber with the reversible glove and grasped the patient's sex organ. He was so weak now that the chamber nurses had to steady him or he would have fallen flat on his face. The pretty young doctor's own face flushed as she felt the intensity of the patient's orgasmic twitches begin all over again just from her gentle touch on his privates. This time he ejaculated a very tiny amount of seed. But his penis spasmed in Dr. Harm's gloved hand for a very long time.

As the Gräfin and Dr. Harm continued to observe his treatment regimen, the chamber nurses subjected the patient to two more orgasms. Between them they lifted him up and held him off his feet while he sagged weakly, his penis still jerking and twitching—constantly on the verge of orgasm. Then one or the other would raise a thigh up between his legs from underneath to prod his genitals, or they would hold his scrotum. Either proved enough to provoke his fourth and fifth orgasms.

Finally the Gräfin ordered the demonstration to a close and ordered a reluctant Liesl to raise the oxygen level and turn on powerful ventilation fans to dissipate the gas. The patient had to be literally carried from the chamber by his rubber-clad nurses. Dr. Harm noticed that his face was now as soft and unlined as that of a young man one-third his age. The Gräfin said that five orgasms were the maximum that a patient should be subjected to unless his heart rate and rhythm were monitored closely with electrodes during the process.

Of course these demonstrations were all it took to finally persuade an already-intrigued Dr. Gerda Harm to sign on at the Gräfin's Rubber Sanitarium. She took her stringent duties there most seriously indeed and proved soon to be an expert at relieving her patient's tensions in many imaginative—and quite often bizarre—ways.

Chapter II

The patient sat "bottomless" in a leather wing chair in Dr. Gerda Harm's inner office. His only garment was a black rubber straitjacket that pinioned his arms securely to his sides. His heart beat rapidly in anticipation, for the nurses who relieved him of his clothing and fastened him naked in the straitjacket assured him that Dr. Harm would begin his masturbation therapy in a few moments. The patient was quite infatuated with Dr. Gerda Harm. The fact that this sweet-faced young woman —with wide blue eyes, full lips, and the most curvaceous buttocks and hips he had ever seen—had chosen to reduce the stress of her male patients using sexual-release therapy—truly fascinated him.

Dr. Gerda Harm walked down the white-tiled corridor

of The Rubber Sanitarium's central clinic. She paused for a moment as a stern-faced nurse in a white rubber uniform dress—so abbreviated that her bottom was half-bare—strutted past in black patent leather high-heeled oxfords. The nurse pushed a reclining wheelchair on which a naked straitjacketed patient was fastened down. Dr. Gerda Harm smiled as the nurse nodded to her respectfully. The nurse and her patient were headed for the sanitarium's enclosed courtyard garden for the patient's daily constitutional. Dr. Gerda Harm had no doubt that once outside, even this snooty-faced nurse would find numerous excuses to play coy little games with her patient's sexual organ.

Ten minutes later, Dr. Gerda Harm had changed from her high-heeled dress pumps and lab coat and paused for a moment to gaze out the window of her outer office down upon the enclosed courtyard garden of The Rubber Sanitarium. She had made many enhancements of her own design to the Gräfin's institution, and she was more than a little proud of her efforts—justifiably so. The daily garden "constitutional" was one of them.

Below her second-story window, the nurses of The Rubber Sanitarium pushed their straitjacketed patients about the shaded lawns and past the intricate sun dappled flower beds in the especially designed reclining wheelchairs. For the most part, of course, the patients were not invalids and did not require the wheelchairs from any medical necessity. Rather, Dr. Gerda Harm felt the use of the wheelchairs was desirable to further enforce the sanitarium's regimen of absolute relaxation.

The nurses were clad in form-fitting white rubber dresses with high collars and elbow-length gloves. They wore black patent leather oxfords with six-inch heels. The heels were so high that they gave the nurses a hip-wiggling, almost lewd gait as they pushed the wheelchairs to and fro, round and round the grounds.

If a patient showed any sign of an erection his nurse would stop pushing him, pause to stand beside him—bending excitingly, at the waist as she did so—and then relieve him through a bit of expert masturbation. Dr. Gerda Harm noted with satisfaction that several of the patient's abdomens were already messy with spilled seed. The nurses were performing their masturbatory duties in most admirable fashion. The smug-faced nurse whom she had just seen in the corridor outside her office had already relieved her patient of his seed for the first time. His penis was limp and his abdomen was gooey and glistening.

The patient in Dr. Gerda Harm's inner office was beginning to show signs of sexual arousal. His penis thickened a bit. Soon his pretty doctor would come in to masturbate him! He rather enjoyed his predicament. A copy of the *Daily Telegraph* was spread out on the floor at his feet. The patient was rather suspicious that it had been placed there to catch his seed. His penis thickened a bit more. The nurses of The Rubber Sanitarium had shaved his private area bare shortly after his admittance and his genitals were now as hairless as an infant's.

His attention became occupied with a strange device placed on the floor before him. He wondered what it was. The device consisted of a darkly varnished wooden box perhaps eighteen inches square. A narrow rubber hose extended from a fixture in the side of the box to a black rubber sleeve—about four inches long—which rested on a narrow table beside the patient's chair. The top of the varnished wooden box was equipped with a foot pedal and what appeared to be some sort of gauge.

Then the door opened to admit Dr. Gerda Harm!

The patient gaped and his penis thickened and raised until he sported a full erection. Dr. Gerda Harm presented quite a sight indeed! She wore a single tight garment that was part apron, part blouse, and part skirt. It was fashioned wickedly from glossy form-fitting black rubber. Its long sleeves ended seamlessly in matching black rubber gloves. In front, the apron-dress was quite modest—save for its extreme tightness—for it covered her from chin to knee. From behind, however, Dr. Gerda Harm's apron-dress was most scandalous. It covered her only down to the hollow of her back! The broad, full curves of Dr. Gerda Harm's bottom were presented bare to the world! Her tight apron-dress was fastened down to its hem by two straps. One passed behind just below her bare backside. The other ran back just above and behind her knees. Dr. Gerda Harm's prim little feet were clad in stylish black patent leather oxfords with seven-inch heels. The patient marveled at the smooth curves of his doctor's calves and thighs. And the sight of his doctor's big nude bottom practically made the poor fellow drool and swoon. The outrageous height of her heels and the extreme tightness of her rubber apron-dress turned each step Dr. Gerda Harm took into a lewd hip-wiggling prance.

Dr. Gerda Harm took a few mincing steps forward to stand—in a strange way almost prudishly—in front of her patient with her hands resting authoritatively upon the full curves of her shiny rubber-clad hips. "I see you are ready for your masturbation therapy!" she said sweetly, her eyes appraising her patient's now-rigid male organ saucily. "I see also that you're intrigued with my masturbation machine. Its use was once demonstrated upon habitually addicted degenerate Onanists on the midway of the Chicago Exposition. And now, some eighty years later, it will be used to drain you of your seed. Somehow appropriate, don't you think?" She moved still closer to her patient and picked up the rubber sleeve that was attached by the hose to the box upon the floor.

Then, very clinically, as if it were the most natural thing in the world, Dr. Gerda Harm reached down to take her patient's male sac. Then, with her other rubber-gloved hand, she slipped the suction sleeve down over the tip of his excited sex organ and worked it back against his abdomen.

As Dr. Gerda Harm straightened up and turned about to strut back to the masturbation machine, her patient's fevered gaze was locked upon her bare buttocks. It was as if he was desperately trying to commit each broad out-thrust curve to memory. Now imprisoned in the tight grasp of the suction sleeve, his penis throbbed, hugely erect, its swollen head now turning a strangled shade of purple-red.

Dr. Gerda Harm stood over the masturbation machine. Now facing her patient, she raised one daintily shod foot—a trifle awkwardly, due to the extreme tightness of her rubber apron-dress—to the masturbation machine's foot pedal. Then, bending forward with her gleaming rubber-gloved hands resting on her thighs for support, she began to work her foot up and down rhythmically. Each up-and-down cycle of the pedal was accompanied by a faint hissing sound.

"The box contains a pneumatic cylinder that I am charging with air pressure now," Dr. Gerda Harm explained to her straitjacketed patient. "When the gauge tells me that the cylinder is fully charged, I'll turn the release lever and a steady stream of compressed air will flow down the hose to the sleeve I have placed about your sexual organ—where, by means of a reciprocating valve, an inner cuff will move back and forth to stimulate you until you emit your seed. I am sure that you will find the sensations to be most compelling indeed. One charge will operate the suction sleeve for a full six minutes. Most patients never require a second charge to bring them to orgasm."

Dr. Gerda Harm's feminine charms were certainly not lost upon her patient as she worked the pedal up and down. The play of light on the shiny rubber apron-dress and gloves of his lovely doctor captivated him, and the bare curves of her flawless legs enthralled him. Dr. Gerda Harm was a lovely, sweet-faced young woman with an expression both intelligent and fastidious—perhaps bordering on outright conceit. To see such an exquisite young woman clad so bizarrely—and performing such outrageous acts on him—made the patient's head spin.

At last Dr. Gerda Harm finished priming the device and bent forward to turn the release lever before straightening up, her feet together primly, arms folded across her breasts, to watch the effects of her masturbation-machine on her patient. Her mien was a trifle self-righteous and accusatory—almost as if she herself were immune to the baser pleasures to which she happily addicted her male patients.

The poor fellow began panting almost at once as the device worked his organ up and down with precisely measured strokes. The only sounds in the room were the patient's heavy breathing and the rhythmic hiss and click of the masturbation-machine itself. Dr. Gerda Harm noted with satisfaction that the masturbation therapy was proceeding most gratifyingly indeed.

"Are the sensations compelling?" Dr. Gerda Harm asked her patient, her eyes registering the now-drooling tip of his sexual organ. She watched him now as he sat panting and squirming in his straitjacket with no little amusement.

Her patient finally managed a stuttering reply between panting moans. "The...sens...sensations are m-most compelling indeed!" He paused to gasp and writhe convulsively against the bonds of his straitjacket for a bit and then continued. "I have ne-never experienced s-such feelings b-before!"

Dr. Gerda Harm was secretly satisfied. "Well, sit still then and simply let nature take its course," she said bossily. "I am sure that the *Daily Telegraph* will prove most suitable in protecting my office floor from being soiled with your discharge of seed."

Even as a physician of no mean ability, Dr. Gerda Harm was not above acting on an occasional wicked notion. And, she did so now. In order to hasten her patient's orgasmic crisis—and perhaps in so doing prove to herself the mettle of her masturbation machine—she decided that her patient might need a bit of additional inspiration. So, as if bored with the whole process and waiting for it to reach its inevitable conclusion, she turned her back to her patient—thus exposing the charms of her bare posterior—this time for a rather more extended period. Her excuse for this lewdly provocative act was the charade of pretending to withdraw a volume of medical esoterica from the recessed bookshelves in the wall beyond.

Thus bending ever so slightly at the hips in order to present her posterior in the most alluring manner possible, Dr. Gerda Harm opened the glass door, withdrew a volume from a lower shelf, and pretended to study it. The audible gasps and heavier panting of her patient from behind her confirmed to Dr. Gerda Harm that her efforts were well spent.

Dr. Gerda Harm's recessed bookshelf was filled with volumes penned by such sexologists as Moll, Tissot, Havelock Ellis, Krafft-Ebing, Henry, Reischler, and Stekel. With their litany of case histories of masturbatory addiction, these volumes had inspired her myriad bizarre plans for the masturbatory training of patients at the Gräfin's Rubber Sanitarium.

Now her patient's crisis was imminent. The machine worked him incessantly, its tempo never varying its hisses and clicks punctuating his pleasure like a metronome. The patient's eyes were locked feverishly on the broad, full cheeks of Dr. Gerda Harm's bare bottom as his penis spasmed in the suction sleeve of the masturbation machine. The bloated swollen tip of the patient's male organ expanded visibly, and he moaned aloud. A moment later, thick jets of her patient's seed spurted from the tormented tip of his sex organ and spattered the *Daily Telegraph*—liberally soaking the text and picture of the feature article—as well as the headline.

Dr. Gerda Harm allowed herself a satisfied smile as she heard the audible plops of her patient's seed as it spurted down upon the newspaper before him. Each drop of seed that soiled the *Daily Telegraph* was as much a tribute to his doctor's big, bare bottom as it was a testimony to the efficacy of the masturbation machine.

Dr. Gerda Harm, turned about just in time to see the last weak strings of her patient's essence drool from the tip of his male organ and hang swaying nearly down to the newspaper on the floor. She turned the release lever on the machine back to closed, then stepped forward, her high-heeled patent leather oxfords and her rubber apron-dress catching the light most alluringly as she did so. Once again she bent over and held her patient's testicles, this time to remove the pneumatic sleeve from his messy—and now softening—sexual organ.

Dr. Gerda Harm left him there, sitting weakly in a daze and all astonished at the intensity of his orgasm. As she strutted through the door into her outer office to summon two or three nurses to clean up and remove him, her patient's eyes were still locked on the broad cheeks of Dr. Gerda Harm's big, bare bottom. The wiggle and sway of her buttocks as she stepped through the door seemed somehow to mock his now-softened penis in a most impudent fashion indeed.

Dr. Gerda Harm was more than a little pleased with her efforts. When the Gräfin returned, she would have much to show her. Though hardly more than an erotic curiosity from a bygone era the masturbation machine would fascinate her as would the rubber immersion spa, face-sitting therapy performed most suitably by especially selected big-bottomed nurses and, of course, the sensory-deprivation closets, cylinders, and vats (used to enforce the absolute stress-free relaxation of the rubber-enclosed patients) would all impress her fashionable employer. Of this Dr. Gerda Harm had no doubt whatever!

MASQUERADE

AMERICA'S FASTEST GROWING EROTIC MAGAZINE

SPECIAL OFFER
RECEIVE THE NEXT TWO ISSUES FOR ONLY $5.00—A 50% SAVINGS!

A bi-monthly magazine packed with the very best the world of erotica has to offer. Each issue of *Masquerade* contains today's most provocative, cutting-edge fiction, sizzling pictorials from the masters of modern fetish photography, scintillating and illuminating exposés of the world-wide sex-biz written by longtime industry insiders, and probing reviews of the many books and videos that cater specifically to your lifestyle.

Masquerade presents radical sex uncensored—from homegrown American kink to the fantastical fashions of Europe. Never before have the many permutations of the erotic imagination been represented in one publication.

THE ONLY MAGAZINE THAT CATERS TO YOUR LIFESTYLE

Masquerade/Direct • 801 Second Avenue • New York, NY 10017 • FAX: 212.986.7355
E-Mail: MasqBks@aol.com • MC/VISA orders can be placed by calling our toll-free number: 800.375.2356

☐ 2 ISSUES $10 *SPECIAL* $5!

☐ 6 ISSUES (1 YEAR) FOR $30 *SPECIAL* $15!

☐ 12 ISSUES (2 YEARS) FOR $60 *SPECIAL* $25!

NAME _____

ADDRESS _____

CITY _____ STATE _____ ZIP _____

E-MAIL _____

PAYMENT: ☐ CHECK   ☐ MONEY ORDER   ☐ VISA   ☐ MC

CARD # _____ EXP. DATE _____

No C.O.D. orders. Please make all checks payable to Masquerade/Direct. Payable in U.S. currency only.

MASQUERADE BOOKS

MASQUERADE

ROBERT SEWALL
THE DEVIL'S ADVOCATE
$6.95/553-0
Clara Reeves appeals to Conrad Garnett, a New York district attorney, for help in tracking down her missing sister, Rita. To Clara's distress, Conrad suspects that Rita has disappeared into an unsavory underworld dominated by an illicit sex ring. Clara soon finds herself being "persuaded" to accompany Conrad on his descent into this modern-day hell, where unspeakable pleasures await....

LUCY TAYLOR
UNNATURAL ACTS
$6.95/552-2
"A topnotch collection" —*Science Fiction Chronicle*
Unnatural Acts plunges deep into the dark side of the psyche and brings to life a disturbing vision of erotic horror. Unrelenting angels and hungry gods play with souls and bodies in Taylor's murky cosmos: where heaven and hell are merely differences of perspective; where redemption and damnation lie behind the same shocking acts.

OLIVIA M. RAVENSWORTH
THE DESIRES OF REBECCA
$6.50/532-8
Beautiful Rebecca follows her passions from the simple love of the girl next door to the relentless lechery of London's most notorious brothel, hoping for the ultimate thrill. Finally, she casts her lot with a crew of sapphic buccaneers, each of whom is more than capable of matching Rebecca lust for lust....

THE MISTRESS OF CASTLE ROHMENSTADT
$5.95/372-4
Lovely Katherine inherits a secluded European castle from a mysterious relative. Upon arrival she discovers, much to her delight, that the castle is a haven of sensual pleasure. Soon, Castle Rohmenstadt is the home of every perversion known to man—and under the iron grip of an extraordinary woman.

GERALD GREY
LONDON GIRLS
$6.50/531-X
In 1875, Samuel Brown arrived in London, determined to take the glorious city by storm. And sure enough, Samuel quickly distinguishes himself as one of the city's most notorious rakehells. Young Mr. Brown knows well the many ways of making a lady weak at the knees, and uses them not only to his delight, but to his enormous profit! A rollicking tale of cosmopolitan lust.

ATAULLAH MARDAAN
KAMA HOURI/DEVA DASI
$7.95/512-3
"Mardaan excels in crowding her pages with the sights and smells of India, and her erotic descriptions are convincingly realistic."
—Michael Perkins,
The Secret Record: Modern Erotic Literature
Two legendary tales of the East in one spectacular volume. *Kama Houri* details the life of a sheltered Western woman who finds herself living within the confines of a harem—where she discovers herself thrilled with the extent of her servitude. *Deva Dasi* is a tale dedicated to the cult of the Dasis—the sacred women of India who devoted their lives to the fulfillment of the senses—while revealing the sexual rites of Shiva.

J. P. KANSAS
ANDREA AT THE CENTER
$6.50/498-4
Kidnapped! Lithe and lovely young Andrea is whisked away to a distant retreat. Gradually, she is introduced to the ways of the Center, and soon becomes quite friendly with its other inhabitants—all of whom are learning to abandon restraint in their pursuit of the deepest sexual satisfaction. Soon, Andrea takes her place as one of the Center's greatest success stories—a submissive seductress who answers to any and all!

VISCOUNT LADYWOOD
GYNECOCRACY
$9.95/511-5
Julian, whose parents feel he shows just a bit too much spunk, is sent to a very special private school, in hopes that he will learn to discipline his wayward soul. Once there, Julian discovers that his program of study has been devised by the deliciously stern Mademoiselle de Chambonnard. In no time, Julian is learning the many ways of pleasure and pain—under the firm hand of this beautifully demanding headmistress.

CHARLOTTE ROSE, EDITOR
THE 50 BEST PLAYGIRL FANTASIES
$6.50/460-7
A steamy selection of women's fantasies straight from the pages of *Playgirl*. These tales of seduction—specially selected by Charlotte Rose, author of such bestselling women's erotica as *Women at Work*—are sure to set your pulse racing.

A DANGEROUS DAY
$5.95/293-0
From the best-selling author who brought you the sensational *Women at Work* and *The Doctor Is In*. And if you thought the high-powered entanglements of her previous books were risky, wait until Rose takes you on a journey through the thrills of one dangerous day—the ultimate day off.

MASQUERADE BOOKS

N. T. MORLEY

THE LIMOUSINE
$6.95/555-7
Brenda was enthralled with her roommate Kristi's illicit sex life: a never ending parade of men who satisfied Kristi's desire to be dominated. While barely admitting she shared these desires, Brenda issued herself the ultimate challenge—a trip into submission, beginning in the long, white limousine where Kristi first met the Master. Following in the footsteps of her lascivious roommate, Brenda embarks on the erotic journey of her life....

THE CASTLE
$6.95/530-1
A pulse-pounding peek at the ultimate vacation paradise. Tess Roberts is held captive by a crew of disciplinarians intent on making all her dreams come true—even those she'd never admitted to herself. While anyone can arrange for a stay at the Castle, Tess proves herself one of the most gifted applicants yet....

THE PARLOR
$6.50/496-8
Lovely Kathryn gives in to the ultimate temptation. The mysterious John and Sarah ask her to be their slave—an idea that turns Kathryn on so much that she can't refuse! But who are these two mysterious strangers? Little by little, Kathryn not only learns to serve, but comes to know the inner secrets of her stunning keepers.

J. A. GUERRA, EDITOR

COME QUICKLY:
For Couples on the Go
$6.50/461-5
The increasing pace of daily life is no reason to forgo a little carnal pleasure whenever the mood strikes. Here are over sixty of the hottest fantasies around—all designed to get you going in less time than it takes to dial 976. A super-hot volume designed especially for modern couples on a hectic schedule.

ERICA BRONTE

LUST, INC.
$6.50/467-4
Lust, Inc. explores the extremes of passion that lurk beneath even the coldest, most businesslike exteriors. Join in the sexy escapades of a group of high-powered professionals whose idea of office decorum is like nothing you've ever encountered! Business attire is decidedly *not* required for this unflinching look at high-powered sexual negotiations!

VANESSA DURIES

THE TIES THAT BIND
$6.50/510-7
From the first page, this chronicle of dominance and submission will keep you gasping with its vivid depictions of sensual abandon. At the hand of Masters Georges, Patrick, Pierre and others, this submissive seductress experiences pleasures she never knew existed.... One of modern erotica's best-selling accounts of real-life dominance and submission.

M. S. VALENTINE

THE GOVERNESS
$6.95/562-X
Lovely Miss Hunnicut eagerly embarks upon a career as a governess, hoping to escape the memories of her broken engagement. Little does she know that Crawleigh Manor is far from the upstanding household it appears. Mr. Crawleigh, in particular, devotes himself to Miss Hunnicut's thorough defiling. Soon, the young governess proves herself worthy of the perverse master of the house—though there may be even more depraved powers at work in gloomy Crawleigh Manor....

ELYSIAN DAYS AND NIGHTS
$6.95/536-0
From around the world, neglected young wives arrive at the Elysium Spa intent on receiving a little heavy-duty pampering. Luckily for them, the spa's proprietor is a true devotee of the female form—and has dedicated himself and his staff to the pure pleasure of every lovely lady who steps foot across Elysium's threshold....

THE CAPTIVITY OF CELIA
$6.50/453-4
Celia's lover, Colin, is considered the prime suspect in a murder, forcing him to seek refuge with his cousin, Sir Jason Hardwicke. In exchange for Colin's safety, Jason demands Celia's unquestioning submission.... Sexual extortion guarantees her lover's safety—and soon, she finds herself entranced by the demands of her captor....

AMANDA WARE

BINDING CONTRACT
$6.50/491-7
Louise was responsible for bringing many prestigious clients into Claremont's salon—so he was more than willing to have her miss a little work in order to pleasure one of his most important customers. But Eleanor Cavendish had her mind set on something more rigorous than a simple wash and set. Sexual slavery!

BUY ANY 4 BOOKS & CHOOSE 1 ADDITIONAL BOOK, OF EQUAL OR LESSER VALUE, AS YOUR FREE GIFT

MASQUERADE BOOKS

BOUND TO THE PAST
$6.50/452-6

Anne accepts a research assignment in a Tudor mansion. Upon arriving, she finds herself aroused by James, a descendant of the mansion's owners. Together they uncover the perverse desires of the mansion's long-dead master—desires that bind Anne inexorably to the past—not to mention the bedpost!

SACHI MIZUNO
SHINJUKU NIGHTS
$6.50/493-3

A tour through the lives and libidos of the seductive East. No one is better that Sachi Mizuno at weaving an intricate web of sensual desire, wherein many characters are ensnared and enraptured by the demands of their carnal natures.

PASSION IN TOKYO
$6.50/454-2

Tokyo—one of Asia's most historic and seductive cities. Come behind the closed doors of its citizens, and witness the many pleasures that await. Lusty men and women from every stratum of society free themselves of all inhibitions....

MARTINE GLOWINSKI
POINT OF VIEW
$6.50/433-X

The story of one woman's extraordinary erotic awakening. With the assistance of her new, unexpectedly kinky lover, she discovers and explores her exhibitionist tendencies—until there is virtually nothing she won't do before the horny audiences her man arranges!

RICHARD McGOWAN
A HARLOT OF VENUS
$6.50/425-9

A highly fanciful, epic tale of lust on Mars! Cavortia—the most famous and sought-after courtesan in the cosmopolitan city of Venus—finds love and much more during her adventures with some of the most remarkable characters in recent erotic fiction.

M. ORLANDO
THE ARCHITECTURE OF DESIRE
Introduction by Richard Manton.
$6.50/490-9

Two novels in one special volume! In *The Hotel Justine*, an elite clientele is afforded the opportunity to have any and all desires satisfied. *The Villa Sin* is inherited by a beautiful woman who soon realizes that the legacy of the ancestral estate includes bizarre erotic ceremonies. Two pieces of prime real estate.

CHET ROTHWELL
KISS ME, KATHERINE
$5.95/410-0

Beautiful Katherine can hardly believe her luck. Not only is she married to the charming and oh-so-agreeable Nelson, she's free to live out all her erotic fantasies with other men. Katherine's desires are more than any one man can handle—luckily there are always plenty of men on hand, ready and willing to fulfill her needs!

MARCO VASSI
THE STONED APOCALYPSE
$5.95/401-1/mass market

"Marco Vassi is our champion sexual energist." —VLS

During his lifetime, Marco Vassi's groundbreaking erotic writing was praised by writers as diverse as Gore Vidal and Norman Mailer, and his reputation as an indefatigable champion of sexual experimentation was worldwide. *The Stoned Apocalypse* is Vassi's autobiography; chronicling a cross-country trip on America's erotic byways, it offers a rare glimpse of a generation's sexual imagination.

ROBIN WILDE
TABITHA'S TICKLE
$6.50/468-2

Tabitha's back! The story of this vicious vixen didn't end with *Tabitha's Tease*. Once again, men fall under the spell of scrumptious co-eds and find themselves enslaved to demands and desires they never dreamed existed. Think it's a man's world? Guess again. With Tabitha around, no man gets what he wants until she's completely satisfied—and, maybe, not even then....

ERICA BRONTE
PIRATE'S SLAVE
$5.95/376-7

Lovely young Erica is stranded in a country where lust knows no bounds. Desperate to escape, she finds herself trading her firm, luscious body to any and all men willing and able to help her. Her adventure has its ups and downs, ins and outs—all to the pleasure of the increasingly lusty Erica!

CHARLES G. WOOD
HELLFIRE
$5.95/358-9

A vicious murderer is running amok in New York's sexual underground—and Nick O'Shay, a virile detective with the NYPD, plunges deep into the case. He soon becomes embroiled in an elusive world of fleshly extremes, hunting a madman seeking to purge America with fire and blood sacrifices. Set in New York's infamous sexual underground, and peopled with thrilling characters.

MASQUERADE BOOKS

CLAIRE BAEDER, EDITOR
LA DOMME: A Dominatrix Anthology
$5.95/366-X

A steamy smorgasbord of female domination! Erotic literature has long been filled with heart-stopping portraits of domineering women, and now the most memorable have been brought together in one beautifully brutal volume. A must for all fans of BD/SM fiction.

CHARISSE VAN DER LYN
SEX ON THE NET
$5.95/399-6

Electrifying erotica from one of the Internet's hottest authors. Encounters of all kinds—straight, lesbian, dominant/submissive and all sorts of extreme passions—are explored in thrilling detail.

STANLEY CARTEN
NAUGHTY MESSAGE
$5.95/333-3

Wesley Arthur discovers a lascivious message on his answering machine. Aroused beyond his wildest dreams by the acts described, he becomes obsessed with tracking down the woman behind the seductive voice. His search takes him through strip clubs, sex parlors and no-tell motels—before finally leading him to his randy reward....

AKBAR DEL PIOMBO
THE FETISH CROWD
$6.95/556-5

A triple treat! A full-fledged trilogy presented as a special volume guaranteed to appeal to the modern sophisticate. Separately, *Paula the Piquôse*, the infamous *Duke Cosimo*, and *The Double-Bellied Companion* are rightly considered masterpieces, rife with wit, intelligence, and stunning eye for sensuous detail.

DUKE COSIMO
$4.95/3052-0

A kinky romp played out against the boudoirs, bathrooms and ballrooms of the European nobility, who seem to do nothing all day except each other. The lifestyles of the rich and licentious are revealed in all their glory.

A CRUMBLING FAÇADE
$4.95/3043-1

The return of that incorrigible rogue, Henry Pike, who continues his pursuit of sex, fair or otherwise, in the most elegant homes of the most debauched aristocrats. Ultimately, every woman succumbs to Pike's charms—and submits to his whims!

CAROLE REMY
FANTASY IMPROMPTU
$6.50/513-1

Kidnapped and held in a remote island retreat, Chantal finds herself catering to every sexual whim of the mysterious and arousing Bran. Bran is determined to bring Chantal to a full embracing of her sensual nature, even while revealing himself to be something far more than human....

BEAUTY OF THE BEAST
$5.95/332-5

A shocking tell-all, written from the point-of-view of a prize-winning reporter. And what reporting she does! All the secrets of an uninhibited life are revealed, and each lusty tableau is painted in glowing colors.

DAVID AARON CLARK
THE MARQUIS DE SADE'S JULIETTE
$4.95/240-X

The Marquis de Sade's infamous Juliette returns—and emerges as the most perverse and destructive nightstalker modern New York will ever know. Her insatiable hungers come to dominate Manhattan's underground, and one by one, the innocent are drawn in by Juliette's empty promise of immortality, only to fall prey to her deadly lusts.

ANONYMOUS
THE MISFORTUNES OF COLETTE
$7.95/564-6

An epic tale of one young woman's deliciously erotic suffering at the hands of the sadistic men and women who take her in hand. Beautiful Colette is passed from one tormentor to another, until it becomes clear that she is destined to find her greatest pleasures in punishment—a destiny her admirers are only too willing to help her fulfill!

SUBURBAN SOULS
$9.95/563-8/Trade paperback

One of the century's most sought-after titles. Focusing on the May–December sexual relationship of nubile Lillian and the more experienced Jack, all three volumes of *Suburban Souls* now appear in one special edition—guaranteed to enrapture modern readers with its lurid detail.

LOVE'S ILLUSION
$6.95/549-2

Elizabeth Renard yearned for the body of rich and successful Dan Harrington. Then she discovered Harrington's secret weakness: a need to be humiliated and punished. She makes him her slave, and together they commence a thrilling journey into depravity that leaves nothing to the imagination!

BUY ANY 4 BOOKS & CHOOSE 1 ADDITIONAL BOOK, OF EQUAL OR LESSER VALUE, AS YOUR FREE GIFT

MASQUERADE BOOKS

NADIA
$5.95/267-1
Follow the delicious but neglected Nadia as she works to wring every drop of pleasure out of life—despite an unhappy marriage. A classic title providing a peek into the secret sexual lives of another time and place.

NIGEL McPARR
THE TRANSFORMATION OF EMILY
$6.50/519-0
The shocking story of Emily Johnson, live-in domestic. Without warning, Emily finds herself dismissed by her mistress, and sent to serve at Lilac Row—the home of Charles and Harriet Godwin. In no time, Harriet has Emily doing things she'd never dreamed would be required of her—all involving shocking erotic discipline.

THE STORY OF A VICTORIAN MAID
$5.95/241-8
What were the Victorians really like? Chances are, no one believes they were as stuffy as their Queen, but who would have imagined such unbridled libertines? Nigel McParr now lays bare everything we thought we'd never know. One maid is followed from exploit to smutty exploit, as all secrets are finally revealed!

TITIAN BERESFORD
CHIDEWELL HOUSE AND OTHER STORIES
$6.95/554-9
What are the deliciously dastardly delights that keep Cecil a virtual, if willing, prisoner of Chidewell House? One man has been sent to investigate the sexy situation—and reports back with tales of such depravity that no expense is spared in attempting Cecil's rescue. But what man would possibly desire release from the breathtakingly corrupt Elizabeth?

CINDERELLA
$6.50/500-X
Beresford triumphs again with this intoxicating tale, filled with castle dungeons and tightly corseted ladies-in-waiting, naughty viscounts and impossibly cruel masturbatrixes—nearly every conceivable method of erotic torture is explored and described in lush, vivid detail.

JUDITH BOSTON
$6.50/525-5
Edward would have been lucky to get the stodgy companion he thought his parents had hired for him. But an exquisite woman arrives at his door, and Edward finds his lewd behavior never goes unpunished by the unflinchingly severe Judith Boston

THE WICKED HAND
$5.95/399-6
With a special Introduction by *Leg Show*'s Dian Hanson.
A collection of fanciful fetishistic tales featuring the absolute subjugation of men by lovely, domineering women. From Japan and Germany to the American heartland—these stories uncover the other side of the "weaker sex."

NINA FOXTON
$5.95/443-7
An aristocrat finds herself bored by the run-of-the-mill amusements deemed appropriate for "ladies of good breeding." Instead of taking tea with proper gentlemen, naughty Nina "milks" them of their most private essences. No man ever says "No" to Nina!

TINY ALICE
THE GEEK
$5.95/341-4
A notorious—and uproarious—cult classic. *The Geek* is told from the point of view of, well, a chicken who reports on the various perversities he witnesses as part of a traveling carnival. When a gang of renegade lesbians kidnaps Chicken and his geek, all hell breaks loose. A strange but highly arousing tale, filled with outrageous erotic oddities, that finally returns to print after years of infamy.

P. N. DEDEAUX
THE NOTHING THINGS
$5.95/404-6
Beta Beta Rho has taken on a new group of pledges. The five women will be put through the most grueling of ordeals, and punished severely for any shortcomings. Before long, all Beta pledges come to crave their punishments!

LYN DAVENPORT
THE GUARDIAN II
$6.50/505-0
The tale of submissive Felicia Brookes continues in this volume of sensual surprises. No sooner has Felicia come to love Rodney than she discovers that she must now accustom herself to the guardianship of the debauched Duke of Smithton. Surely Rodney will rescue her from the domination of this stranger. Won't he?

DOVER ISLAND
$5.95/384-8
On a island off the west coast, Dr. David Kelly has planted the seeds of his dream—a Corporal Punishment Resort. Soon, many people from varied walks of life descend upon this isolated retreat, intent on fulfilling their every desire. Including Marcy Harris, the perfect partner for the lustful Doctor....

MASQUERADE BOOKS

GWYNETH JAMES
DREAM CRUISE
$4.95/3045-8
Angelia has it all—a brilliant career and a beautiful face to match. But she longs to kick up her high heels and have some fun, so she takes an island vacation and vows to leave her inhibitions behind. From the moment her plane takes off, she finds herself in one steamy encounter after another!

LIZBETH DUSSEAU
THE APPLICANT
$6.50/501-8
"Adventuresome young women who enjoys being submissive sought by married couple in early forties. Expect no limits." Hilary answers an ad, hoping to find someone who can meet her special needs. The beautiful Liza turns out to be a flawless mistress, and together with her husband, Oliver, she trains Hilary to be the perfect servant.
SPANISH HOLIDAY
$4.95/185-3
Lauren didn't mean to fall in love with the enigmatic Sam, but a once-in-a-lifetime European vacation gives her all the evidence she needs that this hot, insatiable man might be the one for her....

ANTHONY BOBARZYNSKI
STASI SLUT
$4.95/3050-4
Adina lives in East Germany, where she can only dream about the freedoms of the West. She begins to despair of ever living in a more sexually liberated world. But then she meets a group of ruthless and corrupt STASI agents. They use her body for their own gratification, while she opts to use her sensual talents in a final bid for total freedom!

JOCELYN JOYCE
PRIVATE LIVES
$4.95/309-0
The lecherous habits of the illustrious make for a sizzling tale of French erotic life. A widow has a craving for a young busboy; he's sleeping with a rich businessman's wife; her husband is minding his sex business elsewhere! Uninhibited sexual entanglements run through this tale of upper-crust lust!
SABINE
$4.95/3046-6
There is no one who can refuse her once she casts her spell; no lover can do anything less than give up his whole life for her. Great men and empires fall at her feet; but she is haughty, distracted, impervious. It is the eve of WW II, and Sabine must find a new lover equal to her talents and her tastes.

THE JAZZ AGE
$4.95/48-3
The time is the Roaring 20s. An attorney becomes suspicious of his mistress while his wife has an interlude with a lesbian lover. A romp of erotic realism from the heyday of the flapper and the speakeasy—when rules existed to be broken!
THE WOMEN OF BABYLON
$4.95/171-3
"She adored it. Oh, what an amusement! she thought. Axel Gruning was now one of her conquests...." With lusty abandon, some very independent women set their sights on ensnaring the hearts—and more—of every man in sight!

SARAH JACKSON
SANCTUARY
$5.95/318-X
Sanctuary explores both the debauchery of court life and the privations of monastic solitude, leading the voracious and the virtuous on a collision course that brings history to throbbing life.
THE WILD HEART
$4.95/3007-5
A luxury hotel is the setting for this artful web of sex, desire, and love. A newlywed sees sex as a duty, while her hungry husband tries to awaken her to its tender joys. A Parisian entertains wealthy guests for the love of money. Each episode provides a perverse new variation.

SARA H. FRENCH
MASTER OF TIMBERLAND
$5.95/327-9
A tale of sexual slavery at the ultimate paradise resort—where sizzling submissives serve their masters without question. One of our bestselling titles, this trek to Timberland has ignited passions the world over—and stands poised to become one of modern erotica's legendary tales.

MARY LOVE
ANGELA
$6.95/545-X
Angela's game is "look but don't touch," and she drives everyone mad with desire, dancing for their pleasure but never allowing a single caress. Soon her sensual spell is cast, and she's the only one who can break it!
MASTERING MARY SUE
$5.95/351-1
Mary Sue is a rich nymphomaniac whose husband is determined to declare her mentally incompetent and gain control of her fortune. He brings her to a castle where, to Mary Sue's delight, she is unleashed for a veritable sex-fest!

BUY ANY 4 BOOKS & CHOOSE 1 ADDITIONAL BOOK, OF EQUAL OR LESSER VALUE, AS YOUR FREE GIFT

MASQUERADE BOOKS

THE BEST OF MARY LOVE
$4.95/3099-7

One of modern erotica's most daring writers is here represented by her most scalding passages. Mary Love leaves no coupling untried and no extreme unexplored in these scandalous selections from *Mastering Mary Sue, Ecstasy on Fire, Vice Park Place, Wanda,* and *Naughtier at Night.*

WANDA
$4.95/002-4

Wanda just can't help it. Ever since she moved to Greenwich Village, she's been overwhelmed by the desire to be totally, utterly naked! By day, she finds herself inspired by a pornographic novel whose main character's insatiable appetites seem to match her own. At night she parades her quivering, nubile flesh in a non-stop sex show for her neighbors. An electrifying exhibitionist gone wild!

AMARANTHA KNIGHT
The Darker Passions: THE PICTURE OF DORIAN GRAY
$6.50/342-2

Knight's take on the fabulously decadent tale of highly personal changes. One woman finds her most secret desires laid bare by a portrait far more revealing than she could have imagined. Soon she benefits from a skillful masquerade.

THE DARKER PASSIONS READER
$6.50/432-1

The best moments from Knight's phenomenally popular Darker Passions series. Here are the most eerily erotic passages from her acclaimed sexual reworkings of *Dracula, Frankenstein, Dr. Jekyll & Mr. Hyde* and *The Fall of the House of Usher.*

The Darker Passions: THE FALL OF THE HOUSE OF USHER
$6.50/528-X

Two weary travelers arrive at a dark and foreboding mansion, where they fall victim to the many bizarre appetites of its residents. The Master and Mistress of the house of Usher indulge in every form of decadence, and initiate their guests into the many pleasures to be found in submission.

The Darker Passions: DR. JEKYLL AND MR. HYDE
$4.95/227-2

It is a story of incredible transformations. Explore the steamy possibilities of a tale where no one is quite who—or what—they seem. Victorian bedrooms explode with hidden demons!

The Darker Passions: FRANKENSTEIN
$5.95/248-5

What if you could create a living human? What shocking acts could it be taught to perform, to desire? Find out what pleasures await those who play God....

The Darker Passions: DRACULA
$5.95/326-0

"Well-written and imaginative...taking us through the sexual and sadistic scenes with details that keep us reading.... A classic in itself has been added to the shelves."   —*Divinity*

The infamous erotic revisioning of Bram Stoker's classic.

THE PAUL LITTLE LIBRARY
SENTENCED TO SERVITUDE
$8.95/565-4/Trade paperback

One of infamous Paul Little's most fierce and compelling novels. A haughty young aristocrat learns what becomes of excessive pride when she is abducted and forced to submit to unthinkable ordeals of sensual torment. Trained to accept her submissive state, the icy young woman soon melts under the relentless heat of her owners....

ROOMMATE'S SECRET
$8.95/557-3/Trade paperback

What are the secrets young ladies hide—even from their trusted roommates? Here are the many exploits of one woman forced to make ends meet by the most ancient of methods. From the misery of early impoverishment to the delight of ill-gotten gains, Elda learns to rely on her considerable sensual talents.

LOVE SLAVE/PECULIAR PASSIONS OF MEG
$8.95/529-8/Trade paperback

Two classics from erotica's most popular author! What does it take to acquire a willing *Love Slave* of one's own? What are the appetites that lurk within *Meg*? The notoriously depraved Paul Little spares no lascivious detail in these two relentless tales!

CELESTE
$6.95/544-1

It's definitely all in the family for this female duo of sexual dynamics. While traveling through Europe, these two try everything and everyone on their horny holiday.

ALL THE WAY
$6.95/509-3

Two excruciating novels from Paul Little in one hot volume! *Going All the Way* features an unhappy man who tries to purge himself of the memory of his lover with a series of quirky and uninhibited lovers. *Pushover* tells the story of a serial spanker and his celebrated exploits.

THE DISCIPLINE OF ODETTE
$5.95/334-1

Odette was sure marriage would rescue her from her family's brutal "corrections." To her horror, she discovers that her beloved Jacques has also been raised on discipline—an upbringing he's intent on sharing with Odette. A shocking erotic coupling!

MASQUERADE BOOKS

THE END OF INNOCENCE
$6.95/546-8
The early days of Women's Emancipation are the setting for this story of some very independent ladies. These women were willing to go to any lengths to fight for their sexual freedom, and willing to endure any punishment in their desire for total liberation. A shockingly sexy historical romp.

TUTORED IN LUST
$6.95/547-6
This tale of the initiation and instruction of a carnal college co-ed and her fellow students unlocks the sex secrets of the classroom.

THE BEST OF PAUL LITTLE
$6.50/469-0
Known for his fantastic portrayals of punishment and pleasure, Little never fails to push readers over the edge of sensual excitement. His best scenes are here collected for the enjoyment of all erotic connoisseurs.

THE PRISONER
$5.95/330-9
Judge Black has built a secret room below a penitentiary, where he sentences his female prisoners to hours of exhibition and torment while his friends watch. Judge Black's brand of rough justice keeps his captives on the brink of utter pleasure!

TEARS OF THE INQUISITION
$4.95/146-2
A staggering account of pleasure and punishment, set in an age of corruption and brutal abuses of power. "There was a tickling inside her as her nervous system reminded her she was ready for sex. But before her was…the Inquisitor!"

DOUBLE NOVEL
$4.95/86-6
The Metamorphosis of Lisette Joyaux tells the story of a young woman initiated into an incredible world world of lesbian lusts. *The Story of Monique* reveals the twisted sexual rituals that beckon the ripe and willing Monique.

CAPTIVE MAIDENS
$5.95/440-2
Three beautiful young women find themselves powerless against the debauched landowners of 1824 England. They are banished to a sex colony, and corrupted by every imaginable perversion.

SLAVE ISLAND
$5.95/441-0
A leisure cruise is waylaid by Lord Henry Philbrock, a sadistic genius. The ship's passengers are kidnapped and spirited to his island prison, where the women are trained to accommodate the most bizarre sexual cravings of the rich, the famous, the pampered and the perverted.

ALIZARIN LAKE
CLARA
$6.95/548-4
The mysterious death of a beautiful woman leads her old boyfriend on a harrowing journey of discovery. His search uncovers a woman on a quest for deeper and more unusual sensations, each more shocking than the one before!

SEX ON DOCTOR'S ORDERS
$5.95/402-X
A chronicle of selfless devotion to mankind! Beth, a nubile young nurse, uses her considerable skills to further medical science by offering incomparable and insatiable assistance in the gathering of important specimens. Soon she's involved everyone in her important work—including the horny doctor himself.

THE EROTIC ADVENTURES OF HARRY TEMPLE
$4.95/127-6
Harry Temple's memoirs chronicle his incredibly amorous adventures—from his initiation at the hands of insatiable sirens, through his stay at a house of hot repute, to his encounters with a chastity-belted nympho, and much more!

MORE EROTIC ADVENTURES OF HARRY TEMPLE
$4.95/67-X
Harry Temple's lustful adventures continue. this time he begins his amorous pursuits by deflowering the ample and eager Aurora. Harry soon discovers that his little protégée is more than able to match him at every lascivious game and very willing to display her own talents. An education in sensuality that only Harry Temple can provide!

MISS HIGH HEELS
$4.95/3066-0
It was a delightful punishment few men dared to dream of. Who could have predicted how far it would go? Forced by his wicked sisters to dress and behave like a proper lady, Dennis Beryl finds he enjoys life as Denise much more!

JOHN NORMAN
TARNSMAN OF GOR
$6.95/486-0
This controversial series returns! Tarl Cabot is transported to Gor. He must quickly accustom himself to the ways of this world, including the caste system which exalts some as Priest-Kings or Warriors, and debases others as slaves. The beginning of the mammoth epic which made Norman a controversial success—as well as a household name among fans of both science fiction and dominance/submission.

BUY ANY 4 BOOKS & CHOOSE 1 ADDITIONAL BOOK, OF EQUAL OR LESSER VALUE, AS YOUR FREE GIFT

MASQUERADE BOOKS

OUTLAW OF GOR
$6.95/487-9
Tarl Cabot returns to Gor, to reclaim both his woman and his role of Warrior. But upon arriving, he discovers that his name, his city and the names of those he loves have become unspeakable. Cabot has become an outlaw, and must discover his new purpose on this strange planet, where danger stalks the outcast, and even simple answers have their price….

PRIEST-KINGS OF GOR
$6.95/488-7
Tarl Cabot searches for his lovely wife Talena. Does she live, or was she destroyed by the all-powerful Priest-Kings? Cabot is determined to find out—even while knowing that no one who has approached the mountain stronghold of the Priest-Kings has ever returned alive….

NOMADS OF GOR
$6.95/527-1
Cabot finds his way across Gor, pledged to serve the Priest-Kings in their quest for survival. Unfortunately for Cabot, his mission leads him to the savage Wagon People—nomads who may very well kill before surrendering any secrets….

ASSASSIN OF GOR
$6.95/538-7
Assassin of Gor exposes the brutal caste system of Gor at its most unsparing: from the Assassin Kuurus, on a mission of bloody vengeance, to Pleasure Slaves, tirelessly trained in the ways of personal ecstasy. From one social stratum to the next, the inhabitants of Counter-Earth pursue and are pursued by all-too human passions—and the inescapable destinies that await their caste…

RAIDERS OF GOR
$6.95/558-1
Tarl Cabot descends into the depths of Port Kar— the darkest, most degenerate port city of the Counter-Earth. There, among pirates, cutthroats and brigands, Cabot learns the ways of Kar, whose residents are renowned for the iron grip in which they hold their voluptuous slaves….

ELAINE PLATERO
LESSONS AND LOVERS
$4.95/196-9
"Stunned by her spanking, Hettie felt like a sex-doll for the other two, a living breathing female body to demonstrate the responses and vulnerabilities of womankind to a young man who was hungry for knowledge…." When a repressed widow, her all-too-willing manservant, a voluptuous doctor and an anxious neophyte take a country weekend together, crucial lessons are learned by all— through the horny formulas of Sexual Geometry!

SYDNEY ST. JAMES
RIVE GAUCHE
$5.95/317-1
The Latin Quarter, Paris, circa 1920. Expatriate bohemians couple with abandon—before eventually abandoning their ambitions amidst the intoxicating temptations waiting to be indulged in every bedroom.

GARDEN OF DELIGHT
$4.95/3058-X
A vivid account of sexual awakening that follows an innocent but insatiably curious young woman's journey from the furtive, forbidden joys of dormitory life to the unabashed carnality of the wild world.

DON WINSLOW
THE FALL OF THE ICE QUEEN
$6.50/520-4
Rahn the Conqueror chose a true beauty as his Consort. But the regal disregard with which she treated Rahn was not to be endured. It was decided that she would submit to his will, and learn to serve her lord in the fashion he had come to expect. And as so many had learned, Rahn's depraved expectations have made his court infamous.

PRIVATE PLEASURES
$6.50/504-2
Frantic voyeurs, licentious exhibitionists, and everyday lovers are here displayed in all their wanton glory—proving again that fleshly pleasures have no more apt chronicler than Don Winslow.

THE INSATIABLE MISTRESS OF ROSEDALE
$6.50/494-1
Edward and Lady Penelope reside in mysterious Rosedale manor. While Edward is a true connoisseur of sexual perversion, it is Lady Penelope whose mastery of complete sensual pleasure makes their home infamous. Indulging one another's bizarre whims is a way of life for this wicked couple….

SECRETS OF CHEATEM MANOR
$6.50/434-8
Edward returns to his late father's estate, to find it being run by the majestic Lady Amanda. Edward can hardly believe his luck—Lady Amanda is assisted by her two beautiful, lonely daughters, Catherine and Prudence. What the randy young man soon comes to realize is the love of discipline that all three beauties share.

KATERINA IN CHARGE
$5.95/409-7
When invited to a country retreat by a mysterious couple, two randy young ladies can hardly resist! But do they have any idea what they're in for? Whatever the case, the imperious Katerina will make her desires known very soon— and demand that they be fulfilled…

MASQUERADE BOOKS

THE MANY PLEASURES OF IRONWOOD
$5.95/310-4

Seven lovely young women are employed by The Ironwood Sportsmen's Club, where their natural talents in the sensual arts are put to creative use. A small and exclusive club with seven carefully selected sexual connoisseurs.

CLAIRE'S GIRLS
$5.95/442-9

You knew when she walked by that she was something special. She was one of Claire's girls, a woman carefully dressed and groomed to fill a role, to capture a look, to fit an image crafted by the sophisticated proprietress of an exclusive escort agency.

MARCUS VAN HELLER
KIDNAP
$4.95/90-4

P.I. Harding is called in to investigate a mysterious kidnapping case involving the rich and powerful. Along the way he has the pleasure of "interrogating" an exotic dancer named Jeanne and a beautiful English reporter, as he finds himself enmeshed in the sleazy international underworld.

ADAM & EVE
$4.95/93-9

Adam and Eve long to escape their dull lives by achieving stardom—she in the theater, and he in the art world. They throw aside all inhibitions, and Eve soon finds herself spread-eagle on the casting couch, while Adam must join a bizarre sex cult to further his artistic career.

N. WHALLEN
TAU'TEVU
$6.50/426-7

In a mysterious and exotic land, the statuesque and beautiful Vivian learns to subject herself to the hand of a domineering man. He systematically helps her prove her own strength, and brings to life in her an unimagined sensual fire.

ALEXANDER TROCCHI
YOUNG ADAM
$4.95/52-1

Two British barge operators discover a girl drowned in the river Clyde. Her lover, a plumber, is arrested for her murder. But he is innocent. Joe, the barge assistant, knows that. As the plumber is tried and sentenced to hang, this knowledge lends poignancy to Joe's romances with the women along the river whom he will love then… well, read on.

ISADORA ALMAN
ASK ISADORA
$4.95/61-0

Six years' worth of Isadora's syndicated columns on sex and relationships. Alman's been called a "hip Dr. Ruth," and a "sexy Dear Abby," based upon the wit of her advice. Today's world is more perplexing than ever—and Alman is just the expert to help untangle the most personal of knots.

THE CLASSIC COLLECTION
THE ENGLISH GOVERNESS
$5.95/373-2

When Lord Lovell's son was expelled from his prep school for masturbation, his father hired a very proper governess to tutor the boy—giving her strict instructions not to spare the rod to break him of his bad habits. But governess Harriet Marwood was addicted to domination.

PROTESTS, PLEASURES, RAPTURES
$5.95/400-3

Invited for an allegedly quiet weekend at a country vicarage, a young woman is stunned to find herself surrounded by shocking acts of sexual sadism. Soon her curiosity is piqued, and she begins to explore her own capacities for delicious sexual cruelty.

THE YELLOW ROOM
$5.95/378-3

The "yellow room" holds the secrets of lust, lechery, and the lash. There, bare-bottomed, spread-eagled, and open to the world, demure Alice Darvell soon learns to love her lickings.

SCHOOL DAYS IN PARIS
$5.95/325-2

Few Universities provide the profound and pleasurable lessons now in fashion in after-hours study—particularly if one is young and available, and lucky enough to have Paris as a playground. Here are all the randy pursuits of young adulthood.

MAN WITH A MAID
$4.95/307-4

The adventures of Jack and Alice have delighted readers for eight decades! A classic of its genre, *Man with a Maid* tells a tale of desire, revenge, and submission. Over 200,000 copies in print!

MASQUERADE READERS
INTIMATE PLEASURES
$4.95/38-6

Indulge your most private penchants with this specially chosen selection. Try a tempting morsel of *The Prodigal Virgin* and *Eveline*, or the bizarre public displays of carnality in *The Gilded Lily* and *The Story of Monique*. Many other selections guaranteed to have you begging for more!

BUY ANY 4 BOOKS & CHOOSE 1 ADDITIONAL BOOK, OF EQUAL OR LESSER VALUE, AS YOUR FREE GIFT

MASQUERADE BOOKS

CLASSIC EROTIC BIOGRAPHIES

JENNIFER AGAIN
$4.95/220-5

The uncensored life of one of modern erotica's most popular heroines. Once again, the insatiable Jennifer seizes the day and extracts every last drop of sensual pleasure!

JENNIFER III
$5.95/292-2

The adventures of erotica's most daring heroine. Jennifer has a photographer's eye for details—particularly of the male variety! One by one, her subjects submit to her demands for pleasure.

PAULINE
$4.95/129-2

From rural America to the royal court of Austria, Pauline follows her ever-growing sexual desires as she rises to the top of the Opera world. "I would never see them again. Why shouldn't I give myself to them that they might become more and more inspired to deeds of greater lust!"

RHINOCEROS

JOHN NORMAN
IMAGINATIVE SEX
$7.95/561-1

In 1974, the author of the controversial Gor novels unleashed his vision for an exciting sex life for all. *Imaginative Sex* outlines John Norman's philosophy on relations between the sexes, and presents fifty-three scenarios designed to reintroduce fantasy and intimacy to the bedroom.

KATHLEEN K.
SWEET TALKERS
$6.95/516-6

"If you enjoy eavesdropping on explicit conversations about sex... this book is for you." —*Spectator*

Kathleen K. ran a phone-sex company in the late 80s, and she opens up her diary for a very thought provoking peek at the life of a phone-sex operator. Transcripts of actual conversations are included.   Trade /$12.95/192-6

THOMAS S. ROCHE
DARK MATTER
$6.95/484-4

"*Dark Matter* is sure to please gender outlaws, bodymod junkies, goth vampires, boys who wish they were dykes, and anybody who's not to sure where the fine line should be drawn between pleasure and pain. It's a handful."—Pat Califia

"Here is the erotica of the cumming millennium.... You will be deliciously disturbed, but never disappointed."
—Poppy Z. Brite

NOIROTICA: An Anthology of Erotic Crime Stories (Ed.)
$6.95/390-2

A collection of darkly sexy tales, taking place at the crossroads of the crime and erotic genres. Here are some of today's finest writers of sexual fiction, all of whom explore the murky terrain where desire runs irrevocably afoul of the law.

ROMY ROSEN
SPUNK
$6.95/492-5

Casey, a lovely model poised upon the verge of super-celebrity, falls for an insatiable young rock singer—not suspecting that his sexual appetite has led him to experiment with a dangerous new aphrodisiac. Soon, Casey becomes addicted to the drug, and her craving plunges her into a strange underworld, where the only chance for redemption lies with a shadowy young man with a secret of his own. A thrilling tale from one of our hottest young talents.

MOLLY WEATHERFIELD
CARRIE'S STORY
$6.95/485-2

"I was stunned by how well it was written and how intensely foreign I found its sexual world.... And, since this is a world I don't frequent... I thoroughly enjoyed the National Geo tour."
—bOING bOING

"Hilarious and harrowing... just when you think things can't get any wilder, they do." —*Black Sheets*

"I had been Jonathan's slave for about a year when he told me he wanted to sell me at an auction. I wasn't in any condition to respond when he told me this…" Desire and depravity run rampant in this story of uncompromising mastery and irrevocable submission. A unique piece of erotica that is both thoughtful and hot!

CYBERSEX CONSORTIUM
CYBERSEX: The Perv's Guide to Finding Sex on the Internet
$6.95/471-2

You've heard the objections: cyberspace is soaked with sex, mired in immorality. Okay—so where is it!? Tracking down the good stuff—the real good stuff—can waste an awful lot of expensive time, and frequently leave you high and dry. The Cybersex Consortium presents an easy-to-use guide for those intrepid adults who know what they want. No horny hacker can afford to pass up this map to the kinkiest rest stops on the Info Superhighway—sure to provide hours of sexy entertainment.

MASQUERADE BOOKS

AMELIA G, EDITOR
BACKSTAGE PASSES
$6.95/438-0
Amelia G, editor of the goth-sex journal *Blue Blood*, has brought together some of today's most irreverent writers, each of whom has outdone themselves with an edgy, antic tale of modern lust. Punks, metalheads, and grunge-trash roam the pages of *Backstage Passes*, and no one knows their ways better...

GERI NETTICK WITH BETH ELLIOT
MIRRORS: Portrait of a Lesbian Transsexual
$6.95/435-6
The alternately heartbreaking and empowering story of one woman's long road to full selfhood. Born a male, Geri Nettick knew something just didn't fit. And even after coming to terms with her own gender dysphoria—and taking steps to correct it—she still fought to be accepted by the lesbian feminist community to which she felt she belonged. A true tale of struggle and discovery.

DAVID MELTZER
UNDER
$6.95/290-6
The story of a 21st century sex professional living at the bottom of the social heap. After surgeries designed to increase his physical allure, corrupt government forces drive the cyber-gigolo underground—where even more bizarre cultures await him.

ORF
$6.95/110-1
He is the ultimate musician-hero—the idol of thousands, the fevered dream of many more. And like many musicians before him, he is misunderstood, misused—and totally out of control. Every last drop of feeling is squeezed from a modern-day troubadour and his lady love.

LAURA ANTONIOU, EDITOR
NO OTHER TRIBUTE
$6.95/294-9
A collection sure to challenge Political Correctness in a way few have before, with tales of women kept in bondage to their lovers by their deepest passions. Love pushes these women beyond acceptable limits, rendering them helpless to deny anything to the men and women they adore.

BY HER SUBDUED
$6.95/281-7
These tales all involve women in control—of their lives, their loves, their men. So much in control that they can remorselessly break rules to become powerful goddesses of the men who sacrifice all to worship at their feet.

TRISTAN TAORMINO & DAVID AARON CLARK, EDS.
RITUAL SEX
$6.95/391-0
The many contributors to *Ritual Sex* know—and demonstrate—that body and soul share more common ground than society feels comfortable acknowledging. From memoirs of ecstatic revelation, to quests to reconcile sex and spirit, *Ritual Sex* provides an unprecedented look at private life.

TAMMY JO ECKHART
AMAZONS: Erotic Explorations of Ancient Myths
$7.95/534-4
The Amazon—the fierce, independent woman warrior—appears in the traditions of many cultures, but never before has the full erotic potential of this archetype been explored with such imagination and energy. Powerful pleasures await anyone lucky enough to encounter Eckhart's legendary spitfires.

PUNISHMENT FOR THE CRIME
$6.95/427-5
Peopled by characters of rare depth, these stories explore the true meaning of dominance and submission. From an encounter between two of society's most despised individuals, to the explorations of longtime friends, these tales take you where few others have ever dared....

AMARANTHA KNIGHT, ED.
SEDUCTIVE SPECTRES
$6.95/464-X
Breathtaking tours through the erotic supernatural via the imaginations of today's best writers. Never have ghostly encounters been so alluring, thanks to a cast of otherworldly characters well-acquainted with the pleasures of the flesh.

SEX MACABRE
$6.95/392-9
Horror tales designed for dark and sexy nights—sure to make your skin crawl, and heart beat faster.

BUY ANY 4 BOOKS & CHOOSE 1 ADDITIONAL BOOK, OF EQUAL OR LESSER VALUE, AS YOUR FREE GIFT

MASQUERADE BOOKS

FLESH FANTASTIC
$6.95/352-X
Humans have long toyed with the idea of "playing God": creating life from nothingness, bringing life to the inanimate. Now Amarantha Knight collects stories exploring not only the act of Creation, but the lust that follows.

GARY BOWEN
DIARY OF A VAMPIRE
$6.95/331-7
"Gifted with a darkly sensual vision and a fresh voice, [Bowen] is a writer to watch out for." —Cecilia Tan
Rafael, a red-blooded male with an insatiable hunger for the same, is the perfect antidote to the effete malcontents haunting bookstores today. The emergence of a bold and brilliant vision, rooted in past and present.

RENÉ MAIZEROY
FLESHLY ATTRACTIONS
$6.95/299-X
Lucien was the son of the wantonly beautiful actress, Marie-Rose Hardanges. When she decides to let a "friend" introduce her son to the pleasures of love, Marie-Rose could not have foretold the excesses that would lead to her own ruin and that of her cherished son.

JEAN STINE
THRILL CITY
$6.95/411-9
Thrill City is the seat of the world's increasing depravity, and this classic novel transports you there with a vivid style you'd be hard pressed to ignore. No writer is better suited to describe the extremes of this modern Babylon.

SEASON OF THE WITCH
$6.95/268-X
"A future in which it is technically possible to transfer the total mind...of a rapist killer into the brain dead but physically living body of his female victim. Remarkable for intense psychological technique. There is eroticism but it is necessary to mark the differences between the sexes and the subtle altering of a man into a woman." —The Science Fiction Critic

GRANT ANTREWS
ROGUES GALLERY
$6.95/522-0
A stirring evocation of dominant/submissive love. Two doctors meet and slowly fall in love. Once Beth reveals her hidden desires to Jim, the two explore the forbidden acts that will come to define their distinctly exotic affair.

MY DARLING DOMINATRIX
$7.95/566-2
When a man and a woman fall in love, it's supposed to be simple, uncomplicated, easy—unless that woman happens to be a dominatrix. This highly praised and unpretentious love story captures the richness and depth of this very special kind of love without leering or smirking.

SUBMISSIONS
$6.95/207-8
Antrews portrays the very special elements of the dominant/submissive relationship with restraint—this time with the story of a lonely man, a winning lottery ticket, and a demanding dominatrix.

LAURA ANTONIOU writing as "Sara Adamson"
THE MARKETPLACE
$6.95/3096-2
The volume that introduced the Marketplace to the world—and established it as one of the most popular realms in contemporary SM fiction. The thrilling overview of this ultimate slave-ring.

THE SLAVE
$6.95/173-X
One talented submissive longs to join the ranks of those who have proven themselves worthy of entry into the Marketplace. But as all applicants soon discover, the price is staggeringly high....

THE TRAINER
$6.95/249-3
The Marketplace Trilogy concludes with the story of the trainers, and the desires and paths that led them to become the ultimate figures of authority.

JOHN WARREN
THE TORQUEMADA KILLER
$6.95/367-8
Detective Eva Hernandez gets her first "big case": a string of vicious murders taking place within New York's SM community. Eva assembles the evidence, revealing a picture of a world misunderstood and under attack—and gradually comes to understand her own place within it.

THE LOVING DOMINANT
$6.95/218-3
Everything you need to know about an infamous sexual variation—and an unspoken type of love. Warren guides readers through this world and reveals the too-often hidden basis of the D/S relationship: care, trust and love.

DAVID AARON CLARK
SISTER RADIANCE
$6.95/215-9
A meditation on love, sex, and death. The vicissitudes of lust and romance are examined against a backdrop of urban decay in this testament to the allure—and inevitability—of the forbidden.

MASQUERADE BOOKS

THE WET FOREVER
$6.95/117-9

The story of Janus and Madchen—a small-time hood and a beautiful sex worker on the run—examines themes of loyalty, sacrifice, redemption and obsession amidst Manhattan's sex parlors and underground S/M clubs.

MICHAEL PERKINS
EVIL COMPANIONS
$6.95/3067-9

Evil Companions has been hailed as "a frightening classic." A young couple explores the nether reaches of the erotic unconscious in a shocking confrontation with the extremes of passion.

THE SECRET RECORD:
Modern Erotic Literature
$6.95/3039-3

Michael Perkins surveys the field with authority and unique insight. Updated and revised to include the latest trends, tastes, and developments in this misunderstood and maligned genre.

AN ANTHOLOGY OF CLASSIC ANONYMOUS EROTIC WRITING
$6.95/140-3

The very best passages from the world's most enduring erotic writing. "Anonymous" is one of the most infamous bylines in publishing history—and these steamy excerpts show why!

HELEN HENLEY
ENTER WITH TRUMPETS
$6.95/197-7

Helen Henley was told that women just don't write about sex—much less the taboos she was so interested in exploring. So Henley did it alone, flying in the face of "tradition" by writing this touching tale of arousal and devotion in one couple's kinky relationship.

ALICE JOANOU
BLACK TONGUE
$6.95/258-2

"Joanou has created a series of sumptuous, brooding, dark visions of sexual obsession, and is undoubtedly a name to look out for in the future." —*Redeemer*

Exploring lust at its most florid and unsparing, *Black Tongue* is a trove of baroque fantasies—each redolent of forbidden passions.

TOURNIQUET
$6.95/3060-1

A heady collection of stories and effusions from the pen of one our most dazzling young writers. Strange tales abound in this complex and riveting series of meditations on desire.

CANNIBAL FLOWER
$4.95/72-6

"She is waiting in her darkened bedroom, as she has waited throughout history, to seduce the men who are foolish enough to be blinded by her irresistible charms.... She is the goddess of sexuality, and *Cannibal Flower* is her haunting siren song." —Michael Perkins

LIESEL KULIG
LOVE IN WARTIME
$6.95/3044-X

Madeleine knew that the handsome SS officer was a dangerous man, but she was just a cabaret singer in Nazi-occupied Paris, trying to survive in a perilous time. When Josef fell in love with her, he discovered that a beautiful woman can sometimes be as dangerous as any warrior.

SAMUEL R. DELANY
THE MAD MAN
$8.99/408-9

"Reads like a pornographic reflection of Peter Ackroyd's *Chatterton* or A. S. Byatt's *Possession*.... Delany develops an insightful dichotomy between [his protagonist]'s two worlds: the one of cerebral philosophy and dry academia, the other of heedless, 'impersonal' obsessive sexual extremism. When these worlds finally collide...the novel achieves a surprisingly satisfying resolution...." —*Publishers Weekly*

Graduate student John Marr researches the life of Timothy Hasler: a philosopher whose career was cut tragically short over a decade earlier. On another front, Marr finds himself increasingly drawn toward shocking, depraved sexual entanglements with the homeless men of his neighborhood, until it begins to seem that Hasler's death might hold some key to his own life as a gay man in the age of AIDS. Unquestionably one of Samuel R. Delany's most challenging novels, and a must for any reader concerned with the state of the erotic in modern literature.

PHILIP JOSÉ FARMER
A FEAST UNKNOWN
$6.95/276-0

"Sprawling, brawling, shocking, suspenseful, hilarious..." —Theodore Sturgeon

Farmer's supreme anti-hero returns. "I was conceived and born in 1888." Slowly, Lord Grandrith—armed with the belief that he is the son of Jack the Ripper—tells the story of his remarkable and unbridled life. His story begins with his discovery of the secret of immortality—and progresses to encompass the furthest extremes of human behavior.

BUY ANY 4 BOOKS & CHOOSE 1 ADDITIONAL BOOK, OF EQUAL OR LESSER VALUE, AS YOUR FREE GIFT

MASQUERADE BOOKS

FLESH
$6.95/303-1
The author of the mind-blowing classic *The Image of the Beast* returns with one of his most infamous science fiction yarns. Space Commander Stagg explored the galaxies for 800 years, and could only hope that he would be welcomed home by an adoring—or at least appreciative—public. Upon his return, the hero Stagg is made the centerpiece of an incredible public ritual—one that will repeatedly take him to the heights of ecstasy, and inexorably drag him toward the depths of hell.

DANIEL VIAN
ILLUSIONS
$6.95/3074-1
International lust. Two tales of danger and desire in Berlin on the eve of WWII. From private homes to lurid cafés, passion is exposed in stark contrast to the brutal violence of the time, as desperate people explore their darkest sexual desires. A hallucinatory volume of unquenchable desires.

PERSUASIONS
$4.95/183-7
"The stockings are drawn tight by the suspender belt, tight enough to be stretched to the limit just above the middle part of her thighs, tight enough so that her calves glow through the sheer silk..." A double novel, including the classics *Adagio* and *Gabriela and the General*, this volume traces lust around the globe.

ANDREI CODRESCU
THE REPENTANCE OF LORRAINE
$6.95/329-5
"One of our most prodigiously talented and magical writers."
—*NYT Book Review*

By the acclaimed author of *The Hole in the Flag* and *The Blood Countess*. An aspiring writer, a professor's wife, a secretary, gold anklets, Maoists, Roman harlots—and more—swirl through this spicy tale of a harried quest for a mythic artifact. Written when the author was a young man, this lusty yarn was inspired by the heady days of the Sixties. Includes a new introduction by the author, detailing the events that inspired *Lorraine*'s creation.

TUPPY OWENS
SENSATIONS
$6.95/3081-4
Tuppy Owens tells the unexpurgated story of the making of *Sensations*—the first big-budget sex flick. Originally commissioned to appear in book form after the release of the film in 1975, *Sensations* is finally released under Masquerade's stylish Rhinoceros imprint. A rare peek behind the scenes of a porn-flick, from the genre's early, ground-breaking days.

SOPHIE GALLEYMORE BIRD
MANEATER
$6.95/103-9
Through a bizarre act of creation, a man attains the "perfect" lover—by all appearances a beautiful, sensuous woman, but in reality something far darker. Once brought to life she will accept no mate, seeking instead the prey that will sate her hunger for vengeance. A biting take on the war of the sexes.

BADBOY

PETER HEISTER
ISLANDS OF DESIRE
$6.95/480-1
Red-blooded lust on the wine-dark seas of classical Greece. Anacreon yearns to leave his small, isolated island and find adventure in one of the overseas kingdoms. Accompanied by some randy friends, Anacreon makes his dream come true—and discovers pleasures he never dreamed of! A thrillingly erotic glimpse of the gay past.

KITTY TSUI WRITING AS "ERIC NORTON"
SPARKS FLY
$6.95/551-4
The acclaimed author of *Breathless* explores the highest highs—and most wretched depths—of life as Eric Norton, a beautiful wanton living San Francisco's high life. *Sparks Fly* traces Norton's rise, fall, and resurrection, vividly marking the way with the personal affairs that give life meaning. Scaldingly hot and totally revealing.

BARRY ALEXANDER
ALL THE RIGHT PLACES
$6.95/482-8
Stories filled with hot studs in lust and love. From modern masters and slaves to medieval royals and their subjects, Alexander explores the mating rituals men have engaged in for centuries—all in the name of sometimes hidden desires…

MICHAEL FORD, EDITOR
BUTCHBOYS:
Stories For Men Who Need It Bad
$6.50/523-9
A big volume of tales dedicated to the rough-and-tumble type who can make a man weak at the knees. Some of today's best erotic writers explore the many possible variations on the age-old fantasy of the dominant man.

MASQUERADE BOOKS

WILLIAM J. MANN, EDITOR
GRAVE PASSIONS:
Gay Tales of the Supernatural
$6.50/405-4

A collection of the most chilling tales of passion currently being penned by today's most provocative gay writers. Unnatural transformations, otherworldly encounters, and deathless desires make for a collection sure to keep readers up late at night—for a variety of reasons!

J. A. GUERRA, EDITOR
COME QUICKLY:
For Boys on the Go
$6.50/413-5

Here are over sixty of the hottest fantasies around—all designed to get you going in less time than it takes to dial 976. Julian Anthony Guerra, the editor behind the popular *Men at Work* and *Badboy Fantasies*, has put together this volume especially for you—a busy man on a modern schedule, who still appreciates a little old-fashioned action.

JOHN PRESTON
HUSTLING: A Gentleman's Guide to the Fine Art of Homosexual Prostitution
$6.50/517-4

"Fun and highly literary. What more could you expect form such an accomplished activist, author and editor?"—*Drummer*

John Preston solicited the advice and opinions of "working boys" from across the country in his effort to produce the ultimate guide to the hustler's world. *Hustling* covers every practical aspect of the business, from clientele and payment options to "specialties," sidelines and drawbacks.
Trade $12.95/137-3

MR. BENSON
$4.95/3041-5

Jamie is an aimless young man lucky enough to encounter Mr. Benson. He is soon led down the path of erotic enlightenment, learning to accept this man as his master. Jamie's incredible adventures never fail to excite—especially when the going gets rough!

TALES FROM THE DARK LORD
$5.95/323-6

Twelve stunning works from the man *Lambda Book Report* called "the Dark Lord of gay erotica." The relentless ritual of lust and surrender is explored in all its manifestations in this heart-stopping triumph of authority and vision from the Dark Lord!

TALES FROM THE DARK LORD II
$4.95/176-4

THE ARENA
$4.95/3083-0

Preston's take on the ultimate sex club. Men go there to unleash beasts, to let demons roam free, to abolish all limits. Only the author of Mr. Benson could have imagined so perfect an institution for the satisfaction of masculine desires.

THE HEIR•THE KING
$4.95/3048-2

Two complete novels in one special volume. The ground-breaking and controversial *The Heir*, written in the lyric voice of the ancient myths, tells the story of a world where slaves and masters create a new sexual society. *The King* tells the story of a soldier who discovers his monarch's most secret desires.

THE MISSION OF ALEX KANE
SWEET DREAMS
$4.95/3062-8

It's the triumphant return of gay action hero Alex Kane! In *Sweet Dreams*, Alex travels to Boston where he takes on a street gang that stalks gay teenagers.

GOLDEN YEARS
$4.95/3069-5

When evil threatens the plans of a group of older gay men, Kane's got the muscle to take it head on. Along the way, he wins the support—and very specialized attentions—of a cowboy plucked right out of the Old West.

DEADLY LIES
$4.95/3076-8

Politics is a dirty business and the dirt becomes deadly when a political smear campaign targets gay men. Who better to clean things up than Alex Kane! Alex comes to protect the lives of gay men imperiled by lies and deceit.

STOLEN MOMENTS
$4.95/3098-9

Houston's evolving gay community is victimized by a malicious newspaper editor who is more than willing to sacrifice gays on the altar of circulation. He never counted on Alex Kane, fearless defender of gay dreams and desires.

SECRET DANGER
$4.95/111-X

Homophobia: a pernicious social ill not confined by America's borders. Alex Kane and the faithful Danny are called to a small European country, where a group of gay tourists is being held hostage by ruthless terrorists.

BUY ANY 4 BOOKS & CHOOSE 1 ADDITIONAL BOOK, OF EQUAL OR LESSER VALUE, AS YOUR FREE GIFT

MASQUERADE BOOKS

LETHAL SILENCE
$4.95/125-X
Chicago becomes the scene of the right-wing's most noxious plan—facilitated by unholy political alliances. Alex and Danny head to the Windy City to take up battle with the mercenaries who would squash gay men underfoot.

MATT TOWNSEND
SOLIDLY BUILT
$6.50/416-X
Matt Townsend debuts with the tale of the tumultuous relationship between Jeff, a young photographer, and Mark, the butch electrician hired to wire Jeff's new home. For Jeff, it's love at first sight; Mark, however, has more than a few hang-ups. Soon, both are forced to reevaluate their outlooks....

JAY SHAFFER
SHOOTERS
$5.95/284-1
Hot sex for no-nonsense guys. No mere catalog of random acts, *Shooters* tells the stories of a variety of stunning men and the ways they connect in sexual and non-sexual ways. A virtuoso storyteller, Shaffer always gets his man.

ANIMAL HANDLERS
$4.95/264-7
In Shaffer's world, each and every man finally succumbs to the animal urges deep inside. And if there's any creature that promises a wild time, it's a beast who's been caged for far too long.

FULL SERVICE
$4.95/150-0
No-nonsense guys bear down hard on each other as they work their way toward release in this finely detailed assortment of masculine fantasies. One of gay erotica's most insightful chroniclers of male passion.

D. V. SADERO
IN THE ALLEY
$4.95/144-6
Hardworking men—from cops to carpenters—bring their own special skills and impressive tools to the most satisfying job of all: capturing and breaking the male sexual beast.

SCOTT O'HARA
DO-IT-YOURSELF PISTON POLISHING
$6.50/489-5
Longtime sex-pro Scott O'Hara draws upon his acute powers of seduction to lure you into a world of hard, horny men long overdue for a tune-up. Pretty soon, you'll pop your own hood for the servicing you know you need....

SUTTER POWELL
EXECUTIVE PRIVILEGES
$6.50/383-X
No matter how serious or sexy a predicament his characters find themselves in, Powell conveys the sheer exuberance of their encounters with a warm humor rarely seen in contemporary gay erotica.

GARY BOWEN
WESTERN TRAILS
$6.50/477-1
A wild roundup of tales devoted to life on the lone prairie. Some of gay literature's brightest stars tell the sexy truth about the many ways a rugged stud found to satisfy himself —and his buddy—in the Very Wild West.

MAN HUNGRY
$5.95/374-0
By the author of *Diary of a Vampire*. A riveting collection of stories from one of gay erotica's new stars. Dipping into a variety of genres, Bowen crafts tales of lust unlike anything being published today.

KYLE STONE
HOT BAUDS 2
$6.50/479-8
Stone conducted another heated search through the world's randiest gay bulletin boards, resulting in one of the most scalding follow-ups ever published. Sexy, shameless, and user-friendly.

HOT BAUDS
$5.95/285-X
Stone combed cyberspace for the hottest fantasies of the world's horniest hackers. Stone has assembled the first collection of the raunchy erotica so many gay men surf the Net for.

FIRE & ICE
$5.95/297-3
A collection of stories from the author of the infamous adventures of PB 500. Stone's characters always promise one thing: enough hot action to burn away your desire for anyone else....

FANTASY BOARD
$4.95/212-4
Explore the foreseeable future—through the intertwined lives of a collection of randy computer hackers. On the Lambda Gate BBS, every horny male is in search of virtual satisfaction!

THE CITADEL
$4.95/198-5
The sequel to *The Initiation of PB 500*. Micah—now known only as '500'—will face new challenges and hardships after his entry into the forbidding Citadel. Only his master knows what awaits—and whether Micah will again distinguish himself as the perfect instrument of pleasure....

MASQUERADE BOOKS

THE INITIATION OF PB 500
$4.95/141-1

He is a stranger on their planet, unschooled in their language, and ignorant of their customs. But this man, Micah—now known only by his number—will soon be trained in every detail of erotic service. He must begin proving himself worthy of the master who has chosen him....

RITUALS
$4.95/168-3

Via a computer bulletin board, a young man finds himself drawn into a series of sexual rites that transform him into the willing slave of a mysterious stranger. All vestiges of his former life are thrown off, and he learns to live for his Master's touch....

ROBERT BAHR
SEX SHOW
$4.95/225-6

Luscious dancing boys. Brazen, explicit acts. Take a seat, and get very comfortable, because the curtain's going up on a show no discriminating appetite can afford to miss.

JASON FURY
THE ROPE ABOVE, THE BED BELOW
$4.95/269-8

A vicious murderer is preying upon New York's go-go boys. In order to solve this mystery and save lives, each studly suspect must lay bare his soul—and more!

ERIC'S BODY
$4.95/151-9

Fury's sexiest tales are collected in book form for the first time. Follow the irresistible Jason through sexual adventures unlike any you have ever read....

1 900 745-HUNG

THE connection for hot handfuls of eager guys! No credit card needed—so call now for access to the hottest party line available. Spill it all to bad boys from across the country! (Must be over 18.) Pick one up now.... $3.98 per min.

LARS EIGHNER
WHISPERED IN THE DARK
$5.95/286-8

A volume demonstrating Eighner's unique combination of strengths: poetic descriptive power, an unfailing ear for dialogue, and a finely tuned feeling for the nuances of male passion.

AMERICAN PRELUDE
$4.95/170-5

Eighner is widely recognized as one of our best, most exciting gay writers. He is also one of gay erotica's true masters—and American Prelude shows why. Wonderfully written, blisteringly hot tales of all-American lust between oversexed studs.

B.M.O.C.
$4.95/3077-6

In a college town known as "the Athens of the Southwest," studs of every stripe are up all night—studying, naturally. Relive university life the way it was supposed to be, with a cast of handsome honor students majoring in Human Homosexuality.

DAVID LAURENTS, EDITOR
SOUTHERN COMFORT
$6.50/466-6

Editor David Laurents now unleashes a collection of tales focusing on the American South—stories reflecting not only Southern literary tradition, but the many sexy contributions the region has made to the iconography of the American Male.

WANDERLUST:
Homoerotic Tales of Travel
$5.95/395-3

A volume dedicated to the special pleasures of faraway places. Celebrate the freedom of the open road, and the allure of men who stray from the beaten path....

THE BADBOY BOOK OF EROTIC POETRY
$5.95/382-1

Erotic poetry has long been the problem child of the literary world—highly creative and provocative, but somehow too frank to be "art." The Badboy Book of Erotic Poetry restores eros to its place of honor in contemporary gay writing.

AARON TRAVIS
BIG SHOTS
$5.95/448-8

Two fierce tales in one electrifying volume. In Beirut, Travis tells the story of ultimate military power and erotic subjugation; Kip, Travis' hypersexed and sinister take on film noir, appears in unexpurgated form for the first time.

EXPOSED
$4.95/126-8

A unique glimpse of the horny gay male in his natural environment! Cops, college jocks, ancient Romans—even Sherlock Holmes and his loyal Watson—cruise these pages, fresh from the throbbing pen of one of our hottest authors.

BUY ANY 4 BOOKS & CHOOSE 1 ADDITIONAL BOOK, OF EQUAL OR LESSER VALUE, AS YOUR FREE GIFT

MASQUERADE BOOKS

BEAST OF BURDEN
$4.95/105-5

Innocents surrender to the brutal sexual mastery of their superiors, as taboos are shattered and replaced with the unwritten rules of masculine conquest. Intense, extreme—and totally Travis.

IN THE BLOOD
$5.95/283-5

Written when Travis had just begun to explore the true power of the erotic imagination, these stories laid the groundwork for later masterpieces. Among the many rewarding rarities included in this special volume: "In the Blood"—a heart-pounding descent into sexual vampirism.

THE FLESH FABLES
$4.95/243-4

One of Travis' best collections. *The Flesh Fables* includes "Blue Light," his most famous story, as well as other masterpieces that established him as the erotic writer to watch.

SLAVES OF THE EMPIRE
$4.95/3054-7

"A wonderful mythic tale. Set against the backdrop of the exotic and powerful Roman Empire, this wonderfully written novel explores the timeless questions of light and dark in male sexuality. The locale may be the ancient world, but these are the slaves and masters of our time...." —John Preston

BOB VICKERY

SKIN DEEP
$4.95/265-5

So many varied beauties no one will go away unsatisfied. No tantalizing morsel of manflesh is overlooked—or left unexplored! Beauty may be only skin deep, but these a handful of beautiful skin is a tempting proposition.

JR

FRENCH QUARTER NIGHTS
$5.95/337-6

Sensual snapshots of the many places where men get down and dirty—from the steamy French Quarter to the steam room at the old Everard baths. These are nights you'll wish would go on forever....

TOM BACCHUS

RAHM
$5.95/315-5

The imagination of Tom Bacchus brings to life an extraordinary assortment of characters, from the Father of Us All to the cowpoke next door, the early gay literati to rude, queercore mosh rats.

BONE
$4.95/177-2

Queer musings from the pen of one of today's hottest young talents. A fresh outlook on fleshly indulgence yields more than a few pleasant surprises. Horny Tom Bacchus maps out the tricking ground of a new generation.

KEY LINCOLN

SUBMISSION HOLDS
$4.95/266-3

A bright young talent unleashes his first collection of gay erotica. From tough to tender, the men between these covers stop at nothing to get what they want. These sweat-soaked tales show just how bad boys can really get.

CALDWELL/EIGHNER

QSFX2
$5.95/278-7

The wickedest, wildest, other-worldliest yarns from two master storytellers—Clay Caldwell and Lars Eighner. Both eroticists take a trip to the furthest reaches of the sexual imagination, sending back ten stories proving that as much as things change, one thing will always remain the same....

CLAY CALDWELL

JOCK STUDS
$6.50/472-0

Scalding tales of pumped bodies and raging libidos. Swimmers, runners, football players... whatever your sport might be, there's a man waiting for you in these pages. Waiting to peel off that uniform and claim his reward for a game well-played....

ASK OL' BUDDY
$5.95/346-5

Set in the underground SM world, Caldwell takes you on a journey of discovery—where men initiate one another into the secrets of the rawest sexual realm of all. And when each stud's initiation is complete, he takes part in the training of another hungry soul...

STUD SHORTS
$5.95/320-1

"If anything, Caldwell's charm is more powerful, his nostalgia more poignant, the horniness he captures more sweetly, achingly acute than ever." —Aaron Travis

A new collection of this legend's latest sex-fiction. Caldwell tells all about cops, cadets, truckers, farmboys (and many more) in these dirty jewels.

TAILPIPE TRUCKER
$5.95/296-5

Trucker porn! In prose as free and unvarnished as a cross-country highway, Caldwell tells the truth about Trag and Curly—two men hot for the feeling of sweaty manflesh. Together, they pick up—and turn out—a couple of thrill-seeking punks.

SERVICE, STUD
$5.95/336-8

Another look at the gay future. The setting is the Los Angeles of a distant future. Here the all-male populace is divided between the served and the servants—guaranteeing the erotic satisfaction of all involved.

MASQUERADE BOOKS

QUEERS LIKE US
$4.95/262-0

"Caldwell at his most charming." —Aaron Travis

For years the name Clay Caldwell has been synonymous with the hottest, most finely crafted gay tales available. *Queers Like Us* is one of his best: the story of a randy mailman's trek through a landscape of willing, available studs.

ALL-STUD
$4.95/104-7

This classic, sex-soaked tale takes place under the watchful eye of Number Ten: an omniscient figure who has decreed unabashed promiscuity as the law of his all-male land.

CLAY CALDWELL AND AARON TRAVIS

TAG TEAM STUDS
$6.50/465-8

Thrilling tales from these two legendary eroticists. The wrestling world will never seem the same, once you've made your way through this assortment of sweaty, virile studs. But you'd better be wary—should one catch you off guard, you just might spend the rest of the night pinned to the mat....

LARRY TOWNSEND

LEATHER AD: M
$5.95/380-5

John's curious about what goes on between the leatherclad men he's fantasized about. He takes out a personal ad, and starts a journey of discovery that will leave no part of his life unchanged.

LEATHER AD: S
$5.95/407-0

The tale continues—this time told from a Top's perspective. A simple ad generates many responses, and one man finds himself in the enviable position of putting these studs through their paces....

1 800 906-HUNK

Hardcore phone action for real men. A scorching assembly of studs is waiting for your call—and eager to give you the headtrip of your life! Totally live, guaranteed one-on-one encounters. (Must be over 18.) No credit card needed. $3.98 per minute.

BEWARE THE GOD WHO SMILES
$5.95/321-X

Two lusty young Americans are transported to ancient Egypt—where they are embroiled in regional warfare and taken as slaves by barbarians. The key to escape lies in their rampant libidos.

2069 TRILOGY
(This one-volume collection only $6.95)244-2

The early science-fiction trilogy in one volume! Set in the future, the *2069 Trilogy* includes the tight plotting and shameless all-male sex action that established Townsend as one of erotica's masters.

MIND MASTER
$4.95/209-4

Who better to explore the territory of erotic dominance than an author who helped define the genre—and knows that ultimate mastery always transcends the physical.

THE LONG LEATHER CORD
$4.95/201-9

Chuck's stepfather never lacks money or clandestine male visitors with whom he enacts intense sexual rituals. As Chuck comes to terms with his own desires, he begins to unravel the mystery behind his stepfather's secret life.

THE SCORPIUS EQUATION
$4.95/119-5

The story of a man caught between the demands of two galactic empires. Our randy hero must match wits—and more—with the incredible forces that rule his world.

MAN SWORD
$4.95/188-8

The *très gai* tale of France's King Henri III, who encounters enough sexual schemers and politicos to alter one's picture of history forever!

THE FAUSTUS CONTRACT
$4.95/167-5

Two attractive young men desperately need $1000. Will do anything. Travel OK. Danger OK. Call anytime… Two cocky young hustlers get more than they bargained for in this story of lust and its discontents.

CHAINS
$4.95/158-6

Picking up street punks has always been risky, but here it sets off a string of events that must be read to be believed. Townsend at his grittiest.

KISS OF LEATHER
$4.95/161-6

A look at the acts and attitudes of an earlier generation of gay leathermen, *Kiss of Leather* is full to bursting with gritty, raw action. Sensual pain and pleasure mix in this tightly plotted tale.

RUN, LITTLE LEATHER BOY
$4.95/143-8

A chronic underachiever, Wayne seems to be going nowhere fast. He finds himself drawn to the masculine intensity of a dark and mysterious sexual underground, where he soon finds many goals worth pursuing....

BUY ANY 4 BOOKS & CHOOSE 1 ADDITIONAL BOOK, OF EQUAL OR LESSER VALUE, AS YOUR FREE GIFT

ORDERING IS EASY

MC/VISA orders can be placed by calling our toll-free number
PHONE 800-375-2356/FAX 212-986-7355/E-MAIL masqbks@aol.com
or mail this coupon to:
MASQUERADE DIRECT
DEPT. BMMQ97 801 2ND AVE., NY, NY 10017

BUY ANY FOUR BOOKS AND CHOOSE ONE ADDITIONAL BOOK, OF EQUAL OR LESSER VALUE, AS YOUR FREE GIFT.

QTY.	TITLE	NO.	PRICE
			FREE

We never sell, give or trade any customer's name.

SUBTOTAL

POSTAGE AND HANDLING

TOTAL

In the U.S., please add $1.50 for the first book and 75¢ for each additional book; in Canada, add $2.00 for the first book and $1.25 for each additional book. Foreign countries: add $4.00 for the first book and $2.00 for each additional book. No C.O.D. orders. Please make all checks payable to Masquerade/Direct. Payable in U.S. currency only. NY state residents add 8.25% sales tax. Please allow 4–6 weeks for delivery. Payable in U.S. currency only.

NAME _____

ADDRESS _____

CITY _____ STATE _____ ZIP _____

TEL( ) _____

E-MAIL _____

PAYMENT: ☐ CHECK ☐ MONEY ORDER ☐ VISA ☐ MC

CARD NO _____ EXP. DATE _____